Love's Destiny

Elizabeth Meyette

CRIMSON
ROMANCE
Avon, Massachusetts

Published by
Crimson Romance
an imprint of F+W Media, Inc.
10151 Carver Road, Suite 200
Blue Ash, Ohio 45242

www.crimsonromance.com

POD ISBN 10: 1-4405-5062-X
POD ISBN 13: 978-1-4405-5062-1
eISBN 10: 1-4405-5061-1
eISBN 13: 978-1-4405-5061-4

This is a work of fiction.

Names, characters, corporations, institutions, organizations, events, or locales in this novel are either the product of the author's imagination or, if real, used fictitiously. The resemblance of any character to actual persons (living or dead) is entirely coincidental.

Chapter 1

London, April 1774

Emily Wentworth waged a battle between grief and anger. Today grief was winning.

She sat lost in thought, burrowed deeply into the comfort of the brown leather chair, one of two that sat before the large fireplace in the study. It was a room she visited often, one that usually brought a feeling of warmth and closeness to her father when he was away at sea. Today, however, an aching emptiness filled her as it had for the last two weeks since she had received word of her father's death. A violent winter storm had surged across the Atlantic ravaging George Wentworth's ship, the *Spirit*. The few survivors rescued by a passing merchant ship spoke of George's bravery in his futile attempts to save his men and his ship.

Emily gazed around the room that reflected her father. Well-loved books lined the shelves on the walls surrounding the enormous mahogany desk where he pored over ledgers and charts when he was home. Emily smiled as she remembered how he would set them aside when she entered the room.

"Am I bothering you, Father?" she would ask, her timid smile revealing a dimple in each cheek.

"Nothing is as important as you, Em," he would chuckle, falling willingly to her ploy.

They spent hours talking of his voyages, Emily sitting entranced with his tales of the wild animals and exotic people of Africa, of lands scorched under unending heat and sun, of women dressed in beautiful silks in Asia. She imagined she could hear the vendors hawking their wares in crowded markets, the bustle of the people, the lilt and cadence of their languages, the smell of·exotic spices and the aromas of mysterious foods. He also told her stories of the colonies in America and the proud spirit that was the cornerstone of that land. Emily tried to picture the vast territory yet to be settled and the rugged Indians who lived there. She knew some were friendly and helped the British, while others were fierce and terrifying. She wondered about the men and women who would travel across the ocean to live in a land so far from their beloved England.

Emily stared at the embers dying in the hearth. The room took on a chill as the sun settled in the west. Her cheeks were wet, and she realized that she had been crying. Rising, she paced the room. She touched the smoke-stained pipes, always stationed on his desk, and ran her fingertips lightly across the books that lined the shelves. She had read many of them herself, unusual for most girls of her day. George Wentworth had insisted that reading and writing be a part of her education.

"No child of mine is going to be a simpering idiot! There is more to life for Em than embroidery and coquetry," he insisted. "She will receive an education as fine as her brother Andrew's!"

Emily smiled to herself. Father usually got his way, if not with his charm, then with his temper. But her mother, Jessica, had agreed that Emily should be well educated, as she had been herself. Many evenings at supper her parents had drawn her into conversations and asked her to share her opinions. Consequently, at social affairs when the women gathered together, she was bored with their prattle and gossip, sometimes catching her mother's amused glance as they smiled in camaraderie.

"You must not think you are better than others just because you have had the benefit of an education," Jessica would admonish when Emily mocked those "prissy know-nothings." Jessica was always pleasant to the other ladies even though, as Emily suspected, she was often bored, too.

Emily missed the late evening chats they shared after such events. Jessica had died of consumption two years earlier. The family was just recovering from the shock of her death.

"And now they are both gone," Emily whispered.

Jessica's death had brought Emily and her father even closer. Although she was only seventeen, he began to leave much of the running of the house to her, trusting her judgment. Yet, she was still his little girl.

She reached for the open letter on the desk. Her father's solicitor had given it to her after the reading of the will. She knew the words by heart, but she looked at them again as if willing them to change:

My Dearest Emily,

Your reading this means that I am either dead or lost at sea. This must be a difficult time for you and Andrew. Draw on your faith in God and your love for one another to see you through. You have a quiet strength, Em. You helped me through my grief and sorrow at your mother's passing. You are so much like her, not only in looks, but also in courage, gentleness and honesty. Now you must help Andrew. You must be strong for him.

Please know how much I love you both. That is why I have taken measures to see that you and Andrew are properly cared for. I have appointed my dear friend, Captain Jonathon Brentwood of Virginia, as your guardian. He is a good man, Em, and a trusted friend. He saved my life once, and that is why I am entrusting him with the dearest treasures in my life. You and Andrew have brought me more joy than you will ever know. I love you both and will be watching you from the caring arms of our God in heaven.

Your loving father

"Come and eat, darlin'." Etta Mason had come into the room. "You cannot spend all your days hidin' in here and missin' your father," she said gently. The housekeeper put her arm around Emily's shoulders and led her out of the study.

"Oh, Etta, I miss him so," Emily whispered through the lump in her throat, fighting back the tears.

"I know, darlin'," she replied.

Andrew was already at the table. He stood up when Emily entered and held her chair.

"How are you, Em?" he asked. He loved their father very much, but he was aware of the special bond his father and Emily had shared. He wished he could help her.

"Oh, Drew, when is that colonial captain supposed to arrive?" she cried, anger claiming the upper hand now.

"Now, Em, Father would not appoint an ogre to be our guardian. I am sure Captain Brentwood will be a kind man."

Emily looked at her younger brother. He was probably right. At fifteen, Andrew had more common sense than many of the older suitors who had been calling on her.

"You are right. It is just that everything is so different for us now. With no one left in either Father's or Mother's families, we have no choice but to go with this colonial to Virginia. We may have to accept his guardianship, but I do not have to like it!" Her blue-violet eyes sparked with defiance, and her soft full lips set in a firm line.

Andrew smiled to himself. At least thinking about "that colonial captain" had distracted Emily from her somber, brooding mood that had become so common of late. He loved to see her spirit revive. No one liked to tangle with Emily; she had a quick temper and a sharp tongue. Yet she was fair and had a strong sense of justice.

"Well, his letter said he would arrive as soon as his business was settled in France. He thought with fair weather and a good wind he should arrive by the end of this month. I would say another week or two," Andrew answered, watching her eyes and guessing how quickly her mind was working. "Please, Emily, give him a chance. He was Father's friend remember."

"You are right, Drew. I shall try," she smiled fondly at her brother.

*

Emily viewed her reflection in the mirror. Thick dark lashes made a startling contrast to clear, blue-violet eyes. She wrinkled her delicate nose.

"I am too short," she thought. "And my hair . . . I must wear it up."

She pushed her long, thick, tawny-colored hair up from the nape of her neck. Golden highlights danced off it in the evening sun that streamed through the window.

A plan had formed in Emily's mind as the weeks had passed, bringing the inevitable meeting with Captain Brentwood closer. She needed no guardian—why she was seventeen years old. Andrew and she could continue to live here in London. Surely their inheritance would be an adequate income on which they could live comfortably. It was silly to even appoint a guardian for them.

Her heart lifted as she thought of her foolproof plan. That was why she must appear a mature and self-assured woman. But she wrinkled her nose once again at her reflection.

"Bah! I look like a child, and Captain Brentwood will be here any moment." She rang for Mary, her maid. She looked at her reflection pleased with the effect of her hair pulled up and back, making her feel more confident.

Mary scuttled into the room wringing her hands. She had already spent hours assisting her mistress with numerous anxious, and often reassessed, preparations for this meeting

"Quickly, Mary, dress my hair high, and . . . well, sophisticated. I need to look mature . . . older. Oh, you know what I mean."

Mary hesitated. Etta was only the housekeeper, but she clucked over Emily and Andrew like a mother hen. If she did not approve, Mary would really get a dressing down. As gentle as Etta could be with the children, she could be equally stern with the servants.

"Come on, quickly, Mary," Emily insisted. It was time to start asserting her authority and look the part of woman of the house.

Mary did not want to tangle with Emily's temper either, so she quickly picked up the brushes and began to dress the girl's hair.

Emily surveyed the results. Her black, high-necked dress set off her creamy white skin. With her hair piled high on her head, she appeared taller, more dignified. She was sure her plan would work, and in spite of her sadness, her spirits lifted. There was a knock on the door.

"Come in," she called.

Andrew entered. "He should be here . . . Oh, Em, you look so different . . . " Andrew stared at his sister. The transformation was remarkable.

"Do I look older, Drew? Do you think our plan will work?" Her eyes sparkled for the first time in weeks.

"I hope so, Emily. But please do not set your hopes too high. What do you think Captain Brentwood will be like?" Andrew asked.

"Well, he was Father's friend, so perhaps he will be a bit like Father. Perhaps not as robust, perhaps a bit older . . . I do not know. I just hope he agrees to our plan. I do not see why he would not. He probably does not want to be burdened with us any more than we want to be uprooted and moved to those savage colonies." Emily was not to be dissuaded; her plan would work. "We could continue to live here . . . what does it matter to him where we are? I have to convince him that I am capable of running this household and Father's estate."

*

Captain Jonathon Brentwood stared out the window of his coach. Lamplighters were making their way along, igniting the lamps that lined the streets of London. The *clop, clop, clop* of the horse's hooves beat a rhythm against the night as he pondered his new role as guardian of his dear friend's children. It was not a role he relished. And his dealings in Europe were becoming more tenuous as friction mounted between the colonies and England. Most of his time would be spent in the colonies now as trade and prosperity were growing there. And as the rebellion grew, he had other duties to attend.

The timing of this guardianship could not have been worse. But George Wentworth had been a mentor and had become one of his closest friends. Jonathon would honor the promise he had made to him. His experience with children had been limited, and when he was exposed to them, he was bewildered by their endless energy and their proclivity to mischief. He hoped George's children were not quite as lively and imaginative as some he had spent time with. George had told him many stories of Little Em and Andrew. From his stories they sounded well-behaved and mannerly. They certainly would tie him down more than he had been used to in his 28 years of bachelorhood. He had written his sister Joanna explaining the situation. Surely she would help him watch over the children so he could continue sailing. She and her husband lived in Brentwood Manor, the family home. David was a good manager, and the plantation was thriving under him. Jonathon would soon have to take over, but he wanted to sail for a few more years. Well, he would get this situation settled soon, and then he could set sail again.

The coach came to a stop in front of the handsome London townhouse. As he stepped down from the coach, Jonathon noticed an upstairs curtain fall back in place. He took a deep breath, straightened his cravat, and went up to the door.

*

"He is here, Andrew. You go down first. I shall be right there, but let me talk to him alone. I am so nervous; I have eaten nothing all day!" She ran to the mirror as Andrew closed the door. "Oh, dear God, please let this work," she whispered. She lifted her chin peering sideways out of her eyes. Raising one eyebrow, she nodded her head regally. She had been practicing all week. "It must work!"

As she descended the curving staircase she saw a tall figure with broad shoulders and dark hair studying the portrait of Jessica, Emily's mother. Jonathon Brentwood turned and looked up at a younger version of the portrait he had just viewed. Surprise flickered across his face, quickly replaced by a lazy, engaging smile.

"So you are Little Em," he drawled. Not quite, he thought to himself. He gazed at the beautiful tawny-haired girl whose blue-violet eyes threatened to drown him.

Emily was stunned. This was her father's friend? Soft brown eyes gazed at her with amusement. They were set in a bronzed, handsome face. He was dressed in a blue longcoat and cream-colored breeches that enhanced his tall, lean figure. His broad shoulders and brown curly hair tied back at the nape of his neck completed the picture of a strikingly attractive man. Emily's cheeks felt flushed under his close scrutiny, and a strange tingle ran through her body. She reached the bottom of the stairs and looked up into his warm, brown eyes again as she extended her hand.

"Captain Brentwood? I am pleased to meet you." Emily was annoyed at the tremble in her voice. He bent and kissed her hand, his lips brushing softly against her skin. Their eyes met as he straightened. Emily tried to steady herself, unable to make her heart stop beating so hard. She was sure he could hear it. She reminded herself of her plan, and quickly regained her composure, straightening to her full height.

"You must be exhausted after your long, hurried voyage. May I offer you some tea," she paused noting his suppressed smile, "or some brandy?" she added.

"Brandy would be fine. Thank you . . . uh . . . Miss Wentworth," he replied still fighting back the smile.

Emily led him into the parlor and rang for the maid; Etta appeared. Emily knew this would be difficult for Etta still thought of her as a child.

"Two brandies please, Etta." She raised her chin as she had practiced before the mirror. Etta started to protest, but something in Emily's eyes stopped her, and she hurried off to get the drinks.

"Please sit down, Captain Brentwood," Emily said coolly as she sat on the end of the settee. To her confusion, Jonathon sat beside her rather than in the chair she had indicated. A crooked smile played around his lips as though he attempted to hide a joke. He thought of the "Little Em" of George's stories and chuckled to himself. Nothing had prepared him for this beautiful girl who was trying so hard to be a woman.

"We have much to discuss, Miss Wentworth," he said as Etta returned with a tray carrying the decanter and two crystal glasses.

"Indeed we have, Captain," she replied.

Etta set the tray on the table in front of Emily. The housekeeper poured brandy into the glasses, and Emily was grateful for she had no idea what an appropriate amount would have been. She thought Etta rather stingy based on what was in each glass, but she took them and handed one glass to Jonathon.

"Thank you, Etta; that will be all." She turned to Jonathon, dismissing the housekeeper.

"Hmmmph!" Etta grumbled as she left the room.

Jonathon silently saluted Emily and then took a drink from his glass. Emily sipped hers and tried to choke down the spasms of coughing that threatened to overcome her. She had sampled wine before at social gatherings, but had never tasted brandy. Heat spread down her throat and she blinked the tears out of her eyes causing her to miss the fleeting smile that crossed Jonathon's face. It was a few minutes before she caught her breath enough to speak.

"Captain Brentwood, I loved my father very much and always obeyed him as he had my welfare as his concern above all else.

However, with all due respect, sir, I think in this last instance he erred."

Jonathon raised an eyebrow encouraging her to continue.

"I realize you were his dearest friend, and I appreciate your generosity in this matter, but as you can see, sir, I am perfectly capable of taking care of myself and Andrew. I think Father often thought of us as much younger than we actually are and so made provisions that we obviously do not need. With the wealth Father accumulated on his voyages, Andrew and I can continue to live here quite comfortably. Eventually, I will marry, and Andrew will stay on in this house. So you see, Captain Brentwood, I appreciate your willingness to care for us, but it is unnecessary."

She took a deep breath. Would it work? She wanted to squeeze her eyes shut and cross her fingers for good luck. Instead, she maintained her composure though it took all of her strength.

Jonathon continued to look at her with that amused expression. He took another drink of his brandy and, putting down his empty glass he eyed hers and looked at her inquiringly. Emily lifted her glass to her lips and sipped again. It seared her throat and brought tears to her eyes once more. She could not speak for a moment, and when she finally took a breath, the fire returned. She cleared her throat and felt warmth infuse her. Her cheeks felt flushed and her breath came in short gasps. Finally, she spoke.

"Well, Captain Brentwood, do you not agree that this is a simple solution for all of us?" The room seemed very warm.

"Miss Wentworth, I can see that you are a very sensible, as well as capable, young woman . . ."

Emily's spirits soared.

". . . and you are correct when you say that your father thought of you as younger. Why, he would call you 'Little Em' and tell me of how you sat in his lap and begged for stories. Or how you would tease the cook into an extra helping of dessert, and how, on a hot summer's day, you would totter across the lawn with just your . . . ah, well, suffice it to say I was expecting someone much younger."

Emily was blushing furiously at his last reference to her childhood. She avoided his gaze. She had to convince this man that she was mature and responsible enough to be on her own. Goodness, the room felt warm, and it seemed to be tilting a bit. Not thinking, Emily reached for the last of her brandy. Again her throat burned as the fiery liquid made its way down. Finally, she spoke.

"Well, as you can see, Captain, Father was mistaken. I am quite capable of looking after Andrew and myself."

"Yes, I can see that. In fact, you are quite a lovely young woman." Jonathon leaned back against the settee, casually resting one arm behind Emily. He saw through her charade and could not help teasing her for she was so serious. "I imagine you have captured the hearts of all the young men in London. How many suitors have lined up at the door asking for your hand and whispered their undying love in your delicate ear, promising ever to be true?" He had leaned forward and his breath touched her hair, his eyes held hers. His voice was soft and silken as his arm encircled her shoulders. Emily sat gazing at his warm, brown eyes, captivated. The room was warm, and the firelight flickered on their faces.

Suddenly Emily caught herself and sprang from the settee, her head swimming, desperately needing some air.

"It is a beautiful evening, Captain Brentwood. Shall we step out onto the terrace?" she asked trying to steady her trembling. It did not help that the room seemed to be moving, too.

The half-moon perched on a treetop, and the stars sprinkled across the ebony sky. They walked silently out to the garden, the smoky smell of well-stoked fires filling the crisp air. Emily felt a little steadier. They sat on a bench beneath a tall oak.

"May I speak frankly, Captain?"

"By all means, Miss Wentworth," Jonathon smiled.

"I do not want to go to Virginia with you any more than you want to be burdened with me. I fully intend to stay here with my brother. Father's intentions were good, but he was wrong to do this to either of us, and I believe you see the sense in this, too." Emily folded her hands in her lap as if to end the discussion.

"Miss Wentworth, may I also speak frankly?"

"Of course," Emily nodded.

"In the carriage on the way over here, I would have given anything to be rid of this responsibility. But now, having met you, Miss Wentworth, I am not so sure I want to be relieved of my duty. I was expecting a young child. Instead, I find a beautiful young woman who has made it perfectly clear that she does not need me. Yet I find that this is just what I want—for her to need me." Emily could feel her embarrassed blush start at his words. "No, I do not think I will be remiss in my duty. In fact, I am sworn to my promise even more having met you. How can I desert this fair damsel in distress? Why, it is my opportunity to be a knight in shining armor come to rescue a fair maiden." He leaned forward taking her hand. "Is it possible, my lady, that out of many I might claim your heart?" His voice was low; his eyes sparkled. "Oh, but one kiss from your sweet, gentle lips to carry with me forever would be so kind."

Emily felt a new rush of warmth course through her that had nothing to do with the brandy. She knew he was teasing her, yet she tingled with excitement. Just the thought of his soft lips against hers, being held in his strong arms . . . what was she thinking? She stood quickly.

"I fear you mock me, sir, when all I desire is to settle our lives so we can each go our separate ways. Please just agree with me that this solution would be best and we shall be finished with it."

"I do not mock you, Emily," Jonathon spoke softly, "but even if I wanted to, which I do not, I could not agree to your plan."

"Why ever not?" she cried near tears.

"Because your father's will states that I hold everything in trust for you until you marry. Or, if you do not marry, until you reach age twenty-one. I am afraid you cannot be on your own until such time."

Emily's face went white. Tears welled in her eyes, and she turned quickly so he could not see them. It would not do to cry. Not here, not now. Her mind raced. She would be packed off to the colonies, and she was helpless to stop it. What could she do?

"Then I shall marry." She had not realized that she had spoken aloud. Michael Dennings had called quite frequently lately. She was sure he would propose soon. Of course, now he would have to wait until Emily was out of mourning. "That is what I shall do."

Jonathon cleared his throat. "There is one more thing. I must approve the marriage."

"You what?" she shouted. "Do you think, sir, to take my father's place? How dare you come here and tell me what I can and cannot do? Whom I may or may not marry? Who gives you the right?" She shook with rage. Her upswept hair was coming loose; tendrils tumbled and framed her face and shuddered with her anger.

"Your father, Emily."

Emily stared at him, her mouth half open.

"Father?"

"Yes, it is in his will also. Your father loved you very much, Emily. He made it very clear that I was to watch over you and Andrew. You both were so dear to him. I promised that I would take the best possible care of you. George was one of my closest friends; my promise to him means a great deal to me," he said gently.

The loneliness Emily had felt for the past month flooded over her again. Tears stung her eyes and a dull ache settled in the pit of her stomach.

"Excuse me, Captain Brentwood, I am not feeling well. Good night." She swept past him. Jonathon heard her choke back a sob as she ran back in through the terrace doors. He stood there for a moment staring after her, confused. What should he do with this woman-child?

*

Emily peered thoughtfully over her teacup at Michael Dennings as he spoke to her. Many of the matrons in the social circles had already paired them and awaited an impending engagement this season. Michael's sandy-colored hair matched his eyes. Emily had never noticed his eyes before, and if someone had asked her their color, she would have been at a loss to answer. She did remember, however, the soft brown eyes that had warmly perused her during Captain Brentwood's visit.

She must stop comparing them. But she knew that would be difficult, for that was all she had done since Michael had arrived for tea. Of average height, he was shorter than Captain Brentwood, and not nearly so broad in the shoulders. He wore a tan longcoat over a tan vest and matching breeches. So close were they to the color of his hair and eyes that Michael just seemed to run together, nothing distinctive, and a passing stranger would take no notice of him.

Emily had known Michael for years, and, though he was amiable enough, rack her brain as she would, she could not think of a single extraordinary thing he had ever said or done. That was Michael, ordinary and predictable, but a good, safe husband who could keep her in England. And that, thought Emily, is what I need to make him see.

"Do you not agree, Emily?" Michael repeated.

"What? I am sorry, Michael, what did you say?" Emily smiled prettily, and Michael was appeased.

"I said it is dreadful what is occurring in the colonies. Why, they are close to open rebellion!" he answered.

"And I am sailing right into it," Emily murmured.

"I do not like the thought of your traveling over there, Emily. In fact, Mother and I were discussing it just last night. She said it is not proper for a girl of your delicacy and upbringing to be thrust into a savage land. She said it is scandalous for a genteel young lady to go off across the ocean, unescorted, with some sea captain. She said it is a shame you have not been betrothed by now, and if you were not so opinionated, that is ... "

Emily ignored the last remark. She had heard it whispered before. She was more educated than was usual for a young lady of her station; consequently, no man wanted a wife who might have ideas and opinions of her own—not to mention a wife who might be smarter than her husband. She attributed this gossip to jealous girls whose mothers would not allow their education to progress any further than French knots and curtsies.

"Michael, Captain Brentwood is my guardian, so I am properly escorted. Andrew will be with me also. And the colonies are not a savage land anymore. Why, there are large towns such as Boston and Philadelphia, and ships arrive from England frequently. I will not be shut off from the world in some remote and distant land."

What was she saying? This was not at all what she had planned. Why did she suddenly feel defensive about a land she had no desire to see?

"Well, as far as Captain Brentwood is concerned, Mother says he has a reputation with women. She says that having you on his ship is as good as . . ."

"Captain Brentwood has been a perfect gentleman in my presence," Emily snapped. Her cheeks flushed as she recalled his silken voice in the garden and the feel of his strong, firm arm around her shoulders. Michael misread her blush for anger, which was partly true.

"Do not be angry, Emily. I just do not want to see your reputation sullied."

"It is good of you to be so concerned," she retorted.

What was wrong with her? She was ruining her opportunity to stay in England. Yet, as she studied Michael, doubt slowly spread through her. She imagined passing the years as his wife. It would be safe and comfortable, but certainly not exciting. They would live in London and have children. And Mother Dennings would visit on Sundays and expound on her pet theories. Or worse, perhaps she would live *with* them and subject them to daily sermons. And the years would run together, much as Michael's appearance.

Michael had been speaking again, and his last sentence brought Emily back with a start.

"Emily, will you do me the honor of becoming my wife?" He was on one knee in front of her.

"Am I interrupting anything?" Jonathon's clear baritone rang through the room causing Michael to jump to his feet, and startling Emily as much as Michael's proposal had.

"Captain Brentwood," Emily breathed feeling strangely relieved, "do come in."

Michael shot Emily a bemused look. Jonathon strode in and seated himself on the settee beside her. His eyes sparkled when he looked at her, and he took her hand in his own and patted it in a fatherly gesture. She slipped it away.

"Captain Brentwood, may I present Michael Dennings. Michael, this is Captain Jonathon Brentwood." Emily glanced at Michael noting his sour expression. Jonathon extended his hand, which Michael reluctantly shook. The two men sized each other up.

"Well, Captain Brentwood, when do you plan to set sail for Virginia?" Michael finally asked.

"I have some legal matters to which I must attend, and some supplies to order and load. I imagine *we* shall set sail in a fortnight," he stressed the word "we" while looking at Emily. Unable to meet the gaze of either man, she looked down at her hands folded in her lap.

Michael shifted uncomfortably wondering why Emily had invited Captain Brentwood in at such an inopportune moment.

"I imagine you are anxious to get home to see your family and . . . uh . . . dear ones." Michael emphasized the latter cynically.

Jonathon leaned back casually stretching long, lean legs out in front of him.

"Yes, I am anxious to see my sister and her husband. As for the rest of my family, they will be with me on the ship."

Michael glowered at him.

"I think not, Captain Brentwood. I have just asked Emily for her hand in marriage. She will remain in England, where she belongs." He breathed the last decisively.

"No, Michael," Emily whispered. If she had shouted it, the impact could not have been greater. Michael's head whipped sharply back to her; his mouth gaped open. Jonathon searched her eyes. "You are a dear friend, Michael," she continued, "but it would be wrong for both of us if we were to marry."

Michael rose in bewilderment. He looked from one to the other.

"You are responsible for this," he shouted at Jonathon's composed face. He turned to her, "Emily, please reconsider."

"No, Michael. I am sorry," she spoke gently.

Michael shot a baleful glare at Jonathon, then turned on his heel and left. Jonathon looked down at Emily, but she could not meet his gaze. Her head was whirling with the events of the last few minutes. Michael had offered her exactly what she wanted, a chance to remain in England, but she knew it was not right for her. The idea of sailing into an unknown life with the man seated next to her was, somehow, appealing.

"It is just as well," Jonathon teased. "I would not have approved the engagement in any event."

"You arrogant cad," Emily seethed. "How dare you assume what you can and cannot do concerning any matters in my personal life?"

"But you forget, Emily, I am your guardian. Your safety, your health, your happiness are all a precious burden that I will happily carry."

"Who do you think you are that you can presume so much? My happiness will never be dependent on you! I think it is best that you leave at once!"

"Oh, I cannot leave, Em. I am staying for supper."

"You are what? How—?"

"Andrew invited me. He, at least, has some manners." He hid a smile.

"And I do not, I suppose?" Emily rose from the settee placing a hand on each hip. Her blue eyes had darkened to violet with her anger, and a blush heightened in her cheeks. Her jaw was set, and her full soft lips clamped into a firm line.

Jonathon replied easily, "Well, he did have the courtesy to ask a new member of the family to supper. After all, if we are to spend weeks together in the close quarters of a ship, I would deem it necessary to become better acquainted. I am sure that by the end of the voyage we shall know each other *very* well," he smiled wickedly. "But things will go much more smoothly en route if we develop a closer relationship now."

"I have no intention of developing anything with you, Captain Brentwood. And as for the family, I consider all of this to be a totally unnecessary, legalistic mix-up and nothing more. If I never get to know you better, it will be fine with me. Mrs. Dennings was right; you are a rake. Why, you probably have a woman in every harbor. I should have accepted Michael's proposal. He knows how to treat a lady with decency and respect."

"And now you are without the benefit of Mother Dennings' exhortations, too. You've told me of her strong opinions and disdain for anything not of England. Oh, I can picture all of you gathered 'round the cozy hearth listening to her prattle on about the immorality of the savage colonies and their provincialism," he laughed. "No, Em. No such life for you. You have too much spirit, too much drive for what Michael Dennings and his mother could offer."

Emily was startled at how his remarks mirrored her thoughts of just minutes earlier. Could he read her mind?

"And I suppose you could offer so much more? Tell me, sir, would traipsing off to some backward land with you be so much better? Will you then find me a suitable mate who will offer me all I deserve? Hah! You will probably deny me any suitable young gentleman who is courteous and kind. You will keep me a spinster. To what end, sir? What game do you play?" She had paced across the room during her tirade, unaware of admiring eyes that followed her graceful gait.

"Aye, Em, I could offer you more than your Mr. Dennings. I could show you places of such beauty and wonder as to take your breath away. Mountains that soar up and kiss the floor of heaven. Lush forests that stretch as far as the eye can see, full of trees so big that two men with arms outstretched would be hard pressed to span the diameter and touch their fingertips end to end. Our 'backward' land, as you call it, has cities with shops to rival London's. What is more, we judge a man, not by what his ancestors were, but by what he can wrest out of life and shape into his own. A man can build his worth from nothing; he can become wealthy, influential, anything he wants, on his own merit, not someone else's. It is a rich land, Em, full of promise for people with spirit. People like you and Andrew who draw strength from an inner reserve. Come with me because you *want* to, Em. See for yourself what Virginia is like. I believe one day you will love it as I do." Jonathon's eyes were shining as he spoke passionately of his land. Emily felt sudden warmth for him. But he was asking so much.

"I cannot say that I *want* to go, Captain Brentwood, but I have no choice in any event," Emily sighed.

Jonathon saw the confusion in her eyes. She seemed to look deeply into the realm of possibilities before her, and complicating it all was the still-fresh grief for her father. He began to realize his own growing hope that she would indeed *want* to go with him. He understood her pain and the enormity of her decision, for he knew it must be her decision. He tried to lighten her mood.

"Emily, must you be so formal? Please call me Jonathon."

Andrew burst into the room. "I have been down to the wharves, Jonathon. Everything is progressing smoothly. What a beautiful ship the *Destiny* is! Mr. Gates sends word that the mizzenmast is repaired and we should sail on schedule," his eyes danced with excitement.

Jonathon grimaced. They had run into a pirate ship far north of the Barbary Coast, and the *Destiny* had sustained considerable damage. But the pirate ship had suffered her wrath and limped off the worse for wear. Jonathon would have pursued her had he not been on his way to England at the behest of George Wentworth's will. He hoped their crossing to Virginia would be without incident.

"That is good news, Andrew," he replied.

Emily noticed his concern. "Did you encounter trouble, Captain?"

"Nothing we could not handle," he grinned.

Supper was announced, and Jonathon offered his arm to Emily. She could think of no reason to refuse without appearing rude, so she tucked her hand through the crook of his arm. She felt the firm muscles of his forearm through the fabric of his sleeve. She glanced sideways at his strong profile with its aquiline nose and square jaw. He caught her glance and winked at her. She quickly looked away. Why did he disturb her so?

Discussion at the table was lively with Andrew firing a myriad of questions at Jonathon about Virginia. His excitement was apparent, and he was anxious to set sail. Jonathon answered his questions patiently, laughing at his enthusiasm.

"I wish your sister was as eager about this voyage as you are," he laughed gently, glancing at Emily. She had enjoyed listening to his tales of the colonies, but had remained silent for the most part. Now she raised her eyebrows at Jonathon.

"Captain Brentwood, I am leaving everything I know and love. Allow me my reluctance, sir."

"But, Emily, have you not been listening to Jonathon? It sounds like paradise over in Virginia. Can we set sail earlier?" Andrew's eyes shone.

"No, Andrew," Jonathon laughed, "I need time to ready my ship. And to convince your sister that she really *does* want to come."

"You have a difficult task ahead of you, Captain Brentwood," she replied. Andrew chuckled at her proper form of address.

*

Emily watched in the mirror as Mary brushed out her hair. She had to admit that the evening had passed pleasantly enough in Captain Brentwood's company. He had piqued her curiosity with the tales of his homeland. And he was even more handsome, if possible, when he was caught up in stories about Virginia as his eyes sparkled and his smile showed straight, white teeth against skin bronzed by the sun and the sea.

Emily climbed between the lavender-scented sheets and closed her eyes. It had been a trying day. Michael's proposal had been her goal on rising this morning, but the day had not gone at all as she had planned. None of her plans were working out lately. It was as if someone were interfering with her destiny . . . *Destiny.* She slipped off to sleep.

*

Jonathon had stopped off at the Golden Pheasant Inn and sat in the corner table of the common room drinking his ale. He needed time to think before returning to his ship. It had been an enjoyable evening. Andrew was an enthusiastic as well as knowledgeable boy. George Wentworth had hoped Andrew would follow in his footsteps when his education was completed. He was already well versed in the ways of sailing, and seemed to have the natural talent of his father.

Emily was an enigma. She vocalized clearly her reluctance to sail to America, yet her eyes had glowed as she listened to his stories, leaning forward, chin resting in her hand, concentrating on every word, then catching herself, sitting up primly, feigning indifference. He caught her lost in thought once and wondered if she were reconsidering Michael Denning's proposal. He thought not. Searching her eyes today he had seen only firm resolution. No, Michael Dennings was not the man for Emily Wentworth.

"'Scuse me, Captain Brentwood, can I git ya another ale?" A plump, pretty girl was smiling down at him. Millie leaned forward to take his empty tankard revealing much of her ample bosom. "Can I git ya anything else, Love?" she asked invitingly. Jonathon had been at sea a long time, and normally this invitation might not have been unwelcome. But his mind was preoccupied with his new station in life — that of a guardian.

"Not tonight, Millie," he replied. He watched the girl turn and sway her hips provocatively, no doubt in the hopes he would change his mind.

Jonathon rose and went out into the night. Settling George's estate and readying the ship for departure were enough to busy a man. But the problem of what to do with Emily taxed his mind the most.

Chapter 2

Emily pressed back into the deep, blue velvet cushioned seat of the coach. Her throat ached with tightness as she fought off another spell of sobbing and recalled the events of the morning.

Saying good-bye to the loyal household servants she had known all of her life had been difficult enough, but as she turned to Etta, she had broken down uncontrollably. Etta had been like a second mother to her. Ever since her mother's death, Emily had turned to her beloved housekeeper for advice, consolation and care. So many people were being snatched from her life, but Etta was the dearest next to her brother and father, now gone. She had clung to Etta while the older woman stroked her hair.

"There, there, darlin'. It will all work out for the best." Tears streamed down Etta's face, too. She had no say in this matter, and she had to trust that George Wentworth had only the best in mind for his precious children. She instinctively liked Captain Brentwood and was not blind to the effect he had on Emily. In any event, she was powerless to prevent Emily and Andrew from being taken to the colonies. She loved them like her own, and her heart was breaking just as Emily's was. But she had been instructed to stay in England and care for the Wentworths' house and staff. She hugged Emily to herself for the last time.

"This is not good-bye forever, missy. We will be together again," Etta whispered as she pressed her lips against Emily's hair and then let her go.

"Good-bye, Etta," the girl choked out before she ran to the waiting coach. Andrew followed her out, also visibly moved by the farewells. He climbed in across from her. Neither spoke as the driver climbed into his high seat rocking the carriage as his weight shifted. Andrew glanced at Emily and, as one, their heads turned for a last look at the only home they had ever known. The driver slapped the reins and the coach crawled down the road.

A misty drizzle shrouded the silent carriage, and leaden clouds hung low in the gray sky. Puddles parted before the lumbering wheels, and then flowed back together after the coach passed, unmindful of the disturbance. The streets were empty on this early morning, the scene matching the somber mood of the lovely girl who stared, unseeing, at the dismal town.

A contrasting energy pervaded the atmosphere at the waterfront. Men scurried about loading cargo, yelling orders, climbing up and down the gangplank, the rigging and the decks as they readied the ship and made last-minute preparations for the journey.

Emily gazed out at the ship that would take her away from everything she knew, her secure, familiar world. The *Destiny*, a three-masted merchant ship, carried twelve guns. Windows lined the raised quarterdeck and the bowsprit sloped gracefully up from the forecastle. Fully loaded with cargo and provisions, she sat low in the water. Emily was impressed with the ship's beauty and the efficiency of her crew, but she felt detached from it all, like an observer who would be totally unaffected by what was happening.

She noticed a familiar coach waiting by the gangplank, Michael Dennings' coach. She leaned back and closed her eyes, drained, unable to face him. Her coach halted a few steps away and rocked as the driver descended. He opened the door and pulled down the steps to allow them to alight from the carriage. Michael was there at once offering his hand up to Emily, a look of grim determination on his face. Emily sighed, took his hand, and descended. He looked down at her.

"Emily, I must protest. You cannot board that ship."

"Can I not, Michael?" she asked, feeling defeated and very tired.

"No! I insist that you come back with me right now. I repeat my offer of marriage. This is terribly wrong, and you know it."

Emily caught a movement above Michael's shoulder and, looking up, saw Jonathon leaning on the ship's rail. Dressed in a deep green coat, crisp white cravat and tan breeches, he looked the part of a sea captain—at ease on the ship, yet obviously in command. His thick hair was tousled in the wind that swept across the water. She saw white teeth flash in a smile at her, and she could not deny the fluttering sensation in her stomach or the sudden weakness in her knees. Nonetheless, she raised her chin and affected an air of indifference. A strange excitement tickled within her as she sensed her resistance to this voyage waning.

She looked at Michael. "Perhaps this is not as wrong for me as you might think, Michael. I would not be a wife content to live under the domineering rule of your mother. We would both suffer were we to wed, for you would find me rebellious and strong-willed," she paused glancing up at the still-smiling Jonathon, "much as the colonies to which I sail. Perhaps I am better suited to them than to London. You will always be my dear friend. Good-bye, Michael." Rising on her toes, she placed a kiss on his cheek. Head held high, she turned and climbed the gangplank.

"Emily, please—" Michael called after her, but she did not turn back. She heard the coach door slam and the wheels start down the cobbled street. She continued up to the ship. She had burned her bridges and was on her way to a new world.

*

Jonathon approached spreading his arms wide. "Welcome aboard the *Destiny*, Em," he grinned. "Your beauty does her great honor."

Emily shot him a scathing look. "I hope she is a swift vessel for I want to be away quickly," she said coolly.

"Swift she is, my lady, and sound. We shall have a pleasant voyage made more so by your presence," he bowed, smiling broadly. Though she knew that he was teasing her, Emily felt pleased, and strangely warmed by his words.

She brushed past him with a derisive laugh. "Spare me your false flattery, Captain Brentwood." She walked along the deck noting that the ship was well tended. Oiled wood gleamed and neatly coiled ropes lay along the deck. Sailors who passed touched their caps and smiled a welcome, but none lingered, for they knew their tasks and went about them. As she passed, though, many paused a moment to take note of her. Andrew had followed her aboard and was greeting Jonathon. As the two looked across the deck where Emily strolled, Jonathon clapped Andrew on the shoulder.

"Do not worry, Drew; she will overcome her disinclination to depart. Much as she wants us to believe her reluctance, she would die of boredom with Michael Dennings. Note her eyes; you may catch a glimpse of anticipation. Now, shall we get to work?"

Andrew smiled up at the Captain. "Aye, sir."

With the last of the provisions loaded, the crew hastened to raise anchor and set sail. Though each man had his own duties, they worked in a rhythm that mimicked a well-trained militia. One by one the sails were raised as men climbed rigging, set ropes and made ready. Slowly the *Destiny* began to glide through the water. Emily watched as everything familiar to her faded in the distance. The rain had ceased, but the air was heavy with moisture. The mist surrounded Emily and joined the salty tears on her cheeks. Her throat ached with sobs to which she would not yield. A heaviness lay on her chest crushing her with the weight of her own sorrow. Quickly brushing the tears away, she squared her shoulders and set her jaw. She would face this new life challenge with courage and dignity. She became aware of the activity around her.

Men hurried about climbing the masts, working the rigging, and setting the proper sails. Emily turned, searching for her brother. At first, she did not recognize him as he had changed from his breeches and longcoat to loose pants and a heavy woolen shirt conducive to tending a ship. She almost passed him thinking he was one of the crew.

"Andrew?" she gasped.

"How do I look, Em?" He laughed.

"Whatever are you doing dressed like that?"

"Jonathon said I could join his crew. By the time we reach Virginia, I shall be a seasoned sailor." He puffed out his chest proudly.

"Where is Captain Brentwood?"

"May I be of some assistance, Miss Wentworth?" A tall, lean man approached. His gray hair curled about the nape of his neck, and a beard of the same color lent him a distinguished look. "I am Mr. Gates, second in command."

"I am looking for Captain Brentwood," she answered. "Would you please take me to him?"

"Of course." He gestured toward the quarterdeck, and Emily followed him there. They reached the door of the Captain's cabin; Mr. Gates rapped loudly. Jonathon bade them enter, and after doing so they stood and waited for him to finish writing and look up.

"Captain, Miss Wentworth asked to see you," Mr. Gates informed him.

As Jonathon rose, a crooked smile crossed his face. "Mr. Gates, Miss Wentworth is always welcome in my quarters." He eyed her from head to toe causing Emily to blush profusely. Mr. Gates cleared his throat strangling a chuckle.

"Aye, Captain," he said, looking at Jonathon expectantly.

"Thank you, Mr. Gates. That will be all." The door closed quietly.

Although small, the room was handsomely furnished. A large mahogany desk covered with charts and ledgers commanded one corner lit by windows that lined the wall behind it. The dreariness of the day was chased out with cozy lanterns. A single bed fit snugly against one bulkhead and precious space had been made at its head for numerous books. An ornately decorated sea chest and a small armoire held Jonathon's personal things, and a table and two chairs completed the furnishings. All were polished to a high sheen, and the room was invitingly neat and clean.

"Will you join me in a brandy? I know your penchant for the drink," Jonathon grinned wickedly.

Emily glared at him, painfully reminded of her inability to manage that libation on their first meeting.

"No, thank you, Captain. I have come to talk about Andrew. He tells me that you have allowed him to join the crew. I must protest for he is too young to be climbing around working a ship. I fear for his safety."

"He is a good sailor. He has been working the ship since I put in to port. Let him be, Em. Your father would have brought him along on his next voyage, in any case."

"Please, Captain Brentwood, I have lost everyone who is dear to me save Andrew. If anything should happen to him, I do not know what I would do. Please do not allow him to do anything dangerous."

"For a sea captain's daughter, you are a mite skittish," he mocked.

"The sea claimed my father, Captain," she replied. Jonathon looked into her eyes for a long moment.

"All right, Em. I shall make sure he is careful."

Emily nodded her thanks and swept out of the room. Jonathon tossed down his brandy. It was going to be a long voyage.

*

The drizzle lasted into the next week. When the sun broke through one afternoon, Emily realized that her spirits lifted as well. The fresh, salty air was invigorating and she enjoyed feeling its full effects as she strolled along the deck. The gentle creaking of the wood and rigging became a comforting sound, and she quickly acclimated her step to the rolling of the ship. She had often visited her father's vessel, the *Spirit*, when it was in port, and being on the *Destiny* brought memories of happier times vividly to her mind. Instead of making her melancholy, however, these memories helped Emily to feel more at home.

She walked along the deck watching the steady motion of the sea. The sun was descending in the western sky, painting the horizon with a soft, rosy glow.

"It will be a fair day tomorrow." Mr. Gates was at her elbow. "Sometimes, Miss Wentworth, we need only watch the signs to know if we sail to fair or foul," he smiled at her.

"What if you do not know what the signs are, Mr. Gates? What if you have never been to sea before?" she asked, wondering at his meaning.

"Then you must trust your instinct. You must reach deep inside for your answer. But many times we refuse to listen, even to ourselves and what we know to be true," he replied.

"Perhaps we learn as we go along, Mr. Gates."

"Perhaps, Miss Wentworth." He tipped his cap and moved on. Emily stared after him, slightly disturbed, but unable to put her finger on the reason.

She walked slowly to her cabin, reluctant to go below. But she had not much time to freshen up for supper. She, Andrew and Mr. Gates joined Jonathon in his cabin for the evening meal. Although close quarters, the conviviality of the men made the meals enjoyable and Emily found she looked forward to these times.

Her cabin was smaller than Jonathon's and the space was again used as economically as possible. A bunk tucked into one bulkhead, and a small armoire, table and chair took another. Darkening windows gave evidence of the setting sun so Emily lit the lantern above the table. She chose a muslin gown of deep burgundy, having saved her finer dresses for her arrival in Virginia. This dress had a square neckline edged in ivory lace. The tight fitting bodice flattered her slender waist and shapely bosom. She brushed her hair until it shone in the lantern light and tied it back with a burgundy ribbon. Wisps of her honey-colored hair escaped the ribbon and settled about her face, try as she did to capture and hold them back. Sighing, she gave up the effort, unaware of the softness they lent to her loveliness.

A tap sounded on the door. "Em, may I come in?"

She opened the door and Andrew stepped in. Emily gasped as she was struck by his rugged good looks. He wore light blue breeches and a royal blue coat over a spotless white shirt. His face was tanned and his hair bleached by the sun. He flashed a white smile and bowed low.

"May I escort you to supper, my lady?" His eyes danced as he straightened and offered her his arm.

"Thank you, kind sir," she answered, her lilting laughter filling the cabin. She slipped her arm through his, and they walked the short distance to Jonathon's cabin.

*

Jonathon and Mr. Gates rose simultaneously and almost collided as each reached to hold Emily's chair. Mr. Gates deferred and Jonathon took Emily's arm and seated her. The meal passed quickly with good conversation. Emily enjoyed Mr. Gates's yarns, although she suspected he embellished them. Many of his stories were sprinkled with the heroic deeds of Jonathon, who seemed uncomfortable when these were mentioned. He deftly steered the conversation away from himself and gave Mr. Gates a disparaging look. Andrew began to stifle yawns until Jonathon finally ordered him to bed.

"A sailor's day starts early, Andrew. You had better get some rest or you will be of no use to me," Jonathon gently chided.

"If you will excuse me, Captain, I will also retire," Mr. Gates said.

"Of course, Mr. Gates. Good night to you both." He turned to Emily, "May I interest you in a stroll before you retire, Emily?"

"Thank you, Captain Brentwood. That would be fine."

As agreeable as supper had been in Jonathon's cabin, the night was exquisite and Emily was happy to be out on deck. Stars were splashed across the sky like diamonds across black velvet, and a gentle breeze came from the southwest. Emily took a deep breath and let it out slowly.

"I love the sea," she said as they walked along.

"You are your father's daughter," Jonathon laughed.

"How did you meet my father?"

"George and I had seen each other many times in many ports. Our paths seemed destined to cross," Jonathon mused. "I came across the *Spirit* being set upon by two pirate ships. They were either side of her, and she was hard-pressed to defend herself, let alone attack. We had the element of surprise on our side, and, together with the *Spirit*, we sank both pirate ships. Your father was seriously injured and the *Spirit* badly in need of repair. We brought George aboard the *Destiny* and Mr. Gates, a man of many talents, doctored him. Your father then rested with us while the *Spirit* was in port for repairs. We had long nights of discussion finding many similar likes and convictions. I admired your father a great deal, Emily. From then on when we met ashore, we made a point of continuing our friendship. He spoke of you and Andrew at length; he was very proud of you both, although he admitted that you could be a 'spirited vixen'," he laughed softly.

Emily lifted her chin and looked away. "I thank you for helping him, Captain. He never spoke of the incident. We owe you a great deal it would seem, and all you get for your kindness is another burden." She leaned against the rail and looked out at the sea. Emily did not like this feeling of indebtedness and wished somehow that she could free herself from the bond that tied her to this man. George Wentworth had prided himself on being a self-made man, answerable to no one. He had stressed the importance of independence to both of his children. Now, helpless to free herself of this shackle, she began to see how important that feeling of independence was.

Jonathon stood next to her leaning sideways against the rail, studying her profile. "You owe me nothing, Emily, but I would ask one favor."

She stared ahead. What would he ask? Legally he held everything of hers, her property, and any wealth she might have inherited. What else was there for her to give? Suddenly Mrs. Dennings's disapproving face loomed in her mind, and her cheeks took on a reddish hue. Angrily she turned to him.

"Just what do you propose, sir?" she asked indignantly. "You see, I own very little with which to bargain. You hold everything material I have."

Realizing her train of thought, Jonathon's gaze started at her face and lazily ran the full length of her. Emily pulled her cape closer, feeling as if he had seen through every article of clothing she was wearing.

"You think me a rake, Miss Wentworth," he stated. "What you value so highly is not to what I refer." His eyes sparkled with mirth.

"Oh!" she snapped, her eyes blazing. She turned back to the railing, her lips set in a tight line.

"No, Emily, the favor I ask is this—that you give Virginia a chance. Look at her with an open heart; she is beautiful, Em. She is wild and spirited. Give her a chance."

The breeze teased the curls around Emily's face and her blue eyes searched Jonathon's.

"That is what you would ask of me?" she whispered.

Jonathon was caught with her beauty. No, she was not George Wentworth's "Little Em" anymore. She was fast becoming that mature, independent woman she had hoped would rescue her from this situation. He had best watch himself or she might convince him, too. The tender look on her face tempted him sorely and her soft, full lips, parted in question, begged to be kissed. The feelings she was beginning to stir in him made Jonathon uneasy.

"That is all for now, Miss Wentworth," he leered roguishly, breaking the spell.

"You are insufferable," she retorted and turning, walked quickly to her cabin. The sound of his laughter floated behind her on the breeze.

*

The weeks passed smoothly with continued good winds and fair weather. Jonathon was finding it more and more difficult to be around Emily in such close proximity without being affected by her beauty. The sun had lightened her hair to a golden radiance, and, though she was careful to shade it, her complexion was imbued with a healthy, tanned glow. She had adjusted her gait to the motion of the ship, but it did not hide the lithe grace with which she moved. Jonathon was not the only man on board who paused in his labors to watch her progress along the deck. But the men were respectful to her and tried to make her voyage as comfortable and amiable as possible, many entertaining her with stories and pleasantries just for the reward of her dimpled smile. One evening when it rained lightly, the crew tripped over each other setting out buckets to catch the rainwater for her bath. Jonathon good-naturedly watched his men do this, but there was an unspoken law that no man would cross the line to questionable behavior.

Jonathon puzzled over his role as Emily's guardian. What she had said that first night he had met her was true—she was a woman, not a child. Yet, there was an innocence about her that wanted protecting. He was aware of a growing feeling of attachment to both Andrew and Emily. The promise he had made to George was sacred to him, and he would see it through as best he could, in spite of Emily's protests.

Emily's awareness of Jonathon was no less marked. She covertly watched him from behind lowered lashes as he stood at the helm directing the men, who would snap into action at a word. Though the crew was well trained, there was a pride each man held in his own worth that Jonathon had helped to instill. They were a loyal crew, he a demanding yet fair captain.

He was not above throwing himself into a task if needed, and Emily watched him once when the wind shifted suddenly requiring swift action. He stripped to his breeches and sprang in with the others to get the ship on an even keel. His broad chest was matted with thick, curly hair, and the muscles in his arms and back rippled with strength as he adjusted the rigging. His long, solid legs stood firm as he braced them against the deck. The men around him scrambled to their tasks following his orders, and soon the *Destiny* was clipping along in full accord with the wind. Jonathon turned and, too late, Emily lowered her eyes. A devilish grin spread across his face as he sauntered toward her.

"Are you so enamored of me that I am not safe from your scrutiny?" he teased.

"Captain Brentwood, I was interested only in the working of your ship." She turned so that he could not see the rosy hue that diffused across her cheeks.

"I am disappointed. I thought it was I you were appraising. Is there any hope that one day I will favorably catch your eye, my lady? Dare I hope for an ardent look, a gentle touch, mayhap a stolen kiss from one such as lovely as she who tempts me from afar?" He leaned toward her and whispered, "Will I stand a chance against all those eligible young men in Virginia who will clamor about you for your slightest word, a glance from those eyes that challenge the beauty of the finest sapphire?"

Emily's cheeks darkened as he spoke and she tried to quell the pleasurable feeling his words evoked. His breath brushed her ear and sent shivers down her spine.

"Excuse me, Captain; it is becoming quite windy up here." Not turning to look at him, she hurried to her cabin.

*

Spring on the Atlantic sometimes brought extremes in the weather. Once the drizzle that bade them farewell from London had ceased, they were blessed with fair weather for two weeks. But as the third week began, clouds moved in and the sea took on a churning, surging disquiet. Everyone around Emily was caught up with securing the ship for what promised to be a severe storm.

Lightning flashed in the distant clouds, and the remote rumble of thunder caused urgency in movement among the crew. Jonathon hurried across the deck to Emily, a look of concern creasing his brow.

"You had best go below, Emily. It is dangerous to be about during a storm at sea," he said.

Emily felt anxious, but she did not want Jonathon to sense her fear.

"As you wish, Captain."

The tossing ship made it difficult for her to remain seated comfortably anywhere in her cabin. Her heart pounded, and she kept wiping the sweat from the palms of her hands as she awkwardly paced the length and breadth of her quarters. In spite of herself, Emily began to wonder what her father's thoughts and feelings were as his ship was beset by that fatal storm. She pictured him bravely giving orders, urging his men on, boosting their morale. She closed her eyes and ground her fists against them at the thought of him being swept into the sea. It was a vision she had been fighting for a month or more, and, try as she would to erase it, it haunted her waking and sleeping.

Fear gripped Emily and she decided to join Andrew in his cabin. She steadied herself along the walls as she made her way to his quarters, pausing when the ship lurched, then moving on. She knocked at his door and, getting no answer, rapped louder and called his name. Receiving no reply, she entered his room and proved her growing fear. He was not there. She spun about and ran toward the ladder. Clambering up it, she lost her balance when the *Destiny* dipped suddenly. She regained her footing and sped to the main deck.

Drenching rain combined with the waves that spilled over the sides of the ship and made the deck dangerously slippery. She searched for her brother, but rain-soaked men with dripping hair and clothes that clung to their bodies were everywhere. Lightning streaked across the murky sky as thunder deafened Emily's call. She quickly, but cautiously, explored the entire deck, jostling among the men, trying to keep her footing. Suddenly a firm grip encircled her arm and swung her around.

"You little fool! Did I not tell you to get below?" Jonathon yelled above the din. His sodden clothes clung to his lean form and his hair dripped down his face and neck.

"Where is Andrew?" she cried.

"Where he belongs, in his cabin," Jonathon bellowed.

"No, he is not! I was just there!" she wailed in dismay.

Jonathon cursed. "Get below. I will find him and order him down, too," he shouted and swiftly turned and left. Emily started for the quarterdeck but was stopped by a sudden loud crack. Looking up to where the sound came from, she screamed in horror. Andrew was high up the mizzenmast; it had just snapped and was tumbling toward the raging sea.

Everything seemed to happen slowly, as if in a dream, Emily's agonized scream hovering in the air before her. The mast seemed to drift downward, then caught for a moment, and it seemed Andrew would fall to the deck—a long fall, but at least safe from the angry ocean.

Emily ran forward, but it was as though she was caught in a nightmare. Her slippers lacked traction on the rain-soaked deck, and she made no headway. The slick wood made her feet slide from underneath her, and she fell with a thud that knocked her breath from her.

"Andrew!" she tried to scream, scrambling toward where he was falling. Then she watched in horror as the mast snapped completely, and the sea claimed Andrew.

Jonathon saw what had happened also, and stripping hastily, he kept his eyes on the spot where Andrew entered the water. Grabbing a sturdy rope, he tied it about his waist while some men secured the other end to a winch. Tucking a knife between his teeth, he dove into the roiling water and was lost beneath the waves.

Emily regained her footing and scrambled to her feet clutching the railing for support. She desperately scanned the ocean's surface. Soon, she caught sight of Jonathon's dark hair bobbing in the ocean close to where Andrew was struggling to stay afloat. Long, powerful strokes brought Jonathon to the boy quickly, but Andrew was caught in the rigging that stretched to the ship like an enormous, tangled spider's web. Jonathon deftly cut the ropes that bound Andrew, but in the process, sliced his own hand. He wrapped his arm about the youth who was weakening fast, and some of the men began to pull them toward the *Destiny*.

Shock and exertion overcame Andrew, and he lost consciousness. The icy water had cooled his body to a pale, deathly hue, and when they lifted him onto the deck, Emily was sure she had lost another loved one. Pain wrenched her heart and she felt as if her knees would buckle beneath her. Jonathon half climbed, half fell onto the deck and, weak and gasping, looked worriedly over at the boy.

Mr. Gates took charge ordering them both be taken below and cared for. He turned compassionately to the stricken girl whose limp hair hung dripping about her terrified face. Gently he wrapped his sodden cloak around her trembling shoulders and led her below.

*

Gates brought Emily into her cabin and urged her down on the chair.

"Get changed, child. You will need your strength to tend your brother."

Blue-violet eyes searched his for proof of his lie. Finding none, she whispered, "You mean, he is not dead?"

"Near death, perhaps, but he is strong and healthy and with proper care, he will pull through," he smiled. "But I shall need your help, Miss Wentworth. You must be strong for him," he echoed her father's words, then slipped from the cabin.

Emily sat dazed trying to comprehend that Andrew was alive. Shakily, she stripped off her wet clothes and, after toweling her hair, changed into a dry dress. The ship still rocked with the storm, but it seemed a little steadier now. The lightning and thunder were quieting their fearful tirade. Her strength reborn with the news of her brother, Emily hurried to his quarters.

Mr. Gates was there tending him, and Jonathon, still in his soaking breeches with a piece of cloth ripped from his shirt wrapped tightly around his hand to stanch the flow of blood, watched with concern. He did not notice Emily until she came to stand beside him to look down at Andrew. A deathly pallor suffused the boy's face and his breathing was shallow. Mr. Gates was checking his pulse and layers of blankets lay over his slender frame.

"His pulse is strengthening. He will need to be kept warm and given nourishment as soon as he is able to take it." He looked up at Emily. "He will recover with proper care and plenty of rest. But you, young lady, need a good stiff drink."

"Brandy is the lady's preference, Mr. Gates," Jonathon said as the other man went to the door.

"You!" Emily turned on him, her pent up fear looking for release. "This is all your fault. If you had not put it into his head that he was a sailor. You gave me your word that he would stay out of danger. Is this what your word is worth, Captain Brentwood?" she asked sweeping her hand toward the bunk.

"I kept my word, Miss Wentworth. I had ordered him below just as I did you. He had no business being up there, but I was too busy tending my ship to be playing nursemaid to two errant children!" he stormed.

"I am not a child!" Emily shouted furiously.

"As I recall, you were also wandering about on deck after I had given you orders to go below."

"I will not be ordered about by you, Captain Brentwood! I am not one of your sailors! And I am not a child!"

"While you are on my ship, Miss Wentworth, you will do as I say." He towered over her, and then overcome with weariness and weak from loss of blood from his injured hand, Jonathon began to sway dizzily. He reached a hand out to steady himself and, seeing his condition, Emily caught him with her shoulder beneath his arm to brace him. The contact of her soft bosom against his hard chest startled her, and looking up, she caught a mischievous gleam in his eye.

"No, you are no child, Emily," he grinned at her.

Mr. Gates coughed softly behind them, and then stepped forward to relieve Emily of her burden. She gratefully accepted the brandy he offered as she relinquished with equal gratitude the heavy form of the injured captain. Mr. Gates half carried him out of the cabin.

Emily's hand trembled as she raised the glass to her lips and took a long sip. The fiery liquid lent its usual warmth and she choked down the threatening coughs. Her mind whirled with confusion as she looked down at her brother. As worried as she was about him, she was also distressed at the emotions that tumbled within her as a result of her close contact with the dashing sea captain. She shook her head to banish those thoughts from her mind and, sitting beside Andrew, gently took his hand.

The rest of the day flew as Emily cared for her brother. Following Mr. Gates's orders, she kept him warm and, propping his head up on her arm, pressed warm broth to his lips. She forced herself to keep busy, concentrating on Andrew and his needs, so that further thoughts of Captain Brentwood would not seep into her mind.

*

By nightfall the storm had spent its rage and dwindled to a constant, steady rain. Thunder could still be heard in the distance, but it cast no threat toward the ship. Men had worked throughout the day to salvage and repair the mast.

Emily had stayed by Andrew's side throughout the afternoon, and at suppertime Mr. Gates arrived with a tray for her.

"I shall watch him for a while, child. You need to eat and rest," he said gently.

Emily's back ached and her eyes felt heavy, but she was reluctant to leave her brother. She took the tray and began to eat.

"Thank you, Mr. Gates; I did not realize how hungry I am. But I think I shall just stay here awhile. Andrew may awaken, and I would like to be here."

"You must rest, too, if you are to be of any help to Andrew, Miss Wentworth. You will not do him any good if you tire yourself out and have no strength. I shall inform you should he awaken during the night. Now go, child, and lie down," he urged.

Emily turned, and then hesitated. "How is Captain Brentwood?" The question had burned in her all day.

"He will recover. He needs rest, too. We shall watch his hand for putrefaction of the wound. I have some ointments aboard that should help, and if I can keep him down, which I doubt, he will have no trouble at all. I seem to have a couple of patients who resist my ministrations," he said sternly, a twinkle in his eyes betraying him.

Emily grinned. "All right, I shall rest now. But you promise to call me if Andrew awakens, Mr. Gates?"

"I promise, Miss Wentworth," he replied raising his right hand solemnly.

As Emily returned to her cabin, she passed Jonathon's quarters. Hearing movement inside, she impulsively knocked. Instantly she regretted her action. Hoping he had not heard, she turned to walk away, but the door opened and she turned back to look into amused brown eyes.

"I—" Raising her chin she met his gaze. "I wanted to thank you for saving my brother's life," she stated flatly.

"Madam, your sincerity overwhelms me," he replied. "However, if we are to continue this emotional exchange, may we do so within my cabin? I fear my strength is sorely sapped." He did indeed look pale and his mouth was set against any grimace of pain. Emily regretted her brusqueness realizing he was injured and weak because of his rescue of her brother. He stood aside sweeping an arm in invitation. Eyeing him warily, Emily hesitated.

"Do you fear me, Miss Wentworth, even in my weakened condition?" he teased.

"I fear no one, Captain Brentwood!" And tossing her head, she stepped past him into the room. Closing the door behind him, Jonathon followed her. Again Emily was struck with the clean, masculine atmosphere of his quarters. It smelled of polished wood, fine leather and a faint scent of brandy. Jonathon picked up a half-full glass of that drink and saluted her.

"Doctor's orders. It deadens the pain," he indicated his hand. "Will you join me, Miss Wentworth?" he grinned.

"If you intend to humiliate me and insult me, sir, I shall leave immediately." She started toward the door.

Jonathon caught her arm and turned her toward him. Their closeness was disconcerting, and Emily felt flushed as her heart hammered insistently in her chest. He smelled of brandy, and she guessed he had consumed quite a bit that afternoon. His hand encircled her upper arm and was close to brushing against her breast. She could feel his eyes burrowing into her and kept her gaze straight ahead, which had her looking at the thick mat of hair revealed by his half-open shirt.

"Forgive me, Em; it is not my intention to humiliate or insult you. But you persist in your coolness toward me and challenge me at every turn. I do not understand why you dislike me so. Have I given you just cause? Enlighten me so that I can make amends. Have I been cruel or untoward? Tell me how I can attain your good graces. Have I taken liberties and become an object of repulsion to you? Have I not, and earned your scorn? Perhaps if I showed more daring in our relationship I could earn your respect as a man."

Jonathon slid one arm around her waist, the other hand lifted her chin and, as blue eyes looked up into brown, he gently lowered his head and brushed her lips with his. Emily's mind reeled and her body burned with newly awakened desire.

Intending only an innocent kiss, Jonathon was surprised at the impact made by those soft, full lips against his. Combined with the headiness of the brandy he had been drinking, his innocent kiss became intense as his lips moved over hers, searching their sweetness.

Emily became aware of his arms encircling her, pressing her close. She responded instinctively, lost in the spell of his tenderness. His lips parted and she felt his tongue move to open her mouth. Regaining her senses, Emily pulled away and staggered back. To deny she had enjoyed that kiss would have been a lie. He knew that too. She looked up at him in surprise and dismay, her breasts heaving as she gasped for air.

"Emily—" Jonathon began, but she swirled and fled from the room.

Reaching her quarters, Emily slammed the door and stood with her back pressed against it, lest he try to follow. Her body betrayed her with its sensual, pleasurable glow. She felt her hot, flushed cheeks with trembling hands. Her mind tumbled, confused, and she could feel the pressure of his arms around her like a brand. Her lips ached for more of his kiss, and she grew angry at their betrayal. She denied to herself that she was willing in his arms, and suddenly realized in horror that her arms had reached up along his shoulders in welcome.

Throwing herself on the bunk, Emily sobbed into her pillow. Her world was turning upside down. She had lost her parents, left her homeland, almost lost her brother, and now this colonial was launching an attack on her senses. And physically, she seemed more than willing to comply. Was she some sort of wanton woman? She should have married Michael Dennings and been assured a respectable life in London. But, as many times as Michael had stolen kisses, they had never set her on fire the way Jonathon's had. She warmed even now as she remembered it. Exhausted, Emily drifted off to sleep. Somewhere in that hazy dreamworld, strong arms held her close and soft lips urged a welcoming response. Anyone peeking in on the sleeping girl would have noticed a delicate smile on her lips.

*

Morning dawned sunlit and warm, belying the previous day's storm. A gentle tapping on her door brought Emily to full consciousness. Rising, she realized she was still in the rumpled clothes she had worn the previous night, and her hair was a mass of golden tangles. Visions of her encounter with Jonathon assailed her, and she halted before the door afraid that he might be on the other side.

"Miss Wentworth, are you awake?" Mr. Gates called.

Relief swept her and she answered, "Yes, Mr. Gates. Is Andrew all right?"

"He is conscious, but very weak. I wanted to keep my promise to you." She heard the amusement in his voice.

"I shall be there shortly. Thank you, Mr. Gates," Hastily she doffed her clothes and sparingly used her precious rainwater to freshen up. Pulling a comb through them, she managed her tousled locks and in a moment had them pulled back in a shining cascade down her back. Tears stung her eyes in witness to the quick, but determined styling. She donned a light blue muslin frock that mirrored her eyes. Realizing that she was dressing hurriedly for Andrew, but carefully for Jonathon, she slammed down the ribbons she was about to arrange in her hair, afraid to admit to herself that she was taking more care than making haste.

Her heart pounded faster as she reached her door and realized she might come face to face with Jonathon. Inevitably she would have to face him today, but she did not know what she would say. Her cheeks burned at the thought, but deep inside a glimmer of excitement thrilled at it. Setting her lips in a grim line, she flung open the door ready to do battle. No one was about. With a sinking feeling, she hurried to Andrew's cabin.

On entering she was surprised to see Andrew much as she had left him the previous night. But as she neared the bed she was aware of his deep, even breathing. His coloring had improved, too, but he was sleeping deeply. She looked questioningly at Mr. Gates.

"He was awake for only a moment, lass. He will be slipping in and out for a day or more. But a promise is a promise," his eyes twinkled.

"Let me relieve you now, Mr. Gates, so you can rest," Emily offered.

"Aye, lass, it is a fine, fair day. Most of us will be resting after the raging tempest we experienced yesterday," he replied. "Call if you need me, child." Rising he went to the door where he paused and turned. Looking closely at Emily he asked, "Did you sleep well, child?"

Unconsciously raising a hand to her lips, Emily wondered frantically if she had been branded by Jonathon's kiss.

"You look a bit flushed, but very refreshed," he explained.

"Oh, I slept very well, thank you, Mr. Gates," she said quickly.

Still watching her, Gates weighed her words. Then nodding, he turned and left.

Emily sank back in the chair. She looked down at Andrew sleeping peacefully. She shuddered as she recalled the events of yesterday and the deathly pallor that had covered his face. She closed her eyes to block that picture, but Andrew's face became her father's and an ache began in Emily's stomach. The familiar tightness clutched her throat. Tears streamed down her face and dropped onto her clenched hands. Loneliness and confusion overwhelmed her.

"Em?" She heard a whisper like a sigh of a summer's breeze. "Em?" Opening her eyes she saw her brother's lips move. Brushing the tears away she leaned close to him.

"Andrew, I am here."

Struggling to open his eyes, Andrew whispered, "What happened. . .?"

"Andrew, you must rest, please, just rest." Emily whispered. "You were on the mizzenmast during the storm. It snapped and you fell into the sea. Captain Brentwood saved you."

"Jonathon . . . yes, Jonathon . . ." he mumbled and drifted back into oblivion.

The mention of Jonathon's name brought the memory of soft lips against hers and Emily shifted in her seat. She still had to face him today and had not yet settled on what to say. Trying to decide filled the rest of her morning.

*

Refreshed after some food and relieved of her watch over Andrew early in the afternoon, Emily decided, encounter or not, she was in dire need of some fresh air. Bracing herself for the inevitable meeting, she climbed the ladder to the main deck. It was quiet on deck today. Most of the men were taking a well-deserved rest after the frantic rush of yesterday. As few hands as possible were guiding the ship on the gentle breeze. Emily made a brief sweep of the deck trying to sight Jonathon before he spotted her. Forewarned is forearmed she thought. But he was nowhere in sight. Relief mixed with a twinge of disappointment filled Emily as she strolled.

As clear as the sky and as bright as the sun were, a choppiness of the water gave evidence of the previous day's violent storm. The air was cool against her skin, but the sun tempered it with warmth. Emily reveled in the free open feeling after being in confining cabins for so long. She watched the men work with none of the urgency that had spurred them on the day before. The rhythmic rise and fall of the ship was bracing and soon the turbulent emotions that had caused her to despair earlier were eased and calmed.

That day and the next, tending Andrew occupied her. Gradually he came to awaken for longer intervals. Emily busied herself with spooning broth into his mouth at every opportunity and reassuring him gently whenever he rose to consciousness. Walking on deck when she had a brief respite, Emily had the opportunity to convince herself that what had happened in Jonathon's cabin was entirely his fault and that her reaction should be one of justified indignation. She even prepared a little speech to reprimand him and cause him to beg her forgiveness. But she grew frustrated when he did not appear.

As she was tending Andrew that evening, Mr. Gates came in and checked the boy over carefully.

"Andrew is doing well. This rest is what he needed more than anything. He will be weak for quite some time. Continue to spoon feed him, Miss Wentworth, though soon he will be feeding himself." He smiled at her reassuringly.

"Thank you for all that you have done, Mr. Gates," and trying to sound nonchalant, she paused. "How is Captain Brentwood? I have not seen him on deck."

Mr. Gates peered at her for a moment. "I wondered if you had forgotten about him, lass. He is not faring as well as Andrew, I am afraid. He would not rest and is now lying with a fever." Emily looked at him with large, fearful eyes. "He has been calling your name, missy. Perhaps if you spoke to him it would help bring him out of this."

"He called my name?" she exclaimed. "I do not understand, sir."

Again Mr. Gates studied her. "Do you not, lassie?"

Emily looked down at her folded hands. "Will he recover, Mr. Gates?"

"It is hard to say right now. He has a strong will to survive. But remember, lass, he was in that icy water as well as your brother, and with a nasty gash in his hand, too."

Suddenly Emily was filled with remorse for the way she had treated the man who had saved not only her brother's life, but once her father's as well.

"I shall go to him if you think it will help, Mr. Gates."

"It cannot hurt, lassie, and it was your name he was calling."

Emily was shocked when she entered Jonathon's quarters. He lay on his bunk plucking at the sheet and mumbling incoherently. His forehead was beaded with perspiration, and the light sheet that covered him was damp. The crewman beside his bed rose and left at a nod from Mr. Gates. Striding over to the bed, Gates wrung out a cloth from a bucket of water nearby and gently washed the sweat from Jonathon's face. A worried frown puckered his brow, and he turned to the girl.

"This fever could last the week or it could break today. The sooner it breaks the better. He needs liquids and cool water compresses. If the truth be known, lass, I need you more here than in your brother's cabin." He looked at her pleadingly.

"He saved my brother's life as well as my father's, Mr. Gates. I shall do anything I can," she answered.

"That is the girl. I shall get some fresh water; you see if you can get him to swallow a couple drops of the drinking water. I shall be back soon. And do not worry; we shall keep a close watch on Andrew." He left the cabin and Emily turned to her task.

Sitting beside his bed, she looked down at Jonathon's flushed, sweaty face. His dark hair clung to his head, and his lips moved in an inaudible litany. His fingers plucked at the sheets, and he turned his head from side to side.

Pouring a little water into a cup, Emily reached beneath Jonathon's head and propped it against her arm. She held the cup to his lips and, though much of it dribbled down his chin, she thought some of it went into his mouth. Gently easing his head down, she withdrew her arm. Finding a clean cloth, she wiped his brow, his cheeks, and his neck, and wrung it out again and placed it on his forehead. Her tender care seemed to have a calming effect. Mr. Gates returned with fresh water and some food for Emily.

"Your presence seems to have made a difference already, Miss Wentworth," he commented.

Emily continued her routine throughout the day. She began talking gently about anything that came to mind, for the sound of her voice seemed to calm Jonathon, too. Emily was surprised when someone came in to light the lantern and bring her food. She had been so involved in tending Jonathon that she had not noticed the sun slipping into the arms of the sea.

Jonathon had quieted considerably and at times even appeared to sleep comfortably. When his inaudible ravings began, Emily talked to him in gentle, soothing tones, as to a frightened child. Once she caught herself holding his strong, lean hand. Another time she bent close to his ear and stroked his forehead. She studied his face as he slept and was struck by his incredible handsomeness. Dark eyebrows arched over deep, brown eyes, which, although closed now, were etched in Emily's memory. High cheekbones framed a straight, aquiline nose, and his soft lips hid straight, white teeth. Emily stared at his lips, now parched and dry, and remembered the feel of them against her own. She was overcome with an urge to bend down and press her lips against his once again. Before she knew what was happening, she realized she had leaned over him. Pausing, she looked at his face then gently brushed her lips against his. Drawing away she felt embarrassed, as though she had taken advantage of him.

"I *am* a wanton woman," she thought, for she had longed for responding lips to answer, for arms to encircle her and draw her down to him. She felt an unfamiliar longing, an ache she did not comprehend. She stared at Jonathon.

"What madness have you brought upon me?" she whispered.

One of the crew relieved her for the night and before she went for her nightly stroll, she looked in on Andrew. She was surprised to find him awake and felt guilty when she realized she had not inquired about him all day.

"How are you feeling, Andrew?" she asked.

"Oh, I shall be back on deck in no time," he smiled wanly.

"Not if you value your life, for I will see you shot at sunrise!" his sister scolded. "You rest now, Drew. I shall be back in the morning."

"I hear you are tending Jonathon," he smiled, but his voice betrayed his weakness.

"Mr. Gates said I was needed more there than with this reckless boy who got what he deserved," she teased sternly. Bending over, she kissed his forehead. "Thank God you are all right," she whispered. Andrew closed his eyes and slept.

Emily set out for a short stroll on deck, but realizing how tired she was, went below to prepare for bed.

*

Emily continued her routine with Jonathon the next day. His ramblings were not so frequent, and his color seemed improved. Mr. Gates came in often and encouraged her assistance. That afternoon Jonathon's fever broke, and he fell into a deep, uninterrupted sleep. Mr. Gates's face showed immense relief, and he credited Emily's care for the quick improvement.

"I could not have run this ship and given the Captain such careful attention, Miss Wentworth," he explained. "You may have just repaid him for your brother's life."

"I am glad I could help, Mr. Gates," she replied sincerely. "Shall I continue as before?"

"No, you may go to your brother now. I shall have the men look in on Captain Brentwood when I am not with him."

"As you wish," she replied, strangely disappointed.

Andrew looked much stronger and was happy to see Emily.

"How is Jonathon?" he asked.

"The fever has broken and he is resting quietly. Mr. Gates says he is past the most dangerous point now. His hand seems to be healing well, also," Emily answered.

"Em, why do you dislike Jonathon?" Andrew asked.

"It is not that I dislike him, Drew, it is just that . . . well, he was thrust upon us at such an awful time. Perhaps I connect him with Father's death somehow. And he holds everything we own—we shall always have to answer to him. We do not need a guardian, and I resent having one. He tries to take Father's place. And he thinks I am a child," she finished lamely.

Andrew looked at her strangely. "Em, he was not thrust upon us; we were thrust upon him. And he had nothing to do with Father's death. If anything, Father knew he could rest easily because Jonathon would care for us. Perhaps we do not need a guardian, but I do not think Jonathon proposes to take Father's place. And, Emily, I have seen the way Jonathon looks at you. He does not think you are a child." Andrew had countered her every argument.

Emily blushed at his last sentence, realizing its truth. He certainly had not kissed her in a fatherly fashion. Looking at her brother, she appreciated once again his astuteness.

"Well, then, I do not know why I dislike him. I just know that he always laughs at me," she said defensively.

"He does not laugh at you, Em. It is just that you take everything so seriously; he sees the humor in things."

"Well I see nothing humorous about being snatched from our homeland, whisked onto a ship, and sailed across an ocean to be deposited in a foreign land. And we do not have any say in the matter," she fumed.

"Well, you could have married Michael and his mother," Andrew teased mischievously. He might have gone too far, but Emily needed perspective. He watched her face soften from a glower to an equally mischievous grin.

"One must know one's place in the company of one's elders. Children should be seen and not heard," she mimicked Mrs. Dennings perfectly. Both of them broke into laughter. Emily realized that Andrew was right. It could always be worse.

They chatted through supper and Emily took her evening walk before retiring. On the way to her cabin, she paused at Jonathon's door.

"Captain Brentwood is greatly improved this evening, Miss Wentworth," Mr. Gates spoke from behind her. He carried a cup of broth. "I have some business to attend on deck; could I impose on you to assist him in taking some nourishment?"

Before Emily could refuse, he pushed the cup into her hand and, touching his cap, turned on his heel and left. Butterflies invaded Emily's stomach as her hand reached for the latch. Quietly she entered and saw Jonathon sleeping peacefully. She tiptoed to his bed and watched for a moment to make sure he was asleep. Gently she felt his forehead and was relieved to find it cool and dry. She then sat beside him unsure of what to do. Since he was resting so comfortably, she hated to disturb him. Yet it was important he get some nourishment. She watched the steady rise and fall of his chest and was impressed again by the wide shoulders and well developed muscles. Feeling eyes upon her, she returned her gaze to his face and found Jonathon studying her. She was surprised at how drawn he looked and realized fully for the first time how near death he had been.

"Mr. Gates asked me to bring you some broth," she said feeling a need to explain her presence. "Let me help you."

He closed his eyes in compliance. Emily reached beneath his head as she had done many times before and propped him up on her arm. She held the cup to his lips and was pleased when he sipped some broth. The effort drained Jonathon, and he leaned heavily against her arm. His eyes looked into hers in thanks as she gently laid his head back down.

"You must rest now, Captain Brentwood," she said softly. He closed his eyes, and soon his even breathing signaled his deepening slumber.

Again Emily was seized with the desire to kiss him. She fought it this time and was content to study his striking face. After a while the ache in her back and shoulders urged her to bed and, rising, she picked up the cup. Unthinking, she pulled the sheet a little higher over his shoulders and gently stroked his forehead. Then she turned and left, unaware of brown eyes that followed her.

*

A week brought signs of great improvement in both boy and man. Andrew was sitting up playing cards with Emily and the sailors and chafing at being confined to bed. Jonathon was taking more food and, though exhausted, was in good spirits. His hand was healing well with no sign of putrefying. Emily was free to stroll along the deck more and did so as much as possible. All seemed to be more than ready to sight land, though they knew it would be weeks away.

Mr. Gates approached Emily as she watched the waves in endless fascination. "Excuse me, Miss Wentworth; Captain Brentwood would like a word with you."

Emily headed for Jonathon's cabin wondering what he wanted. She had not seen him since Mr. Gates requested her help with the broth. Reaching his door, she knocked and was surprised at the strength in his voice when he bade her enter. Jonathon, propped to a half-sitting position in his bed, was making notations in a ledger. Looking up he was greeted with the sight of Emily in a yellow dress that drew out the golden highlights in her hair.

"Come in and sit down, Emily," he said.

The only chair was the one by his bed since the others had been moved to Mr. Gates's quarters for dining. Emily complied and sat beside him. She avoided his gaze and cast about the room for something interesting to study. None of it registered in her mind, however, since it was occupied with the awareness of Jonathon's intense scrutiny.

"Emily, I wanted to apologize for what happened in here the other evening. I am afraid I was quite drunk and . . . " he began.

Emily felt the blush creep across her cheeks. "It is all right, Captain Brentwood, I understand," she murmured looking at her hands resting in her lap.

"Perhaps you do not Em, I am not sorry that it happened; I am sorry that I was so drunk that I could not appreciate it as I would have liked. I thought we could repeat the performance so at least I would have the memory to carry with me."

Emily was furious. She started to rise, but he caught her hand. She was surprised at his strength, but knew she could pull away if she chose to. She did not.

"You egotistical, insufferable, arrogant fool!"

"Easy, Em, I am a sick man," he grinned. "I was teasing. I really did intend to apologize, but you seemed so upset by such a little incident, that I thought levity would help the situation. Obviously I erred. Please sit down." Emily sank slowly into the chair. "Let us call a truce, Emily. I shall try to be more serious if you will try to find some redeeming qualities in this egotistical, insufferable fool."

Emily eyed him. So it was just a little incident to him. Of

course, it would be. He had been involved with mature women, probably many experienced lovers, and here she was—young and inexperienced. He probably laughed at the awkwardness of their kiss. And it had set her very soul on fire. *A little incident.*

"Do not worry, Captain Brentwood, beneath that jovial, mocking exterior, I am sure there beats a heart of pure stone. But I shall do my best to find something about you that will win my favor."

"Emily, must we be so formal? Please call me Jonathon. After all, we have become much closer on this voyage. Why, Mr. Gates informs me that it was you who made the critical difference in my healing, that it was your gentle ministrations that chased the demons from my mind and pulled me to the calm, serene waters of recovery. When you save someone's life, the least you can do is call him by his Christian name."

"I did not save your life, Captain Brentwood. I simply held a cup to your mouth and helped you drink," she retorted.

"Oh, that the cup had been your warm, sweet lips, my lady. Surely that, however, would only increase my fever and make me rave with mad cravings of the heart. No, I suppose it is fortunate that the only thing you pressed to my lips was a cold, pewter cup." He tried to look relieved, but let out a low chuckle.

Emily went scarlet. Could it be that he knew of her kiss? Oh, how horrible. She could not meet his eyes.

"Good day, Captain. I have a need of some fresh air," Emily said, rising. She quickly walked to the door and on closing it, flew to her cabin in dismay.

Chapter 3

Both Jonathon and Andrew recovered quickly, and life aboard the *Destiny* returned to normal, including enjoyable repasts in Jonathon's quarters. It was after one of these that Mr. Gates suggested a game of cards. Emily declined, preferring an evening stroll on deck.

As she ascended the ladder, she heard the melancholy tunes of a sea chantey coming from the crew's quarters. Reaching the deck she gasped in wonder catching sight of an enormous golden moon hanging just above the horizon. She was drawn to the railing where she stood, enchanted by the sight. It seemed that if she dove into the sea and swam but a short distance, she would be able to reach up and capture the golden orb. Strains of the sailor's song drifted up to her, and she felt a strange mixture of sadness and joy. Her heart welled up within her, yet tears clouded her eyes. She wondered at this intense feeling of melancholy, and an unfamiliar ache throbbed inside that was not quite loneliness. Somehow she knew the loss of her parents was not the cause; in fact, were they beside her that moment, their presence would not comfort her. Her senses seemed to reach out for a fulfillment of which she had no knowledge. It was a terrible sweet pain, this joy-sorrow. She wanted to keep still for fear it would flee, yet she wanted to banish it with good sense and practicality. She was convinced she was moonstruck. Emily did not understand.

And he was beside her.

"Ah, the sea," Jonathon took a deep breath and then exhaled. Looking down at her, Jonathon was stunned by what he saw in Emily's eyes. The silent, aching appeal was there, albeit unknown to the girl. Jonathon understood.

He realized what a precarious position they were in. She was his ward, his responsibility. He could no more take her into his arms to ease the longing and comfort her than he could turn away and leave her here. But Jonathon was torn between two loves already. One the seductive, undulating call of the sea, a mistress that seeped into his being and lulled him with her vastness and freedom. She could rage at him with a violent tempest or mock him by withholding her breezes as an angry lover looms in silence over her faulted beloved. The other love: his land. Her perfume, the magnolia and lilac, and the sweet smell of freshly plowed fields. She beckoned no less seductively with her wild, wooded acres and gently rolling hills promising majestic mountains beyond, poised as a vain woman allowing him to drink in her beauty. And she could ruin him with floods or drought, destroying in days what took a lifetime to build. Two loves, both addictive, neither controllable.

And beside him, this girl. Beautiful, vulnerable, needing to be held, not realizing her need. Jonathon had avoided emotional entanglements so far; taking his pleasure with women who knew it was only that. Never commitment, never love. But this was not what Emily needed. She needed the love and commitment of a lifetime from a man who would be hers alone. Not the sea's, not the land's.

Jonathon recovered.

"So, Miss Wentworth, soon we will be home."

"Your home, Captain. Mine has been left far behind," she replied in a tight voice.

"When you see Virginia, Emily, you will claim her for your very own. Lazy summer days, gentle breezes that rest soft upon your cheek; rivers that slip through thick forests and burst out over rocks, past emerald green lawns that sweep down from red brick manor houses. Sleepy nights listening to the crickets sing. Em, you can ride for a day and never leave Brentwood land. We shall do that one day; you will not believe how beautiful it is. Wooded hills, and in the west, mountains so high the tops hide in the clouds. I shall show you all of it."

"You sound like a besotted lover," she snapped.

"Of course, when you arrive, Virginia will have a rival to her beauty. Why, the young men will be tripping over each other to win your favor."

"And I am sure you will find each one of them unacceptable as a husband for me. No, you will wait until some doddering old fool with gout and a large purse comes along and marry me off to him so you can increase *my* fortune that *you* hold." Emily looked up at him, her eyes blazing.

"So you think me a scheming opportunist," Jonathon chuckled. "I told you about my land holdings, Em. I am really not that close to starvation that I must steal from innocent young women and doddering old fools."

"Frankly, Captain Brentwood, I think you exaggerate. Perhaps if we ride in a small circle we can ride all day on your land. I shall believe it when I see it; until then I am convinced these are the rantings of a colonial fool. England, in case your memory is poor, is quite beautiful, too." She glared at him. "Good evening, Captain."

Jonathon looked into her eyes. One fire had been extinguished by another—anger. That was good; she would sleep much easier tonight. He watched her walk to the steps leading below. Soon she would see that he was right.

*

There was an undercurrent of energy and anticipation within each man. They had traveled this route enough to know instinctively that they would sight land soon, discounting the endless, unbroken horizon that surrounded them. It seemed to build daily until expectation was almost a tangible entity among them. Coiled ropes were undone and recoiled, polished mahogany was buffed again, secure riggings were rechecked, and throughout it all surreptitious glances took in the western horizon. They smelled land before they saw it.

And at dawn one morning the shout came, "Land 'ho!"

The reined anticipation erupted into boundless energy. Men scrambled up rigging and across decks preparing the ship to enter port, Jonathon among them shouting orders, checking charts and compass. Andrew worked among them readying the *Destiny* for her home harbor while he crushed down his unbearable excitement. Excitement welled up and spilled over in all the men as hearty laughs joined lusty jokes about how the first evening ashore would be spent.

A strangely quiet figure stood at the rail staring at the distant shoreline. Somehow leaving London had seemed unreal. There was always the hope that they would, in fact, return. But the proof of their destination loomed ahead and had to be faced. Emily's emotions churned—apprehension, curiosity, fear and excitement. Would Virginia live up to Jonathon's descriptions? As afraid as she was of finding out, she was also strangely exhilarated.

Andrew came up beside her and squeezed her hand. "What do you suppose it will be like, Emily?"

"From what Captain Brentwood says, it is heaven on earth," she answered dryly.

"Will you ever like him, Em?" Andrew asked looking at his sister curiously.

"I have told you, Andrew, he tries to take Father's place; he fancies himself part of the family." She knew these were lame excuses, but she honestly did not know herself why this colonial sea captain disturbed her so. She turned to look at her brother. "I do not like feeling as if we owe him something. I keep waiting for him to call in the debt," she glanced away, "and I am not sure I am ready to pay his price."

Andrew was bemused. "Em, he was Father's friend. He agreed to this long ago."

Emily looked back at him. "That may be so, Andrew, but he probably agreed thinking that Father would live to a hale and hearty old age. I doubt he ever expected to end up playing nursemaid to two reluctant offspring."

"I am not reluctant, Em. I think Jonathon is a fine man, and a good captain. He does not treat *me* like a child. Why, he says I am as fine a sailor as any of his crew was at the end of their first voyage. When my schooling is done, I shall sail with him again." Andrew's eyes sparkled and Emily had to smile.

"I am glad to see you so happy, Drew."

"But I want you to be happy, too, Em. Since Father's death you seem so restless and preoccupied. Jonathon wants the best for us, just as Father did. He would have approved your marriage to Michael if he thought you would have been happy."

Emily's mouth opened in surprise. "Why do you say that?" she demanded.

"Because he told me so," Andrew replied.

"So now Captain Brentwood thinks to read my mind!" she huffed indignantly. "Oh, that egotistical boor . . . " Her tirade was halted by the sight of the lush, green coastline growing on the horizon. "Oh, Drew, look!" she exclaimed. Suddenly her knees trembled and she lost her cool reserve. What would Virginia hold for her and Andrew? Would they be happy there? Doubt and fear possessed her, and she wanted the ship to turn back. She took a deep breath and composed herself. Sensing a presence beside her, she looked up into warm, brown eyes.

"Remember the favor I asked, Emily," Jonathon said softly. His eyes were tender, and a worried look touched his brow.

"As I recall there were two that were mentioned. To which do you refer, sir?" she questioned imperiously.

"Which do you prefer, Miss Wentworth?" he countered.

She caught Andrew's bewildered look and bit back a retort. "I will try to be open minded about Virginia, Captain," she replied.

They turned to view the enlarging coastline. The emerald green trees were a startling contrast to the clear, blue sky. Emily reluctantly admitted to herself that it was a striking first impression. But, she thought firmly, I would need more convincing than a pretty coastline.

They sailed past Cape Henry and the *Destiny* glided regally toward the York River to drop anchor at Yorktown. The day was hot and clear, the sun lending brilliant color to the passing shore. But Emily was more impressed with the look in Jonathon's eyes. He was home, and he seemed to drink in every detail that he saw. A grin had played about his mouth all day, even when he was caught up in the details of readying his ship for port. As they gracefully neared Yorktown, his happiness was barely checked, and coming up to Emily he stood before her, placing his hands on her shoulders.

"We are home, Em."

But the girl could not speak over the catch in her throat. One of the crew called for Jonathon, and he turned and left. Andrew came up to her and placed an arm around her waist.

"Chin up, Emily," Andrew said tenderly. "We still have each other."

Emily gave him a brave smile and blinked back the tears. They walked to the rail and watched the activity. Men rolled, carted or carried hogsheads of tobacco to be shipped to England. Sailors headed to nearby taverns to quench long overdue thirsts, or tipsily staggered back to ships to sleep off just such quenching. Street urchins ran about trying to earn a coin by performing various chores. Voices ran together in the churning, noisy bedlam.

"It could be a pier in London," Emily thought, "or, for that matter, in any country. People are not so different though oceans separate them."

"May I escort you ashore, Miss Wentworth?" Jonathon's eyes sparkled as he offered her his arm.

"Thank you, Captain. Your Virginia is living up to your mad ranting, thus far. But you still have much to prove, 'Mountains that touch the floor of heaven, vast acres of Brentwood land . . .' "

"So you were listening. I am honored," he bowed.

Emily stopped, embarrassed. "There was precious little else to do on this long, lonely sea voyage, Captain."

"Lonely, Em? With you aboard I was not lonely at all," he grinned. She gave him a withering look.

They descended the gangplank with Andrew and found Mr. Gates. Emily and Andrew studied the busy wharf as the two men spoke. Soon Jonathon returned.

"Would you mind a carriage ride after our long journey? We could stay at the Raleigh Tavern in Williamsburg. I am anxious for news of home, and that is where it is to be found," he said. "Mr. Gates will tend to the ship."

Emily and Andrew agreed, and soon they were bouncing along the road in a carriage. Jonathon sat across from them and Emily often felt his eyes upon her. She continued to look at the passing scenery; elation welling within her at the beauty of the countryside as well as the attention Jonathon paid her.

*

The coach lamps were lit after sunset and candlelight flickered off faces glowing with anticipation, excitement, and curiosity. Finally they reached Williamsburg and the coach halted before the Raleigh Tavern.

Voices filled the common room as debates and discussions held the patrons' attention. One man facing the doorway caught sight of the three arrivals as they entered. Excusing himself, the man rose quickly and approached them.

"Jonathon! I had thought the devil had taken you," he exclaimed, his hazel eyes never leaving Emily. Rusty colored hair framed his handsome, jovial face. He was as tall as Jonathon and as broad in the shoulders.

"Randolph, he would not have me. . . nor you!" Jonathon answered in high spirits. "May I present my w—?"

"Your wife!" Randolph exclaimed. Emily's eyes grew large and Jonathon's mouth dropped. Andrew just laughed. "Where did you find a woman who'd have you?"

"Not my wife. My ward!"

"Your ward?" he asked incredulously. "Then you are a fool, man!" Randolph boomed. Emily looked from one man to the other not sure whether she should be enraged or amused. Jonathon had a wicked twinkle in his eye.

"Perhaps you are right, Randy. Maybe I should reconsider this relationship and set it aright. Picture me around the hearth with my sweet Emily and our brood of children."

Emily blushed furiously and shot him a warning glance.

"So Emily is your name. I thought this raving madman would never get on with the introductions. Emily who?"

"Emily Wentworth, sir. And may I present my brother, Andrew."

Randy bent and kissed her hand, then shook Andrew's. "I am pleased to meet you. I am Randolph William O'Connor." He bowed low. "You are George Wentworth's children?"

Emily nodded.

"I met your father. He was a fine man. I was sorry to hear of his death."

"Thank you, Mr. O'Connor."

"Randy, please. All my friends call me Randy." He slapped Jonathon on the back. "Jonathon does, too."

"A rascal he is and be warned," Jonathon countered. "I am anxious for news, Randy. The rumors I have heard sound ominous."

"Aye, things are moving, Jonathon. Come have an ale and some supper."

Conversation was light over a supper of hearty stew, warm rye bread and ale. Talk centered around plantation life, births, deaths, and marriages. Local politics were alluded to, but Emily sensed beneath it all an urgency to move on to important events that would require more than a light skimming over. The two men, she suspected, would be up the better part of the night delving into discussion, perhaps plans, of a serious nature. Sensing their impatience, and noting Andrew's yawns, she rose to retire. The men rose also, and she took Andrew's arm and bade the other two good-night.

Emily's suspicions proved correct; Jonathon knew exactly where to go to learn the current state of affairs, and the two men joined others and lively discussion ensued. Unfair taxation by parliament in the Stamp Act and the Townshend Acts was the subject of animated debate, and some enthusiastically recalled the answer the colonies had given. The House of Burgesses, Virginia's legislature, was bubbling with unrest and claiming their sole right to levy internal taxes. Thomas Jefferson was writing stirring essays on the God-given rights of man, a concept completely foreign to British rule. And the Royal Governor, Lord Dunmore, had again dissolved the Burgesses who reconvened in the conviviality of the Apollo Room at the Raleigh Tavern, whose motto was written on the mantel: *Hilaritas sapientiae et bonae vitae proles* (Jollity is the offspring of wisdom and good living). The vigorous debate lasted into the early hours of the morning.

*

Dawn was streaking the eastern sky when Emily awoke to a tapping on her door. "Wake up, Emily. We want to get an early start," Andrew called softly.

Emily washed and dressed, noting that the day was already warm and humid. She donned a light silk dress of palest blue with white lace at the bodice and elbow-length sleeves. Brushing her hair, she pulled it up in combs to keep it off her face and neck as much as possible.

This was the day she would meet Jonathon's family. All the doubts and fears that had kept her tossing and turning the night before crept over her again. Taking a deep breath, she smoothed her skirts, straightened her shoulders, and went downstairs.

They ate a hurried breakfast of cold ham, cornbread and fruit and soon were on the road. The countryside was still the flat, green land of the tidewater, but after a time it gave way to gently rolling hills.

As Jonathon told them of plantation life and of his family, Emily's nervousness increased with the miles. Jonathon pointed out places of interest and plantations of friends he had known all his life in this society of the gentleman planter. They stopped to dine at a quaint inn and again ate hurriedly, each anxious either to arrive or to get the dreaded moment over with.

Emily noticed Jonathon's silence after a while and, looking across at him, caught the intense scrutiny with which he was studying the landscape. His eyes glowed with pride, and she knew they had reached his land. For a moment she felt uncomfortable, like someone who has intruded on an intimate moment. But Jonathon turned shining eyes upon her and said simply, "We are home."

Finally the coach turned down a road, and Emily craned her neck to catch her first glimpse of Brentwood Manor. After a time, they broke out of the trees into a circular drive that curved gracefully along lush, green lawns and swept before a stately manor.

Emily caught her breath. "Oh, it is beautiful," she whispered.

Jonathon beamed at her. "I knew you would like it, Emily."

Grinning from ear to ear, Andrew remarked, "You did not do it justice, Jonathon."

The three of them laughed remembering all the times he had described Brentwood Manor—always in superlatives.

Majestic catalpa trees lined the drive and sculpted shrubs hugged the mansion. Made of red brick in the Flemish–bond style, it had two enormous chimneys equidistant from the center of the roof; a pair of large windows flanked either side of the central entrance and five smaller windows lined the upper story. A wing with a slightly lower roofline extended out from each end of the main structure. It was beautiful in its simplicity of design and bore an elegance of time and tradition.

The front door opened and a slender, dark–haired woman appeared, followed closely by a tall, blonde man. Each held a parcel as they stood on the bottom step awaiting the coach.

When Jonathon opened the door and stepped out, the woman jumped into his arms laughing gaily. She had the same warm, brown eyes and thick lustrous brown hair as his, although hers gleamed with auburn highlights. She resembled Jonathon, but her features were delicate, her movements graceful. The man with her shook Jonathon's hand, and then pulled him close and embraced him, patting him heartily on the back. Then they all turned expectantly toward the carriage.

Andrew hopped out first; Jonathon reached up to assist Emily. As she emerged from the coach, she heard the woman gasp softly.

"Joanna, David—may I introduce the newest members of our family: Andrew and Emily Wentworth."

Joanna's eyes revealed a mixture of surprise and amusement. She held out her hand with David's and said warmly, "Welcome to Brentwood Manor." Then, a bit hesitantly, she handed a parcel to Emily and said, "We have a gift for you." David handed a parcel to Andrew.

Emily and Andrew unwrapped their gifts; there was a moment of absolute silence.

In her hands Emily held a beautiful doll with a china head and a watered silk dress. Andrew held a hand-carved sailboat. Emily's eyes rose to meet Joanna's; she did not know quite what to say. Joanna's mouth turned up in a half-smile.

"We were expecting you both to be quite a bit younger," she grinned.

In that moment everyone burst out laughing and the tension was broken. Joanna hooked an arm through Emily's.

"Come in, you all must be exhausted and hungry," she said, and the ladies led the way in.

Their shoes echoed on the highly polished hardwood floor as they entered a high-ceilinged, airy hall. Turning right they came to the parlor. Flowered wallpaper of soft blue and white decorated the walls above the dwarf wainscoting, and Scotch carpet gathered the furniture cozily about the room. A beautiful bronze-skinned servant brought in a tray of tall, cool drinks and sweet cakes and set it on a mahogany drop-leaf table beside Joanna. Emily sat on the settee holding the doll in her lap.

"I am so sorry about your father's death. Jonathon has told us what a wonderful man George Wentworth was," David said kindly.

"Thank you," Andrew replied.

"From Jonathon's letter, we were expecting children," Joanna explained, giving her brother a slight frown, betrayed by the twinkle in her eyes.

"Oh, the doll is beautiful, and I shall always cherish it," Emily smiled.

"And the boat is carved splendidly. I would like to learn that craft myself," Andrew added.

"David did that, Andrew. I am sure he would be happy to teach you," Joanna replied. "Now, how was your voyage?"

They spent an amiable afternoon getting acquainted, and all the doubts and fears Emily had wrestled with melted under the warm and sincere friendship of Joanna and David. She began to relax and found herself enjoying the conversation. Finally Joanna rose and offered to show them to their rooms.

They ascended the broad staircase in the central hall and turned to the right. Emily's room was spacious and cheerful, decorated in dusty rose and cream. The canopy bed curtains and window curtains were of rose chintz with darker rose brocade drapes pulled back on either side of the windows. An ivory bedspread decorated with crewelwork done in dusty rose and deeper pink lay across the four–poster bed, and a fireplace with a carved marble mantel matching the one in the parlor faced it. Emily's things had already been put away and Joanna left her to freshen for supper.

Emily sat on the bed and looked around her new room, in her new home. She thought she should be feeling terribly lonely and resentful right now, but instead there was a tickle of anticipation that one would expect to feel when setting out on an adventure. She tried to conjure up loneliness and resentment, but contentment, even excitement, kept beating them down. David and Joanna were warm and welcoming, and she was afraid she would enjoy all this too readily.

She could not let Jonathon win that easily.

*

With the exception of trying to acclimate to the heat and humidity, Andrew and Emily slipped easily into the routine of Brentwood Manor. Emily loved to walk through the vast, manicured gardens. They matched the symmetrical design of the house, rectangular plots bordered by straight walks. Dogwoods, magnolias, and boxwood filled the garden, and azaleas and roses bloomed gaily, lending a heady scent to the air. Emily even enjoyed visiting the kitchen garden near the outbuildings behind the manor, where the invigorating smells of rosemary, chives, and sage vied for attention. These outbuildings housed the kitchen, blacksmith, meat house, stables, and other services necessary to the running of a vast plantation.

On Sunday morning they rode to the small, nearby church that served the local plantations. The beauty of the land again caught Emily. Jonathon did not exaggerate when he had described it to her. Lush fields billowed out to the horizon along the road, and then gave way to thick forests that shaded their drive. The air was dense with summer dew, and Emily inhaled deeply to savor it. Jonathon had been watching her, and he smiled with delight when he caught her eye. Emily shifted in her seat and tried to appear unaffected by the wonder of his land.

It caused quite a stir in the church when Jonathon arrived with Emily on his arm. Heads turned then bent to a neighbor while whispered speculation ensued. Emily tried nervously to ignore the stares and whispers, and Jonathon squeezed her arm reassuringly.

As they approached the pew that David and Joanna were entering, Emily caught the cold, flinty glare of a woman seated just across the aisle. The woman's gaze was so odious that Emily started and quickly looked at Jonathon who gave the woman a nod and a cool smile.

Throughout the service Emily was aware of many eyes upon her, but the eyes that had glared from across the aisle were burned into her mind.

As they left the church, people came up to welcome Emily and Andrew to Virginia. There was surprise on many faces when Jonathon introduced them as his wards. As Emily was chatting, she noticed the woman who had glared at her approaching. She was tall and slender and carried herself regally. Her golden hair was swept up away from her beautiful face, and she was dressed in a yellow linen gown that accented her shapely figure. She made an exquisite picture.

"Welcome home, Jonathon," she said in a sultry voice. Her lovely green eyes looked deeply into his, then she turned them on Emily, disguising the loathing she had betrayed earlier. "And whom do we have here?" she purred.

"Deidre, may I present Andrew and Emily Wentworth, my wards. This is Deidre Manning," he said to them.

Deidre's eyes widened in shock. Quickly recovering, she laughed softly and said, "Come now, Jonathon, are you becoming domestic after all these years?" She turned sea-green eyes upon him again.

"Their father was my good friend; he died at sea. It was an agreement we made long ago." He turned to the others, "Well, shall we return to Brentwood Manor for one of Dora's delicious Sunday afternoon feasts?" Catching Deidre's eye he added, almost reluctantly, "Would you care to join us, Deidre?"

"Why, thank you, Jonathon. That would be lovely." She took his arm before he could offer it to Emily, and they led the others to the waiting carriages.

*

Dinner was indeed a feast. The aroma of freshly baked bread met them as they entered the dining room. After they were seated, Dora brought out plates overflowing with ham, sausage and meat pies still steaming from the oven. Bowls of fresh fruit, roasted vegetables, sauces, and pickles lined the table. When they finished the first course, apple fritters and raspberry tarts completed the repast.

After dinner they relaxed all afternoon on the veranda. The evening breeze was a welcome relief to the day's heat. The sweet smells from the garden wafted over them in an intoxicating aroma and the stillness signaled the approach of night.

"The House of Burgesses is getting restless," Jonathon told David. "They resent Parliament's interference and are ready to act upon it." He chuckled, "I heard the day of fasting and prayer proposed by the Burgesses was quite a sight; people marching to Bruton Church from all over to show their sympathy and support for the Massachusetts Bay Colony. Closing the Port of Boston in retaliation for their 'tea party' was a dire mistake by Parliament. It will serve only to unite the colonies and that is the last thing England wants."

"The northern colonies are far more restless than Virginia," David replied. "Some of them are talking about independence—"

Emily gasped, "Independence from England?" It seemed unbelievable to her.

"Well, Virginia has not gone that far . . . yet," Jonathon replied slowly. "But Parliament is pushing us to the limit of our endurance." He turned to Emily. "We do not want to separate from the Crown, Em, but Parliament is forcing unacceptable legislation upon us. They are denying basic British rights to us here in America. And Parliament meddles—"

"'Parliament meddles!' This sounds like treason to me, Captain Brentwood," she cried indignantly. "If I had known I was being thrust into a hotbed of sedition, I would never have left England."

"And Mrs. Dennings would be nodding heartily in agreement with your damnation of these loathsome colonies," he retorted.

Emily bit back a curt reply and Deidre smiled smugly at the exchange. Everyone sat in embarrassed silence for a moment and then Deidre rose.

"Jonathon, darling, would you escort me home?" she asked sweetly.

"Of course," he answered, rising.

Deidre's carriage was brought around with Jonathon's horse tethered to it. The couple walked arm in arm down the path and climbed into the carriage. Emily felt a knot in her stomach as Deidre's laughter floated back to them. She watched the carriage roll down the drive, then turning, found Joanna's eyes upon her.

"It must be very difficult for you to hear such talk about your beloved England," she said sympathetically. "We should be more sensitive. Forgive us, Emily."

"Yes, Emily, please forgive us," David added. "But we love Virginia as you do England, and we want to be masters of our own destiny. There is restlessness throughout the colony. People are tired of mercantilism and unfair laws. It seems the more we chafe, the more Parliament suppresses us—" He fell silent at a look at Joanna.

"Who is Mrs. Dennings?" Joanna asked, trying to ease the tension.

"She might have been my mother-in-law," Emily said in a tight voice as she rose. "Excuse me, I think I shall retire."

*

Emily lay awake long into the night listening for Jonathon's return. The moon was high in the early morning sky when she heard the hoofbeats come up the drive and the sound of Jonathon's whistling. She buried her face in her pillow and cried, not really understanding why.

Chapter 4

Jonathon was away for two weeks on a brief voyage north to Manhattan Island. Emily did not want to admit to herself that she missed him, but as the days went on, she realized how accustomed she had grown to his presence. She found herself walking aimlessly through the gardens or staring blankly at the pages of a book, and an empty place nagged at her heart. He returned in the midst of the hottest week of the summer. Andrew and Emily suffered in the oppressive heat and felt listless. In the mornings, Emily kept activities light and effortless, and in the afternoons she often slept. The days ran together in an endless, scorching blur.

The house was wrapped in the stillness of a sultry afternoon. Emily stripped to a light, sleeveless cotton shift and lay on her bed avoiding movement that would make her hotter still. The stifling room, darkened by drawn drapes, became unbearable after a time, so she rose and looked reluctantly at the white blouse and pale green skirt she had discarded earlier.

Moaning, she slipped into her clothes and fastened her blouse quickly. Finding her shoes where she had kicked them lazily into a corner, she slid them on and hurried from the house.

It was an effort to breathe the heavy, humid air as she made her way to the stable. Shadow, a black mare she enjoyed riding, seemed as reluctant as Emily to exert any energy on such a sweltering day. Emily did not have the heart to put a saddle on the horse and daringly decided to ride her bareback. Shadow responded slowly to Emily's nudge, and they ambled off to the river and rode along its bank for a time. There was no breeze to disturb the leaves, and the countryside seemed to be in a state of suspended animation. Shadow and Emily caused the only stirring in the picturesque landscape, and their pace was appropriately languid.

A stream branched off from the river and led into a copse of invitingly shady trees. Emily turned her mount toward it, and they entered a silent cathedral of towering oaks. The shade was cooler, and the water gurgled over smooth, mossy stones. Emily slipped off Shadow, walked to the stream and let the clear water wash over her fingers. The coolness of her retreat was a fleeting relief from her ride in the sunshine, for in here, too, the air was still and hot and heavy.

Emily kicked off her shoes, rolled off her stockings, and stuffed them into her shoes. She pulled the back of her skirt up between her legs, tucked it in at her waist, and then tiptoed into the stream. The icy water caused her to catch her breath, and the stones wobbled beneath her feet as she walked along, smiling in ecstasy. She bent and swished her hands in the water, then cupping them, splashed her face. The water ran in rivulets down her neck. She pulled a handkerchief from her pocket and soaked it, then lifting her long, thick curls, ran the wet cloth across the back of her neck. Wetting the cloth again, she unbuttoned her blouse to a daring depth and patted her handkerchief along her neck, throat, and down across her breasts. The cold water was invigorating, and Emily skipped along in the stream singing merrily.

"I have heard tales of sea nymphs, but I never thought to find one so far inland."

Emily froze. Slowly she turned, and looking up, she saw Jonathon standing near Shadow, a grin covering his face.

"I did not know you had added voyeur to your list of virtues, Captain," Emily tossed at him, too hot to care about her appearance. She continued her ritual with the handkerchief and ignored his presence.

"That looks quite refreshing," he laughed, and stooping, removed his boots and stockings. He doffed his shirt and, clothed only in his breeches, joined her in the stream. He cupped his hands and poured the water over the top of his head several times. Reaching up the last time, he accidentally splashed Emily as she danced by.

"Well!" she cried and devilishly splashed him back.

"Oh, a battle, eh?" Jonathon laughed and, cupping his hands along the surface of the water, soaked her with a wide spray.

Laughing, dodging and attacking, they circled trying to outdo one another. Jonathon's hair hung down his neck in a dripping queue as he stealthily stalked Emily. She stepped away, laughing as she tried to catch her breath. Her wet hair hung down her back in honey-colored ringlets and her blouse clung to shapely breasts that swayed and bounced enticingly. Drops of water glistened on her creamy white skin and Jonathon's gaze was drawn to the deep cleavage revealed by her still-unbuttoned blouse. She was unaware of the lovely picture she made, concentrating only on her prey.

"Aha!" Jonathon yelled as he lunged at her and, missing, fell into the water. Emily sidestepped him deftly, laughing gaily, but she slipped on a mossy rock and lost her balance. Reaching up to break her fall, Jonathon grabbed for her waist, but she could not recover her balance and tumbled in beside him. They sat in the icy water laughing heartily, his arm still around her waist. Emily glanced up meeting his eyes and a tremor of excitement rushed through her. Did his arm tighten around her waist?

"Well, we thought we heard children and we were right," Deidre's voice rang out cynically.

The water-soaked couple looked up to see Deidre and Randy perched high above them on their mounts. Randy was grinning broadly, enjoying the delicious view Emily provided. His shirt was soaked with sweat, and his hair stuck to his neck and forehead. Deidre looked flushed and wilted, perspiration beading on her face, her riding suit damp at the armpits and back—a stark contrast to the cool, refreshed, and sparsely clad Emily.

"Join us for a swim?" Jonathon offered.

Randy appeared ready to dismount, but Deidre grabbed his reins.

"Randolph, we are here for tea, remember?" she asked.

"Yes, Deidre dear, but our host is presently away from the manor and is showing a good deal more sense than we, as is his lovely lady."

Emily blushed at that reference.

"Our host and his *ward*," she stressed the word, "are acting like children, which is appropriate for one, since it is so, but not for the other," she returned haughtily.

Randy looked appreciatively at Emily who was rising from the water with Jonathon's assistance.

"Perhaps I am blind, Deidre, but I do not see a single child down there," Randy replied, gesturing toward the stream. Jonathon nodded in agreement; watching while Emily attempted to discreetly button her blouse.

Deidre swung her horse around angrily and galloped off toward the house. Randy laughed and jumped from his horse.

"Do not leave yet. I have missed all the fun."

So they gave him a proper soaking and afterward lay on the grass to dry off. Rolling toward Emily, Jonathon propped his head on one hand. Emily's hair tumbled wildly about her on the grass and her cheeks were pink from her ride in the sun. Her bosom rose and fell gently with her breathing and she turned luminous blue eyes toward him. Jonathon wished Randy had not stayed — and, at the same time, was immensely grateful that he had.

Similar thoughts ran through Emily's mind as she looked up into gently laughing brown eyes.

"May I beg a ride with you, Miss Wentworth? When I found an enchanting sea nymph in the forest, I slapped Neptune's flank to send him back to the stable for relief of that hot, heavy saddle."

Reluctantly, they all rose to return to the manor. Jonathon clasped his hands as a step for Emily to mount Shadow, and then swung up behind her. He wrapped one arm about her waist and held the reins with the other. Having nowhere else to put her hands, she gently clasped them over the hand that held her waist. She was intensely aware of his lean body pressed against hers, and this closeness caused warmth to course through her. Their thighs lay against each other's atop the horse's sides, and they moved together with the rhythm of its gait. Emily felt exhilarated and hated to see the afternoon end.

Deidre was furious when she saw them arrive together. Rumpled and damp, they joined her and Joanna on the veranda, and Jonathon ordered tall, cool drinks for everyone. Jonathon sat beside Emily on a bench and casually laid his arm behind her. A surge of warmth swept through Emily at his nearness and Deidre shot her a cold look. Joanna laughed when they explained their appearance; she also noticed Deidre's disapproving frown.

"I have brought you something interesting, Jonathon," Randy said, handing him a pamphlet from his saddlebag.

Taking it, Jonathon read the title aloud, *A Summary View of the Rights of British America*.

"It is written by Thomas Jefferson, one of the Burgesses. They have convened in Williamsburg and are chafing at the interference of Parliament," Randy explained.

"Again—the interference of Parliament!" Emily burst out. "How can a government interfere with a colony it rules?"

"Well, the House of Burgesses has completely denied the authority of Parliament over the colonies," he replied.

"Denied the authority? Why that is insane!" she cried.

"Think of it, Em. They have tied our hands in trade, taxed so many commodities, limited our expansion—they will drain us dry and we shall never prosper," Jonathon said.

"But we are loyal British subjects . . ." she sputtered. "Of course we are under the authority of Parliament."

Deidre snorted. "You cannot expect a child to understand the politics of the day, Jonathon, darling. I am sure it is quite beyond her."

Jonathon dismissed her with a scornful look and turned to Emily. "Em, we are loyal British subjects. No one is denying that, but Parliament is too far removed from our needs. They have suspended the legislature in New York and taken drastic measures in Boston."

Emily was disturbed as she listened to their discussion, for they were talking of her beloved England. Jonathon offered her the pamphlet to read, and she accepted it. The restlessness that had crackled in the air in the Raleigh Tavern their first night ashore was present here. And it frightened her.

*

Conversation turned to more agreeable topics as they ate a light supper of eggs, corn meal, and cider. In a more affable mood, they returned to the veranda to watch the stars appear in the deep velvet night. Crickets chirped their soothing symphony as the evening enveloped the group with a welcome, cool breeze. Their voices fell softly upon the night, and candlelight flickered on their faces.

Deidre had taken Emily's place next to Jonathon and locked her arm through his, nuzzling against him so her full bosom pressed against his arm. Emily was reminded of a cat arching its back and rubbing against a table leg. She sat across from them and, looking up, met Jonathon's eyes. There was warmth there as he smiled at her, and her returning smile showed dimples that enchanted. She lowered her eyes and picked up the strands of conversation.

Their laughter floated on the gentle night, and their conversation rose and fell in pleasant tones. Deidre and Randy left, and the others prepared to retire. Joanna and David went up first, soon followed by Andrew. Emily felt as if she, too, should leave, but the night was so lovely. . . and she wanted to stay. In the silence she began to feel uncomfortable and wondered if her decision to stay had been a wise one.

"There was a small smile playing on your lips as you looked at Deidre. May I be so bold to inquire as to your thoughts, Miss Wentworth?" Jonathon asked.

Emily looked at him for a moment, and then said boldly, "She reminds me of a cat. A . . . silky cat."

"Would the adjective you were searching for have something to do with her appetite? And I do not refer to food." He laughed softly.

Emily was grateful for the blackness of the night, for then he could not see her turn scarlet. She did not answer.

"I see. Well, you are right; she is like a cat." He became serious, "And she has particularly sharp claws, Em. Be careful of her."

"Is that a warning, Captain?" she asked lightly. "Why ever should I need to be wary of her? What do I have that she could possibly want?"

It was Jonathon's turn to be silent.

They sat watching the stars, pointing out different constellations and listening to the night sounds that surrounded them. It was peaceful as they talked softly. Emily felt a warmth and closeness toward Jonathon that began to wash away the resentment and suspicion that she had harbored more in her head than in her heart.

"I enjoyed our frolic in the stream today, Emily. You are quite lovely, you know."

Emily's heart lifted at the compliment.

"And you are quite impetuous, Captain," she laughed. "I enjoyed it, too. Especially when you got the soaking you deserved!"

"As I recall, madam, I am not the only one who got soaked. Nor that deserved to!"

"Why, Captain, you cannot mean me!"

They laughed together remembering the gaiety, and their laughter faded to smiles as they remembered lying in the grass.

Emily found Jonathon's eyes upon her and, for a moment, time stopped. Her heart raced in her chest, and her body longed to be in his arms. The memory of his kiss aboard the *Destiny* seeped into her mind; her lips felt the fire as if it had happened just a moment before. She looked down at her hands, and then rose. He rose, too, and stood in front of her.

"Well, I think I shall retire," she said softly.

Clenching his fists at his side, Jonathon fought down the urge to take her in his arms, press her body close, and kiss her long and full.

"Good night, Em."

She chanced a look at him, blue eyes meeting brown, and the flicker of candlelight golden upon her face.

"Good night," she whispered and swept past him.

Jonathon went inside and poured himself a brandy. Returning to his seat on the veranda, he silently toasted Emily. He sat deep in thought until the grandfather clock in the hall struck midnight.

*

Emily was puzzled as she entered the parlor, where Dulcie said Deidre awaited her. The morning sun streamed in, and a light breeze billowed the lace curtains. Muted voices drifted in from the gardens as Joanna supervised the work there.

Deidre maintained a cool, sophisticated mien when Emily appeared, though no doubt anger and jealousy roiled within her. She looked the girl over, taking in her tawny hair, highlighted golden by the sun, and her shapely figure enhanced by the simple, yellow frock she wore. The result of her scrutiny served only to increase her reined emotions.

"Good morning, Deidre," Emily said as she took a seat across from her.

"Well, Emily, you look just lovely today."

Not sure how to take this, Emily merely smiled.

"Quite a contrast to the scene I witnessed yesterday." Deidre lowered her eyelids as if properly scandalized. "That is what I came to talk to you about, my dear. At your age I am sure that you do not understand about. . . well. . . proper decorum. I thought we might have a little chat so I could help you begin to act more. . . uh. . . ladylike." Deidre looked at her feigning concern.

"Just how old do you think I am, Deidre? Why not cease this charade and tell me why you came?"

Deidre, kept her composure momentarily. Then, deciding on a course of action let her guard down, and the motherly smile that had been on her face melted into a sneer.

"All right, Emily, I shall be frank. I have known Jonathon for many years, very *intimately*," she stressed the word. "He is a mature man who appreciates a woman who is. . . shall we say, knowledgeable. I do not wish to see our relationship disturbed by you and your conniving ways. I see your game here; you have wormed your way into this house, and you have set your sights on Jonathon. It does not take much to see through your scheme, and I must compliment you on the success of it so far. But I warn you, Emily, find a nice young man your own age and keep away from Jonathon."

Emily was livid at the woman's impudence, but she sat calmly, not showing her rage. Picking an imaginary piece of lint off her skirt she casually looked at Deidre.

"Tell me this, Deidre. In my grand scheme, as you call it, how did I arrange for my father to drown at sea?"

Deidre recoiled as if she had been slapped. Emily did not intend to let her off that easily.

"Deidre, my dear," she said sweetly, "Jonathon is a man of the world; both of us understand that. I appreciate your jealousy because, as we both know, Jonathon is so. . . virile." She looked down delicately. "I think we should just be grateful for any opportunities we have to. . . enjoy his attentions. . . and leave it at that, do you not agree? Otherwise, we would be opponents, and then it would come down to youth versus experience." Emily looked her squarely in the eye.

"You have not heard the end of this, you little—" Deidre seethed, rising from her chair.

"Are you not staying for tea?" Emily asked brightly as Deidre stormed out of the room.

Emily sat staring ahead of her as she listened to the carriage roll down the drive. Her cool exterior was betrayed by trembling as she sat lost in her thoughts.

"So that is how it is," she whispered. Her heart was heavy as she thought of Jonathon lying in Deidre's arms. Why had she led Deidre to believe that she was also Jonathon's lover? But then Emily recalled the smug, condescending look on the older woman's face, and she knew why. But Deidre's claim did not fit somehow. Jonathon certainly had not acted enamored of Deidre last night. In fact, he seemed a bit put off by her attentions. He certainly was not shy. Was he wanting to keep their liaison a secret? Emily puzzled over this for a while. Finally, rising, she joined Joanna who was carrying in a basket vibrant with freshly cut Rose of Sharon, lobelia, lupine and tuberoses from the garden.

Emily took the flowers while Joanna removed her large sunbonnet.

"Joanna, how long have you known Deidre?"

"As long as I can remember. Our families have been friends for years. In fact, it was expected that she and Jonathon would marry, but she married Robert Manning instead. It caused quite a sensation," Joanna explained as she arranged the flowers in a crystal vase.

"When did Robert Manning die?" Emily asked.

"Oh, about six years ago. They had only been married a few years. They found Robert's body in the river. It was a terrible shock, and Deidre was in such a state that she stayed with us for a short time. You see, she was completely alone as her parents had both died by then."

"And she never remarried?"

"No," Joanna answered absently, intent on rearranging an errant tuberose. Then she turned to look at Emily. "Why?"

"I was just curious."

Joanna looked at her for a moment. "Deidre is a strong-willed woman, and when she does not get what she wants she can be quite disagreeable."

"Is that a warning, Joanna?" Emily asked.

Joanna stopped fixing the flowers and again looked at Emily. "It is information that might be useful."

*

The hazy, hot days of August slipped into September, which brought some relief with cooler temperatures. Emily enjoyed riding more and was becoming quite familiar with the area surrounding the manor. Sometimes Andrew or Joanna would accompany her, and she never ceased to be amazed at the vastness of the tobacco fields that stretched as far as the eye could see. She and Andrew were also learning to shoot pistols; between David and Jonathon, they were getting expert instruction. Andrew enjoyed it immensely and practiced whenever possible. Emily did not enjoy it as much as he, but the others convinced her that it was necessary, especially if she planned to continue riding alone. So she practiced, too, and they both became quite proficient.

Jonathon also invited Emily to enjoy the books in his study, so Emily took advantage of his offer. The titles he owned impressed her; she savored the moments she spent in that room surrounded by knowledge and great thinking set to paper. This is where Joanna found her one afternoon.

"Emily, I would like to speak with you," she said.

Emily set her book down. "Yes, Joanna?"

"I know it is only six months since your father died, Emily, but we would like to introduce you and Andrew to our friends. We thought perhaps a ball in honor of your eighteenth birthday."

Emily's eyes danced. "Joanna, how wonderful of you!" She walked over and hugged her impulsively.

"Oh, I am so glad you approve. David and I were not sure if it was too soon, but Jonathon said we should celebrate your arrival. Now we shall make some plans."

The two of them spent a delightful afternoon drawing up a guest list. With each name, Joanna gave a brief description to help Emily ease into the society to which she now belonged.

*

Emily checked her appearance in the mirror. Her blue eyes sparkled with excitement and her face glowed. Her royal blue gown lay just off her shoulders and revealed the fullness of her creamy white breasts. She wore a sapphire necklace and drop earrings that had been her mother's, and her hair was swept up in curls intertwined with blue ribbon and lace. She twirled about in anticipation, her skirts billowing about her legs. Joanna knocked and entered.

"Emily, you look lovely," she smiled. Joanna wore a sea green gown and emeralds at her throat.

"Thank you, Joanna, as do you. It is wonderful of you to do this."

"Birthdays have always been cause for celebration in our family, and now you are a part of our family. And it is a good way to show you off to our friends."

Emily hugged her. "You have made me feel so welcome here. I thought when I left England that I would never be happy again, but—" Tears filled her eyes.

Joanna hugged her and smiled. "Come, Emily, it is time to go downstairs."

Many of the guests had already arrived, and their laughter, mingled with the strains of La Royale, floated up the stairs as Emily and Joanna descended. Jonathon saw them and waited at the bottom of the steps. His gaze rested on Emily, and an appreciative grin settled on his face. Joanna suppressed a smile, and Emily felt suddenly shy, but warmth surged throughout her. He offered the women his arms and escorted them into the ballroom.

Voices softened to a murmur and Emily saw a sea of faces turning toward her. Jonathon reached to a passing tray; he gave each woman a glass of champagne and took one for himself. He signaled Andrew to join them.

"Ladies and gentlemen, may I present my wards, Andrew and Emily Wentworth, late of London, England, now of Brentwood Manor, Virginia. And I pray you all, drink to the health of Miss Wentworth whose birth we celebrate today."

Emily blushed as the guests drank to her health. Then Joanna began a round of endless introductions. Emily murmured polite replies to the myriad questions posed and found it impossible to remember all the names.

Soon Randy approached and scolded, "Enough, Joanna. Let the girl have some fun, too. She can dance with me."

"Diversion, perhaps, Randolph, but her feet will not find it fun to be trod upon," Joanna teased.

"I was born with light feet and a lilting voice, Mrs. Sutton," he retorted and drew Emily onto the floor.

"You look beautiful, Emily," he smiled down at her.

"Why thank you, Randy. And you are light on your feet."

Randy noticed Jonathon on the far side of the room. Although engaged in what appeared to be deep conversation with Deidre, Jonathon's eyes never left Emily. Deidre noticed, too, and plucked at his sleeve to get his attention. But when Jonathon met Randy's gaze he averted his eyes and finally looked back at Deidre.

The music ended for a brief intermission. People milled about, and Randy led Emily toward the table laden with refreshments. He offered her another glass of champagne, which she accepted gratefully for, although the doors were flung wide, the mild September night and the large crowd caused the room to be quite warm.

"Will the belle of the ball promise a dance to her knight in shining armor?" Jonathon was beside her.

Looking up at him, Emily noticed Deidre behind him. She gave him her warmest smile and replied, "Of course, Jonathon."

His eyebrows shot up in surprise when she used his first name.

"My warmest wishes for your birthday, Emily," Deidre said sweetly, her eyes as cold as ice.

"Why thank you, Deidre," she answered graciously.

A tall, handsome young man approached and said, "Well, Jonathon, will you introduce me to this lovely lady, or do you intend to keep her to yourself?"

Deidre's lips tightened.

"Myself? I have yet to dance with her. It seems the bold rakes that are present tonight," he cast a meaningful glance at Randy, "have been claiming all her dances. Emily, may I present Phillip Beaumont. Phillip, Emily Wentworth."

"I am pleased to meet you, Mr. Beaumont," Emily said extending her hand. Phillip bent and kissed it.

"The pleasure is mine, Miss Wentworth. May I have the honor of the next dance?" he inquired.

"She has promised it to her aging guardian," Randy laughed.

"But you shall follow, Mr. Beaumont." Emily replied.

The room was brightly lit with candles that sparkled off jewels and glowed on faces. The musicians returned, and Jonathon led Emily to the floor. The music began and he slipped his arm around Emily's tiny waist, sending shivers of delight through her. Jonathon held her hand lightly as they glided across the floor.

"You continue to surprise me, Miss Wentworth," he said, a twinkle in his eyes. "That last greeting made me almost hope that your opinion of me might be changing. Perhaps, at last, you have found that one redeeming quality for which you had promised to search."

Emily turned up her nose and looked away.

"But then, perhaps not," he teased. "Although, after the interesting discussion I had with Deidre a while ago, I was sure you must have found something pleasing about me."

She peered at him sideways. "Just what was your discussion about?"

"Well, Deidre seems to feel terribly threatened by you and referred to 'our relationship'—meaning you and me—quite often. She made reference to old lechers and young virgins."

Emily blushed scarlet.

"Someone has led her to believe that. . . well, that I have become more than your guardian," his mouth twitched with a suppressed smile.

Emily looked straight ahead at the lace that cascaded at his throat.

He continued, "I do not know where she ever got that idea, certainly not from the warm and loving way you treat me."

"Captain Brentwood, do you intend to mock me throughout this entire dance?" Emily asked.

"I see we are back to formality. Just answer me this, Emily. What did you and Deidre discuss during her visit?"

Emily looked up at him in surprise.

"Oh yes, she told me about it," he answered her silent question.

"Really, Captain," Emily looked at him. There was a look of concern on his face that Emily did not understand. His brown eyes looked away, flitting across the other dancers. "She told me of your intimate relationship." Emily's heart felt heavy as she again thought of the two of them together.

"Emily—" Jonathon began. The waltz ended, and he saw Phillip approaching to claim the next dance. "We will pursue this later," he whispered urgently. His hand pressed her waist so fleetingly before he released her that Emily wondered if she had imagined it. They turned, and Jonathon presented her to Phillip and watched them dance away.

"How do you like Virginia, Miss Wentworth?" Phillip asked.

"Please, call me Emily."

"Virginia is beautiful, Phillip, just as Cap. . . Jonathon said it would be," she answered.

They chatted as they danced and between the champagne and the closeness of the room, Emily began to feel dizzy.

"Would you mind terribly if we stepped outside, Phillip?" she asked.

"Not at all," he replied and led her from the floor.

The evening air felt cool and refreshing. They strolled along a path and sat on a bench in the garden. The moon was a silver crescent hung against a backdrop of a star-speckled sky. The breeze stirred gently, feeling cool against Emily's skin.

"Tell me about yourself, Phillip."

"I am a student at the College of William and Mary. At present, I am studying at my parents' home here, and after the holidays, I shall return to Williamsburg. I enjoy it there, I have many good friends, and we have a grand time together." He smiled thinking about it. He began to relate stories about their escapades, and Emily laughed with him although a part of her mind wished to be back in the ballroom where Jonathon was. They talked for a while; then Phillip looked a bit self-conscious.

"Emily," he started, "may I call on you?"

Emily looked at her hands; she felt confused. This, of course, was what was supposed to happen—young men coming to call on her. But somehow the prospect of Phillip's attention made her uneasy.

"Of course, Phillip," she said softly. "That would be very nice."

"There is our guest of honor," Jonathon called as he approached them. Phillip rose quickly. "You are disappointing several young men whose arms are aching to lead you in a dance, Emily."

"I needed some air," she replied. "It was very warm in there and—"

"And champagne will do that, as will brandy," he winked at her.

Emily rose and frowned at him. She started to turn to Phillip, but Jonathon stepped forward and offered her his arm. Having no choice, she took it and Phillip followed them in. Jonathon led her right to the dance floor and took her in his arms once more.

"What about all those young men and their aching arms, Captain Brentwood?" Emily asked coolly.

"Their arms can ache a bit longer. Are you pleased with the crop of eligible young men here tonight?" Jonathon teased.

"Most pleased. But were one of them to become enamored of me and ask for my hand, you would probably find a reason not to approve the marriage."

"Probably."

"Then it makes no difference, does it?"

He laughed. "You are charming. Happy birthday, Em. I have a present for you."

She looked up at him. "A present? For me?"

"Yes, but it is in the study, and you will have to see it there. Emily, I want to talk to you about Deidre."

"Captain Brentwood, how you live your life is none of my concern."

"Deidre seems to think it is."

Emily looked away. The music ended and everyone headed for the refreshments. Jonathon lightly held Emily's elbow, and the spot burned where he touched her. He got them each a glass of champagne and, turning to her, saluted and said softly, for her ears only, "To the most beautiful ward a man could have." Their glasses clinked and Emily warmed at his compliment.

"How cozy," Deidre snarled behind them.

Jonathon's eyes never left Emily's as he said, "Would you like to join our toast, Deidre?" Slowly moving his eyes to hers he continued, "It was to Emily's beauty."

Deidre bristled. "How convenient for you, Jonathon, to have such *beauty*," she sneered at the word, "right under your own roof."

Jonathon moved toward Emily and placed his arm around her waist. "Indeed."

Deidre glared at each in turn and left. Jonathon looked down at Emily.

"Well, I did not want to make a liar out of whoever it was that told her we were lovers," he whispered down at her, caressing the last word, his eyes dancing.

Emily squirmed at his words. She had certainly made a mess out of things. The price of letting Deidre continue to believe there was romance between them was allowing Jonathon to act as if there were. And Emily was not sure that she wanted Deidre to think differently—or Jonathon to act differently.

Randy approached and Jonathon slowly removed his arm from Emily's waist.

"Well, as usual, the party at Brentwood Manor has outdone all in the countryside. Emily, may I claim you for the next dance?"

"I would be delighted, Randy," she gave him a dazzling smile. Jonathon looked a bit vexed.

*

The evening flew by and Emily danced with all the young men who attended. She charmed the older ones as well, who were quickly claimed by watchful wives and drawn safely away when the music stopped. Emily noticed that Jonathon danced with Deidre twice, and they seemed involved in a lively conversation. Then they disappeared into the gardens for a large part of the evening. Emily's gay laughter sounded hollow in her ears during their absence.

The guests were thinning out—those who lived in the vicinity leaving in their carriages, and a few who had traveled long distances retiring to the guest rooms.

Jonathon approached Emily, who was saying good-bye to Phillip and his parents. Phillip bent to kiss her hand. When he rose, his eyes held hers.

"Good-night, Emily. I shall be calling soon," he promised.

Jonathon cleared his throat. "Quite so, Phillip. Good night," and he urged the young man to the door. Closing it, he turned to Emily.

"Will you accompany me to the study, Miss Wentworth?" he asked, holding out his arm. His eyes twinkled in anticipation. "Andrew, come along," he called out over his shoulder.

Joanna and David joined them as they entered the study. A large box sat before the desk, and Emily looked from the box to Jonathon. Earlier that morning, Andrew had given her soft, leather riding gloves. At dinner that afternoon, Joanna and David had given her a silk bonnet with satin ribbons that matched her eyes. It had not occurred to her then that Jonathon had not given her a present.

"Go ahead, open it," he laughed.

Emily tore at the wrappings excitedly. Lifting the cover off, she gasped. It was a miniature of her father's ship, the *Spirit*. It was authentic even down to the ropes coiled on the deck. Emily stared at it, tears stinging her eyes.

"Oh, Jonathon," she whispered. "It is beautiful!"

Impulsively she threw her arms around his neck and kissed his cheek. Then, embarrassed, she withdrew them. Softly she said, "You have given me a part of my father to have with me always. Thank you."

Jonathon was grinning from ear to ear, but now he wished he had not invited the others. Perhaps that embrace would have lasted longer.

Chapter 5

The early October morning was crisp and cool. The horses were saddled and stamping their hooves in anticipation as Emily, Jonathon, and Andrew approached the stables. Dora was putting the last of a generous repast in three saddlebags.

"There are only three of us, remember, Dora," Jonathon called to her.

Dora laughed, "But I know how you and Master Andrew can eat, Cap'n Brentwood."

Suddenly they heard a horse approaching and spotted a lone rider coming up the drive. Calvin Wheeler waved his hat and whistled for them to wait.

"Hey, Andrew, are you ready to go hunting?" he asked.

"Is this the day we had planned on? I was just about to take a ride with Jonathon and Emily," Andrew answered, walking to meet him.

"You go ahead if you have made plans, Drew," Jonathon called.

"Wait, perhaps we should go another day when Andrew can . . ." Emily paused.

"Chaperone, Miss Wentworth?" Jonathon whispered so only Emily heard.

Seeing the disappointment on Andrew's face and the challenge on Jonathon's, Emily spoke. "You go ahead with Cal, Andrew."

Grinning from ear to ear, Andrew jumped on his horse. The two boys raced down the drive and were quickly out of sight.

Jonathon turned to Emily. "I have a gift for you," he said, holding out a small package.

Reaching to take it Emily's hand brushed his sending a feeling of excitement through her. Tearing away the wrappings she held up a small compass encased in gold, lapis lazuli and mother of pearl. Smiling in bewilderment, she looked up at him.

"Thank you. It is lovely."

"And it is practical. Now you will see that we will not ride only in small circles on my property all day as you suggested when we were aboard the *Destiny*."

Emily laughed. "You are out to prove all of your boasting, are you not, Captain?"

"Of course, Miss Wentworth."

Jonathon helped her to mount her horse, and they started off in good spirits. As they rode west, Emily was taken with the beauty of the countryside. After a time, rolling hills gave way to steeper foothills, so they forded a stream and rode its path until the sun was high.

Jonathon led the way into the trees, and they came upon a grassy hill dotted yellow with wild sunflowers. Riding to the top they had a sweeping view of a valley, and beyond they could see the land climb toward the mountains. They dismounted and spread out a blanket for their picnic. Before sitting down Emily walked around the hilltop breathing in the fresh air. The land was vast and untamed, its beauty enhanced by wildflowers and ancient trees.

Emily knelt down on the blanket and began to set out the food from the saddlebags Jonathon brought over.

"Dora must have thought the whole household would be coming along," she exclaimed when Jonathon brought over the third one. They laughed and began to eat. The food was delicious— cold chicken, cheeses, corn bread, apples, berries, yams and wine.

Jonathon gazed at the clouds gathering in the western sky. "We shall probably be wet by the time we arrive home."

Emily followed his gaze. "The clouds look far off."

"Sometimes they move in faster than you would think. Distance can be deceiving out here." He turned to look at her. "Do you realize that this is the first time we have ever been alone together, Miss Wentworth?" Jonathon teased.

Emily looked down at her wine glass. "Oh, we have been alone many times."

"I mean all alone. No one in the next room or ship's cabin. Does that frighten you?"

"Should it frighten me? After all you are my guardian." She looked him squarely in the eye, her heart racing.

Jonathon threw his head back and laughed. "You certainly know how to break a mood."

Strangely disappointed, Emily laughed unsurely. "Besides, I am just a child, is that not correct, Captain? Only worth a 'little incident'." She could not hide the harshness in her voice. She began to pick up the food.

Jonathon stared at her. He reached out and stopped her hand, but she continued to look down.

"Have I hurt you that much?" he asked.

She pulled away and continued packing up the saddlebags. "Perhaps I am just becoming cynical."

"Perhaps you have been hurt," he answered. "I am sorry, Em."

Slowly she raised her eyes to his. In them she saw his sincerity and his confusion.

"I wonder if Father was aware of the situation into which he was putting us. I am never sure how I should act." she shrugged. "I feel too old to need a guardian, yet when women like Deidre are around I feel so childish." She stood up and brushed off her skirt.

"When women like Deidre are around you, they pale in comparison." Jonathon stood in front of her placing his hands on her shoulders. "Do you not realize your beauty? You not only are beautiful, you are charming, refreshing—and it is so natural. It is all a part of who you are," he paused. "I am confused about all of this, too, Em. I am afraid to act affectionately for fear I shall get carried away as I did on board the *Destiny*. That was supposed to be an innocent kiss meant to tease you. Believe me, Em, I was as taken by surprise as you were. That is why I am afraid to get too close, why I tease and keep it light. What kind of guardian seduces his ward? George was a good friend—I cared a great deal about him. And I care about you, Em. My greatest desire is to see you happy." He stopped and looked out toward the mountains. "You should be married to one of the fine young men around here—like Phillip Beaumont. But there are times I want to take you in my arms and hold you, to kiss you 'til I take your breath away. I fight these feelings more and more, for if I do give in, I shall lose control and ruin your life." He paused and looked down at her, "That is why I am leaving for a while. I have made plans to sail next week for the Committees of Correspondence." He felt her trembling and saw the tears spring to her eyes.

"Oh, Emily," he breathed, folding her into his arms. Her hair smelled sweet; he felt her tears on his shirt. "You tempt me so."

Lifting her head she looked up at him. "I do not mean to, Jonathon." Her hands rested on his chest, tears brimmed in her eyes, and she tried to force a smile.

He could bear it no longer. Their eyes locked and he slowly bent his head. Tenderly, gently, his lips brushed hers. Suddenly, he pulled away.

"No, Emily, I cannot do this to you. I cannot do it to George."

Emily was breathing deeply, trying to clear her head.

"Jonathon, I do not understand."

"Em, you need someone like Phillip. You would have a good, solid, stable life with him. He would not be off sailing all the time. Oh, Em, it is so wrong."

Emily felt like she was tumbling to the ground. She fought to keep her balance and her stemmed passion turned to rage.

"If you wanted me to have a safe, stable life, why not leave me with Michael Dennings?" she cried. "At least I could have stayed in London. Instead you drag me over to this God-forsaken country!"

"Maybe I should have left you there. I would have considerably fewer problems!" Jonathon stormed. He stooped and began packing the saddlebags roughly. He was churning with unspent emotion. His rage was a wiser choice.

Emily shook the blanket out violently. "Well, then we all would have been a lot happier, is that not so?"

*

They mounted their horses in silence and rode eastward, the clouds gathering behind them. Both were shaken by what had happened. Jonathon was lost in thought trying to sort out where his duties lie and what to do about his feelings for Emily. First he would have to define what those feelings were.

Emily was tense, every muscle tightened in an effort to control the trembling that she first felt on the hilltop and that would not seem to dissipate. She watched Jonathon riding ahead, his broad shoulders and lean body graceful and masculine, moving in unison with his horse. She heard thunder and knew Jonathon was right—they were in for a soaking.

Emily pondered their conversation. She had not thought of Jonathon as being in the same predicament as she was. It was, perhaps, more difficult for him, because if romance did develop between them it would be seen as if he had seduced her. Her body tingled with delight as she remembered the feel of his lips against hers. So lost in thought was she that she had not noticed the nearness of the storm until Jonathon reined Neptune to a halt and turned to her.

"The storm is moving in quickly; we had best take cover. There is a cabin nearby that our overseer sometimes uses when he is hunting. It is rustic, but it will shelter us through this storm," he called back to her.

He turned and headed into the trees; Emily followed. Branches brushed against her face and hair, and brambles poked at her boots. The thunder was growing closer and she could feel Shadow growing skittish. Emily spoke softly to the horse in low, soothing tones, but her mind turned back again to Jonathon.

Their progress through the woods was slow, and the thunder

rumbled above them as lightning streaked the sky. Large droplets of rain began to pommel them and pound the forest floor. The trees were little protection, and Emily knew they would soon be drenched.

Suddenly, a rabbit jumped in front of Shadow at the exact moment lightning struck a nearby tree producing a loud crack of thunder. Emily could not control her horse. Shadow shied and reared and Emily was thrown from her back. Jonathon turned in time to see her hurtle off Shadow and land, twisting, on one leg. She fell to the ground hitting her head on a protruding tree root. Shadow bolted, snorting in fear.

Jonathon galloped back to Emily and dismounted. She was unconscious, and her leg was twisted beneath her. Fearing a broken leg, he searched for some straight, sturdy branches. Ripping his shirt into strips, he constructed a crude, but effective, splint. He lifted Emily gently in his arms, held Neptune's reins, and headed for the overseer's cabin, estimating it to be about a half mile away. The thunder and lightning continued, and the skies opened up pelting them with a stinging torrent of rain. The temperature was dropping with the onslaught of the storm. Jonathon walked carefully so not to trip or slip in the now-softening mud. By the time he reached the cabin, they were drenched to the skin. He tied Neptune to a tree and carried Emily into the cabin.

Emily moaned and slowly opened her eyes as Jonathon placed her on the bed.

"Where am I?" she whispered and tried to rise. She winced in pain as her leg shifted.

"Shhh," Jonathon said softly. "You were thrown from Shadow and hit your head. I think you hurt your leg."

Emily was shaking and her lips quivered with the cold.

"We need to get out of these wet clothes before we catch a chill. The storm will last for a while."

Emily looked at him as if he had lost his mind. "And just what do you suggest we wear, Captain Brentwood? Or is this part of some grand scheme of yours?"

He looked around hopelessly. Emily was right; this cabin was rustic and equipped only for an overnight stay. The bed, at least, had bedclothes that would keep them warm. . . and covered up.

He turned to Emily who was shivering both from the dampness and from the shock of the fall. He knew it was critical to get her warm and dry.

"Come on, Em, you need to warm up. Can you undress if I turn my back? I shall pull the quilt off so you can wrap up in it."

Despite the splint that immobilized her leg, it was painful for Emily to shift as he removed the quilt from under her. It took her several moments just to sit up. She strained to reach the laces along the back of her dress, and each time she balanced to reach around her back, the pressure of the movement hurt her leg. Finally, Jonathon sat beside her on the bed.

"Let me help you, Miss Wentworth."

"I beg your pardon?" Emily exclaimed.

"Well, you seem to be making very little headway," Jonathon laughed softly. "Come, Em, let me help you."

Emily hesitated, but seeing the sense of it, and getting colder by the minute, she relented. He sat beside her and, slowly, she turned her back to him and lifted her tawny locks exposing the laces down the back of her dress.

Jonathon fumbled with the laces, surprised at his awkwardness. This certainly was not his first experience relieving a lady of her frock, yet he felt like a schoolboy. His fingers worked deftly, though they trembled. It is just that they are cold, he thought.

Gradually, Emily's dress opened in the back and her creamy skin was revealed. Jonathon's throat felt dry. As her dress slipped forward, he gently brought the quilt across her lap so Emily could modestly hold it against herself. She slipped the dress forward and Jonathon's eyes swept over her back. Her shoulders glistened in the dim light, and he longed to trace his fingers along the outline of her spine from the nape of her neck to the delicate curve just peeking from the below the waistline of her dress.

He wrapped some of the quilt across her back so she could finish removing the bodice of her dress. Emily looked over her shoulder at him, her eyes smiling her thanks. Fighting the allure she felt for him was difficult enough, but now she felt a new warmth and appreciation for Jonathon because of his gentle ministrations. Moving cautiously and laughing with their awkward pursuit of modesty, they finally removed Emily's wet clothes.

Once she was resting comfortably under the quilt, Jonathon went back outside in the downpour to unsaddle Neptune and bring in the saddlebags. Back inside, he started a fire.

"Now, Miss Wentworth, you must fight your basic instincts and turn your head while I shed my wet clothes."

Emily blushed furiously. "Let me assure you, Captain, I have no interest in watching you disrobe." Emily snapped her mouth shut, surprised by her boldness. Jonathon threw his head back, laughing.

"Whom are you trying to convince, Miss Wentworth?" he smiled devilishly.

"Ooooh," she winced and fell against the pillow, turning her face against the wall.

Jonathon stripped off his wet clothing and wrapped himself in a blanket from the cedar chest. He stoked the fire, which brought a warmth and coziness to the cabin, then brought a chair alongside the bed and looked at Emily. Her face pale and drawn, her eyes bespoke her pain.

Reaching into a saddlebag on the floor, he retrieved a flask. "Here, Em, drink some brandy; it will help the pain."

"Why does brandy always seem to enter into our conversation?" she asked ruefully. She accepted the flask and sipped carefully. "It is horrible stuff," she choked out making a face.

Jonathon laughed. "How does your head feel?"

"Like a drum—it is pounding. My leg feels worse." She tried to move it and winced in pain. Jonathon handed her the flask and she took another sip.

"At that rate, Em, your leg will be healed before you drink enough to ease the pain." She made a face at him and sipped some more. She felt the warmth seep through her body, and it did seem to help somewhat.

"Are you warm enough, Em? The storm brought some cool air with it." Emily nodded and smiled. He continued, "I imagine Shadow will reach the stables soon. When we do not return with him or shortly after, someone will come looking for us."

"Will they think to look here? Your land is so vast they could search for days."

"Hmmm, so you admit to the vastness of my land? You are right, though, Em. They do not know what direction we were headed in, so it could be days." Jonathon raised his eyebrows. "That could be interesting."

"You are terrible!" Emily gasped. "Please get me my clothes."

"They are not dry yet and you do not need damp clothes clinging to that lovely body right now."

Emily felt a rush of warmth at his words. "I did not realize how difficult this situation has been for you. You have been most kind to Andrew and me, and have always acted in a gentlemanly manner."

Jonathon gave her a crooked smile, "Even this afternoon?"

"I was as much at fault as you," she said softly. The brandy warmed Emily all over and the throbbing in her head had lessened considerably. As long as she did not move it, her leg was fairly comfortable. The fire made the room quite cozy and Emily carefully lifted her arms from beneath the blanket and rested them on top, revealing soft, creamy shoulders. Feeling sleepy, she stifled a yawn.

"You need some more rest," Jonathon said. He brushed a strand of hair out of her eyes, and she reached up, caught his hand, and held it.

"Thank you for rescuing me," she murmured sleepily.

"My pleasure, m'lady. I shall see how our provisions are. It is lucky for us that Dora packed enough for a week."

Emily dozed off.

*

When she awakened, the sky was dark and the light of the fire and a single candle cast deep shadows in the one-room cabin. It was rustic, fit for a man concerned only with hunting for a few days, not amenities. But the thick, feather mattress and down pillows were comfortable and, since Jonathon had pulled the bed in front of the hearth, quite warm. Warm enough in fact that in her sleep Emily had let the blanket slip, exposing most of the curve of her round, full breasts. Realizing this she quickly yanked up the blanket and winced as she caught her right foot, sending shards of pain up her leg.

"Time for your medicine, Miss Wentworth," Jonathon said bringing over the flask and gently sitting down beside her. Emily took a couple of sips and coughed, which hurt her head.

"I do not know which is worse, the injury or the cure." She took a couple more sips and handed him the flask. "You could have covered me up, Jonathon," she scolded.

"Why? I was enjoying the view," he grinned. "You are lovely, Em. Enticing."

"And you are a rogue," she said impishly. "May I have my clothes now?"

"I do not know, I rather like you this way. Very natural, do you not agree?" he teased.

"I shall get them myself."

She rose but her head began to throb and when she reached up to her temples the blanket slipped to her waist. Letting out a little scream she flopped back to the pillows and regained her modesty. "Ohhh," she moaned and reached for the flask.

Jonathon burst out laughing. "If you continue to tempt me like this, I shall not be held accountable for my actions."

Emily took several sips this time and snarled, "You love to see me miserable, do you not?"

Chuckling Jonathon rose and brought over the saddlebags. He spread out napkins and some food and wine on a nearby table.

"I do not think I am hungry," Emily said. Her head seemed to float and she was warm all over. "But I do feel much better," she giggled.

Jonathon grabbed the wine bottle and gave her a stern look. "None of this for you, young lady."

She grabbed the flask. "Yes sir, guardian," she saluted letting the blanket slip. "I shall have to quench my thirst medicinally," she slurred and sipped some brandy. And coughed.

"You have had enough, Em," Jonathon said, reaching for the flask.

"Do not be such an old fogey, Jonathon," Emily smirked, pulling the flask away.

Jonathon reached across her but she stretched her arm back and the blanket dropped again to her waist. Firelight flickered across her full pink-tipped breasts. There was a devilish twinkle in her eyes and she giggled again.

"Emily," Jonathon said in a tight voice.

"Yes, Jonathon?" she said, feigning innocence.

He reached over her for the flask and his chest rubbed against her. Her breath was soft against his shoulder.

"Jonathon?" she whispered.

He turned and met her eyes—their twinkle was replaced with a smoldering fire. Her arm slowly lowered the flask to the mattress, snapping the lid closed. She reached up and touched Jonathon's face, gently stroking his cheek. Her eyes traced the line of his jaw and returned to meet his gaze.

"Jonathon," she repeated softly. Her body burned to be next to his, to feel his touch. She tingled with desire and a passion she had never known.

Jonathon stroked her arm, feeling her silken skin beneath his fingers. His body screamed to take her in his arms, his excitement evident and throbbing.

"Emily, no," he whispered huskily.

Her fingers traced his lips and moved to the nape of his neck. She lightly massaged him and gently ran her fingers through his hair. She leaned toward him, her scent warm and sweet. Gently she brushed his lips, her own parted, then his cheek and the line of his jaw. Jonathon's passion rose until he thought he would explode, and all the time his mind screamed, "No!"

Their arms went around each other and their lips met in a hungry, blazing kiss. Emily's skin felt like silk beneath his hands and Jonathon caressed her back. Their mouths locked in a demanding, fierce kiss. Jonathon traced fiery kisses down her throat and shoulders, and then he dipped his head to trace the full curve of her breast. Emily moaned with desire and pulled his head closer, running her fingers through his thick, wavy hair.

Jonathon raised his head and held her away from him.

"Em, I shall hurt you."

"No, Jonathon, I want you."

"I mean your leg," he grinned.

"I do not feel any pain right now, Jonathon."

"I imagine you do not."

He leaned over her and softly brushed her lips with his. His tongue traced over them and slipped into her mouth. She eagerly met it with her own and wrapped her arms around his neck. His hands caressed her back and slid gently to her breasts. He teased her nipples to a taut peak and she shivered in delight. He lifted the blanket and slid in beside her, pressing his lean body close. Emily brushed her hand through the hair on his chest as he nuzzled into her neck. She nibbled on his ear, and her soft breath excited him even more. Jonathon's hands boldly explored, giving Emily such newfound excitement that she trembled. She began to do the same, at first timidly, then with boldness and delight. Finally Jonathon rose above her and carefully eased between her thighs. Emily gasped when she felt him enter her, but the brief pain was quickly replaced with intense pleasure.

Their bodies moved together in a delicious rhythm. Then, wrapped in each other's arms they strained toward that ultimate unity. Emily moaned, amazed at the intensity of the sensations she was experiencing.

"Jonathon. . . oh, Jonathon," she called out, clinging to him, moving with him until they soared in a shimmering explosion of bliss.

Finally spent, they lay with limbs entangled, in the glow of the fire. Jonathon's head rested on Emily's breast, and he traced lazy circles on her stomach. She twined her fingers in his hair and pressed a kiss on his head. Neither spoke for a while.

"How is your leg, Em?" Jonathon finally said.

"Wonderful," she sighed.

He rose up on one elbow and looked at her. Her hair was wildly tossed on the pillow and a rosy hue heightened in her cheeks. Her eyes glowed a soft periwinkle and she smiled gently.

"Really, Jonathon. I am quite comfortable," she said, running a finger down his arm. He bent down and nibbled playfully at her breast, chuckling at the reaction it brought.

"You are excited," he said

"You seem to arouse that reaction in me."

He nuzzled against her neck; his hands gently caressed her. She stroked his hair and sighed in contentment, closing her eyes. Soon their passion raged, and again they satisfied the hunger they both had fought against so long.

"Emily, are you hungry?" Jonathon murmured against her throat after a while.

"Mmmm."

Reluctantly he rose and pulled the table next to the bed. Climbing in beside her, he sliced some cheese and poured the wine. They ate slowly talking softly and sipping wine from the same glass. Neither was very hungry and soon the food was packed away and they lay in each other's arms once more.

"This certainly complicates things," Jonathon thought aloud.

Emily pressed her finger to his lips. "Jonathon, we are here together right now and I have never been so happy in my life. I want to bask in the glow of this joy and worry about complications tomorrow. There is precious little we can do about it tonight."

Jonathon rose up and leered wickedly. "Well there is *one* thing we can do." Emily laughed.

Their fevered, pent-up passion had been sated, and their lovemaking this time was languid. Finally, entwined in each other's arms, they slept deeply.

*

The early morning sun streamed in across the nestled, sleeping couple. Slowly Jonathon awakened, disturbed at something of which he was not quite aware. Suddenly, he reached beneath the bed for his pistol and aimed it as the cabin door opened.

"And we were worried about you," Randy chided.

Jonathon pulled the blanket up around Emily's shoulders as she slowly opened her eyes.

"Jonathon—what is it?" she murmured.

"We have company, Em."

Closing the door, Randy came in, his eyes stormy. "I hate to disturb you two, but Andrew and some others are close behind me. I took the detour to check this cabin. You might want to put some clothes on before they arrive."

"Well not with you standing here we will not. Go tell them we are in need of a wagon. Emily has hurt her leg. And Randy, that is all they need to know."

"I am not daft, man," he snarled. "Emily, are you all right?" he asked, a worried frown creasing his brow.

"Yes, Randy. Jonathon took good care of me."

"I can see that," he snapped and left the cabin.

Jonathon turned to Emily. "I am truly sorry, Em."

"Jonathon, do not be; I am not. Randy is a good friend, he will not say anything." She kissed him gently.

"Before we start something we do not want to stop, we had best get dressed," he said.

Jonathon's shirt was in rags as he had used it for her splint, but he quickly slipped into the rest of his clothes and gently helped Emily into hers amidst much giggling, tickling, and teasing.

"Behave, Jonathon, or the search party will discover more than they are searching for."

Straightening up the cabin, Jonathon did his best to make it appear that Emily had slept in the bed and he on the floor. Soon they heard horses approach and Randy's voice rang out loudly.

"I shall tell them we are here."

Jonathon chuckled at the obvious warning and opened the door. Andrew ran up and the look of relief on his face was touching.

"Em, are you all right?" he asked, running to the bed. "We have been so worried."

She hugged her brother, "Yes, I am well, Drew, except for my leg." Ruefully she pulled back the covers to show him the splint.

"Another group has a wagon and they are not far from here," he answered.

Randy had followed him in and scrutinized the cabin. Grunting in satisfaction, he gave Jonathon a long, cold look that Jonathon returned.

*

Joanna and David hurried out of the house when the party arrived. Tears streaming down her face, Joanna ran up to the wagon where Emily lay on the tick mattress and pillows. Then she looked at Jonathon.

"Are you two all right? It frightened us so when Shadow came charging in last night. Emily, what has happened to you?" she cried.

Emily explained the accident as the men dismounted. Jonathon strode over to the wagon and put down the back. Tenderly he lifted her into his arms, their eyes meeting briefly.

"She needs rest. Randy went for the doctor," he explained.

"Emily, I shall fix you some tea while Jonathon takes you upstairs," Joanna said, looking closely at the two of them. "Then we shall visit and you can tell me all about it." She turned and swept into the house.

Jonathon carried Emily to her room where the bedclothes had been folded back.

"I am beginning to feel like a lecher with the looks people are giving me," he said softly to Emily.

"You are one, Captain Brentwood," she teased.

As he gently laid Emily down on the crisp, fresh sheets, he noticed how drawn her face was. The trip had been difficult for her. He stroked her forehead.

"Em, what can I get for you? Dare I suggest more brandy?"

"Heavens, no!" she protested. "The doctor will be here soon and I can wait until then."

Joanna entered with a tray. "Now, Jonathon, I shall take over from here until Dr. Anderson arrives." She paused. "I would like to speak with you when he arrives, though."

Jonathon winked at Emily as he answered, "Yes, Joanna."

When he left, Joanna turned to Emily. "Dulcie will be up to

give you a soothing sponge bath soon. Have some tea, Emily?" She handed her a cup. "Are you. . . all right, Em?"

"I am well, Joanna, really."

Joanna's wide, brown eyes, so much like Jonathon's, searched hers. Finally she smiled, "I believe you are, Emily."

Jonathon was in his study when Joanna came to speak to him.

"Jonathon, what have you done?" she asked.

"I am not sure I understand what you mean, Joanna," he replied.

"The two people who left yesterday are not the same two people who came back today."

Jonathon looked at his sister. She had always been intuitive and she knew him so well.

"Well, I did not rape her if that is what you mean. It all just. . . happened."

"Jonathon, I know you have not led a celibate life, but Emily is not a. . . well. . . loose woman. Jonathon, good Lord, you are her guardian!"

"Damn it, woman! Do you not think I know that better than anyone?" he yelled. "George Wentworth, my dearest friend, entrusted his daughter to me and I took her to bed!" His voice softened, "But, Joanna, it was not like that."

"Do you love her, Jonathon?" she asked quietly, holding her breath.

"I. . . I do not know. I care very deeply about her—and Andrew. But for so long I have been trying to put my feelings into perspective, trying to act the proper guardian. Yes, I love her, but affectionately—until last night. I am confused, Joanna."

"You will marry her, of course."

Jonathon stared at his sister. "Would that be fair, Joanna? Two lovers claim me already—the sea and Brentwood Plantation. I am spread thinly enough between the two as it is. Would it be fair for Emily to have one–third of me at best—probably less?"

"Perhaps you should have thought of that before giving in to your passion. Tell me this, Jonathon. What husband would you have for her now? And what will he do to her when he discovers on his wedding night that she is not his alone? I understand your love for the sea, but the sea is a fickle lover. If you leave her, other men will take her to their hearts never expecting her to be theirs alone. But if you leave Emily now, I do not know what you will be condemning her to. Think long and hard about this, Jonathon. Ask yourself how Emily feels right now." Silence fell between them.

Finally Joanna walked over and kissed his cheek. "She could do much worse, you know. And so could you."

"Joanna, I have made plans for a brief voyage next week to Massachusetts for the Committees."

"I see," she said thoughtfully. "Jonathon, ten men were on that search party, including Andrew. I do not know how long you can take to make a decision. Randy is a good friend, as are the others, but news has a way of spreading, and they all know you were there together all night. I suggest you think long and hard about this and ask the Lord for direction."

She left him silently staring out the window.

*

Dr. Anderson had given Emily a sleeping draught and wrapped her leg. He announced that it was not broken, rather a severe sprain, and Emily was confined to bed. She slept all afternoon and as the lamps were lit, she roused. Andrew sat with her while she ate a light supper; she soon dozed again. She was vaguely aware of people coming in to check on her, but the moon was high and the house quiet when she became aware of a tall figure beside her bed.

"Jonathon?"

"I am here, Em," he said quietly. Slowly she lifted her hand to him. Taking it, he sat down beside her and placed a kiss on her forehead. She lifted his hand to her lips and kissed it.

"I am so sleepy," she said.

"I know. The rest is good for you," he stroked her hair.

"Jonathon," she murmured and pulled his arm to bring him closer. "Hold me."

He leaned down, gently pulling her toward him, his arms slipping behind her back. Her arms went slowly up around his shoulders and she sighed. He buried his face in her hair and held her close.

"Em, what have I done to you?" he whispered.

Hearing her even breathing, he slowly laid her back on the pillows. She was sleeping soundly; her lips parted slightly, dark lashes against her cheeks. Jonathon wanted to crush her to him. Instead, he placed another kiss on her forehead, covered her, and slipped from the room.

*

It was late morning when Emily awoke the next day. The bright sun splashed in through the chintz curtains and gleamed off the highly polished floor. Joanna was just setting a tray on the bedside table and noticed Emily stir.

"Good morning," she said brightly.

"Good morning, Joanna."

"How are you feeling? Did you sleep well?"

"Well, and yes, in that order." Emily laughed. "My, it must be almost noon!"

"Do not worry. You needed the sleep and the freedom from pain for a while. Andrew would like to come up now. I shall tell him you are awake."

Andrew and Emily spent the remainder of the morning talking about his plans to attend William and Mary College after the Christmas holidays. Emily always enjoyed chats with Andrew, but, throughout their conversation, she kept listening for Jonathon's footsteps in the hall. Twice when Dulcie entered her room, Emily's eyes shot to the door in anticipation, but then showed only disappointment.

She slept a bit in the afternoon, but lay staring at the canopy for the hour before supper. She could not understand why Jonathon had not come in to see her. Perhaps, as she had on the *Destiny,* she was taking what happened between them more seriously than he. Perhaps he considered it only another "little incident." But she had seen the look in his eyes—the tenderness, the passion, the caring. And she thought about how tenderly he had held her just last night. Then where was he?

"Perhaps I have been a fool. I was warned about his reputation with women. Maybe I only believed what I wanted to believe."

Tears streamed down her cheeks and she ached with longing for strong arms to enfold her, for gentle kisses to excite her.

Joanna brought in a tray and she and Andrew ate supper with Emily. David was tending some business at a nearby plantation and would not be back until late. Joanna noticed how quiet Emily was and guessed the reason.

"Jonathon had to go into Williamsburg today," she said casually, pouring more tea into Emily's cup. Setting the silver teapot down, she looked up at the younger girl. "He came in early this morning to say good-bye, but you were sleeping so peacefully that he did not want to disturb you."

The relief was evident on Emily's face. "I see," was all she could say, trying to stifle a cry of joy. Composing herself she asked, "When does he expect to return?"

"Tomorrow evening. He has to prepare to sail next week," Joanna replied.

"I am to go with him, Em," Andrew exclaimed.

"Oh, Drew, you will not do anything foolish this time, will you?" she pleaded.

Joanna looked from sister to brother. "Did something happen on the voyage from England?" she asked. Together they told her of the incident aboard the *Destiny* during the storm and Jonathon's daring rescue that saved Andrew's life.

"I stopped asking Jonathon about his voyages long ago," Joanna laughed. "If I had not, my hair would be pure gray by now!"

The rest of the evening was spent pleasantly playing cards and chatting.

Emily tried to read a book the next day, but at every sound she looked up, listening for Jonathon's step, her heart pounding furiously until the sound faded or proved to be someone else entering her room. Then she would have to reread the page, forcing herself to concentrate.

The dinner hour passed, the lamps were lit and still there was no sign of Jonathon. Emily waited far into the night, staring at the fire in the hearth and reliving those wonderful moments in Jonathon's arms. Slowly her eyes began to get heavy and she could fight sleep no more.

*

Jonathon looked down at the slumbering girl, her hand tucked beneath her cheek, light breath whispering between her parted lips.

"So beautifully peaceful," he thought.

He bent and gently brushed her cheek with his lips. Slowly her eyes opened. He saw the happiness there when she awakened and realized he was beside her. A sleepy grin spread across Emily's face, and he felt a responding one on his.

"Good morning, sleepyhead," he teased. "Is this what a lady of leisure does all day and night?"

"Only when she is left to her own resources, sir."

He sat on the bed beside her. "I had to go into Williamsburg, Em."

"I know. Joanna told me. When do you sail?"

"In six days. It will be a short voyage to Massachusetts, a fortnight, perhaps a month." He brushed a curl from her cheek. "How are you feeling?"

"Confined. The weather has been marvelous they tell me, and I can only glimpse the sunshine."

"I shall carry you down to the veranda tomorrow. Will that lift your spirits?" he asked.

"Oh, Jonathon, could you?" she exclaimed, impulsively throwing her arms around his neck and pulling him down for a kiss on the cheek. She lay back on the pillow, but kept her arms around his neck. They looked steadily into each other's eyes for a long moment. Emily's heart beat wildly. Jonathon reached to her nightgown and slowly pulled the ribbon, untying the bow at the bodice. He gently opened it revealing the deep valley between her breasts. He kissed her softly, and lowering his head, traced a line down her throat to the full curve of her breast. She sighed softly and pressed his head closer with one hand, loosening his shirt with the other. He rose and quickly shed his clothes and Emily saw his handsome figure outlined in the moonlight that streamed in the window. He slipped into bed beside her and Emily felt the hardness of his body against hers. His hands roamed her body, exploring, teasing, caressing, bringing a passion in her that she never expected. And she did the same, delighted at the reaction in Jonathon. Soon they were moving in a frenzied rhythm that signaled the climax of their union before slipping into that peaceful exhaustion that overwhelms lovers and enfolds them in a warm afterglow.

Cradled in Jonathon's arm, her head resting on his shoulder, Emily caught curls of matted hair on his chest and wound them around her finger.

"I shall miss you, Jonathon," she said softly.

"I shall miss you too, love."

Emily thrilled at that name. She traced the line of his jaw with her fingers, then around his chin up to his lips. He kissed them and she turned his head toward her. He leaned down and kissed her and she traced his lips with her tongue. He leaned back on the pillow.

"You are an enchantress, Em."

"You are a rogue, Captain Brentwood," she pulled a hair on his chest. He gently tugged her nipple in return and she giggled softly.

"I must leave you now; it will soon be dawn and Dulcie will be shocked out of her senses if she finds me here." He kissed Emily gently and rose from the bed. Quickly dressing, he bent and pulled the covers up over her.

"Good night, Jonathon."

"Good night, Love."

*

The next day dawned sunny and mild. Emily's spirits lifted at the thought of being outside. Dulcie bathed her and dressed her hair; putting in lavender ribbons to match her gown. It was one of her more revealing ones, cut lower in the bodice with demure lace edging that was merely for decoration.

After breakfast, Jonathon arrived to keep his promise. Seeing her he stopped to take a long admiring look.

"Perhaps we should stay up here, Em."

"I shall die if I stay up here any longer, Jonathon."

"Oh, I could keep you occupied, but if you must be outside, I thank you for the lovely view with which you have gifted me."

He lifted her up effortlessly and carried her down to the veranda. A chaise had been set out for her and Jonathon gently lowered her onto it, gazing down from an advantageous angle at her bosom.

"Oh, Em, you tempt me sorely," he whispered hoarsely.

"Mind your manners, Captain," she scolded.

He placed a blanket around her lap and drew her shawl about her shoulders.

"Are you comfortable, my lady?" he asked.

"This is wonderful. Thank you, Jonathon."

Joanna appeared with a tea tray and they shared a lovely

morning. At everyone's insistence, Emily napped in the afternoon but was allowed to join them for supper.

Jonathon came to her room again after the house was quiet. He slipped between the sheets and took Emily into his arms. They made love in the flickering firelight, speaking softly in the shadows. And they lay together quietly, sometimes talking, sometimes not needing to talk, until Jonathon slipped out of bed and left her room.

Emily had never been so happy in her life.

The days continued thus until the night before Jonathon left. Their lovemaking was especially passionate that night, each knowing it would be a long time before they could be together again. Emily held Jonathon close as he kissed her good night.

"I shall miss you, Jonathon," she said softly.

"I shall miss you, love," he whispered against her lips.

*

Jonathon carried Emily to the veranda the next morning as Andrew carried the last of his own belongings to the carriage. Emily tried to swallow the lump in her throat and to blink back the tears that stung her eyes.

"You will not let Andrew do anything foolish, will you Jonathon?" she asked as he stepped onto the veranda.

"No, Emily. I shall watch out for him." He set her down on the chaise. "And you will take good care of that leg, will you not? We shall be out riding again in no time." He leaned close and whispered, "Perhaps we can ride back to our cabin."

Joanna and David came out to say good-bye. Joanna kissed her brother on the cheek, and David shook his hand and slapped him on the back.

"Have a good voyage, Jonathon," he said, "and be careful." David gave him a long look. Jonathon nodded.

"Ah, well, Andrew, are you ready?" he asked.

"Aye, aye, Captain," he shouted, then bent and kissed Emily's cheek, then Joanna's and shook David's hand. "Take good care of my sister."

"We will, Andrew," Joanna said. She glanced past him at Jonathon who was looking into Emily's eyes. The look held everything he wanted to do at that moment—sweep her into his arms and kiss her long and hard. Instead he bent and kissed her forehead. Joanna let out the breath she had been holding. Jonathon caught her eye.

"Remember what we discussed, Jonathon," she said quietly walking arm in arm with him to the carriage. The two sailors climbed inside and waved until the carriage was down the drive. David kissed Joanna and turned toward the overseer's cabin to attend to the business of the day.

Joanna returned to the veranda and sat down beside Emily, appearing not to notice the young girl's red-rimmed eyes. Joanna turned to a tray and instead of tea, poured a light amber wine into two cups.

"I thought we'd enjoy a change of pace for today. No one need ever know," she said lightly. "Of course we should not make a habit of this," and reaching over she patted Emily's hand affectionately.

Emily looked at her in wonder, and then smiled in gratitude.

"How did you ever know?" she asked.

"Because I know my brother well, and I love David very much," she smiled.

Chapter 6

Phillip Beaumont had been a frequent visitor since Emily's birthday celebration. He often came for tea and stayed for supper as well, playing cards late into the evening. He was an amicable young man with a wry sense of humor, and his exaggerated descriptions of life in law school had everyone holding their sides with laughter. He was quite taken with Emily and enjoyed quiet walks through the gardens with her more than any other activity at Brentwood Manor.

Since Emily's accident, Phillip came almost every day to keep her company. Emily liked Phillip and welcomed his companionship during her convalescence, but she was becoming aware of an underlying tension in these visits. She watched carefully one day trying to ascertain what the change was.

One day when Phillip arrived, he bent to kiss her hand as usual, but he lingered over it, if only for a few seconds. When he looked at Emily, his eyes seemed to bore into her, and he was more intense than usual. Though he still bantered and made her laugh, beneath his smile he seemed always to be studying her.

Emily began to feel uncomfortable around Phillip, sensing a seriousness developing on his part alone. She tried to keep Joanna with them as much as possible and encouraged Phillip to bring others along with him, which he seldom did. Emily knew what was happening and felt panic rise within her at the thought. She wished Jonathon were here.

*

Emily noticed another change at Brentwood Manor. David was acting quite uncharacteristically. At breakfast one morning he appeared with his vest buttoned crookedly. A small smile playing at her lips, Joanna straightened it for him. He then proceeded to pour coffee into an already full cup. Joanna laughed.

"David let me serve you before you do yourself some great bodily harm."

"No!" he almost shouted. Glancing at a surprised Emily, he coughed and said more quietly, "No, I am well, Joanna. Please just sit and relax."

For several days David continued to act in an absentminded way. Emily watched in bewilderment and would have been alarmed but for Joanna's reaction—Joanna seemed to look on in good-natured amusement. If anything she seemed more serene than ever. Finally, Emily could stand it no longer.

"Joanna," she said over their afternoon ritual of tea, "I am worried about David. He does not seem to be himself lately. Perhaps it is not my place to say anything, but you two have become so dear to me, like my own family, that I can keep silent no longer."

"Emily, David is healthy and fit. I realize his actions have been bizarre of late, but that is only because. . . well. . . David is worried about me."

"You? Why you look lovelier than ever! Joanna, is something wrong?"

"No, Emily, something is right. Very right. David and I are expecting a child," she answered, tears of happiness springing to her eyes.

Emily sat up and started to rise, forgetting about her injured leg in the excitement. Joanna came over to her and they embraced happily, laughing and crying at once.

"How wonderful for you, Joanna! I am so happy for you both. No wonder David has been preoccupied lately."

"Well, with good reason, Em. You see, we had a child, but he died in infancy. Since then I have had two miscarriages. We just pray that the Lord will bless us with a healthy baby. Oh, we are so excited, Emily," she smiled. "Our son was beautiful. We believe he was conceived on our wedding night, our very first time together. . ." Joanna continued talking gaily, but Emily did not hear her. The words "our very first time together" rang through her head. Could she, too, be with child? She was astonished that the thought had never crossed her mind before. She and Jonathon had been together several times; the chances were high. Her mind raced. What would he do if she were carrying his child? They had neither spoken of marriage—nor of love—although many times Emily yearned to tell Jonathon of her love for him. But she never did. Emily remembered Mrs. Dennings's dire warning, *He has a reputation with women.* Emily knew that Jonathon was well experienced, but none of these women were his ward, lived under the same roof or, as far as Emily knew, bore his child.

Yes, this was quite a predicament George Wentworth had created. Neither of them had planned their passion in the cabin, and yet it seemed as natural as a stream flowing to the sea. But what now? When Jonathon returned, and that would be soon, would they continue as before?

Emily knew that if she were pregnant, she would not want to trap Jonathon into a marriage he did not want. She was wise enough to know that it would ruin any affection he had for her. If she were not pregnant, it would be wise to discontinue their intimacy and be grateful.

But the thought of never lying in Jonathon's arms again was agony; the thought of carrying his child made her heart leap with joy. Emily wished that Jonathon were there with her at that moment, for if she could look into his eyes, she would know his heart.

Noticing the silence, Emily looked up. Joanna had been studying her for a few minutes. She saw the confusion on Emily's face, and her heart went out to her.

"Do you suspect that you, too, could be with child?" she asked softly.

"I do not know yet," Emily's voice was barely a whisper.

"Oh, Emily," Joanna cried and wrapped her arms around the girl's trembling shoulders.

"I love him so, Joanna, but I know he loves his freedom. He loves the sea and his land; I do not think he has room for a wife."

"Emily, he has said as much. But surely if you carry his child. . . He should never have trifled with you," she said angrily.

"Please, Joanna, it was not only Jonathon's fault. I wanted him, too, and it was quite. . .well, spontaneous. And mutual. But to have him marry me because I carry his child would only lead to resentment. Perhaps he would allow me to return to London with a fabricated husband who left me a widow," she paused a moment. "There is another twist to all of this. I suspect that Phillip is going to propose to me."

Joanna laughed. "That is as obvious as the nose on your pretty little face, Em. Wait!" she cried, her eyes getting large. "Do you love him—or at least find him attractive? Maybe Phillip is the solution to this whole problem."

"Joanna!" Emily gasped. "You cannot think that I would marry Phillip when I carry Jonathon's child. . .if I carry Jonathon's child."

"Well, I thought it might work. Oh, Em, I could throttle my brother right now. I do not know what he thinks and feels. Perhaps he does love you. . ."

"Joanna, please," Emily interrupted. "I cannot bear to think that, for it is what I hope and pray with all my heart. And if I begin to believe it and find it is not so, I fear I would go insane. I will keep the memories of our times together as a precious treasure, but I will allow it no more."

"Times?" Joanna blurted out.

Emily blushed and looked down at her hands.

"Oh, Em, you are hopeless," she wailed and gently patted the girl's shoulder.

*

Finally Emily was allowed to walk, although her ankle ached if she stayed on her feet too long. Jonathon had been away for a little over a month, and Emily found herself growing more and more restless awaiting his return. Anything that sounded like hoof beats brought her to a window at the front of the house. At night she lay in bed longing for the feel of his warm, lean body close against hers, for his gentle touch and low, sweet voice.

Unable to concentrate, she abandoned a book she had been reading. She even felt unsociable and, seeing Phillip riding up the drive instead of Jonathon one afternoon, the disappointment was almost too much to bear. She wanted to flee to her room and beg a headache, but she remained and received him in the sunlit parlor.

"Emily, you look lovely today. It is so good to see you up and about." He took her hand and kissed it slowly, then looked up into her eyes. Emily looked away. He sat beside her on the settee. "Any news of your brother yet?" he asked.

"Nothing," she answered.

"Emily, do you feel up to a brief walk?"

"Yes, that would be nice, Phillip."

The chilly November air was sharp compared to the mild October they had enjoyed. Emily drew her cape closer about her.

"Are you cold, Emily?"

"I do not mind, Phillip. I was beginning to feel cooped up inside. I enjoy the outdoors, even when it is brisk." She smiled at him, "It is so good of you to visit this invalid."

"My pleasure," he beamed. "Perhaps tomorrow I shall bring the carriage and we shall take a ride. Would you feel up to that?"

"Oh, yes, I would." Her only excursion had been a trip to a village so Joanna could buy some lace to trim baby clothes. Emily had waited in the carriage while Joanna shopped, but she had enjoyed the outing and an opportunity to observe the changing countryside preparing for winter. Her spirits lifted at the thought of another excursion the next afternoon.

At supper Emily was bright and talkative with the next day's outing to look forward to, and Jonathon and Andrew's homecoming imminent. Joanna and David noticed her mood change, too.

"You seem quite chipper this evening, Emily," David remarked.

"I have been invited for a carriage ride with Phillip tomorrow and . . . uh, my leg is feeling so much better," she replied. Though she was looking forward to the carriage ride, she knew her spirits lifted at the thought of Jonathon's pending return.

"Well, it is good to see you like this." He smiled and took Joanna's hand gently. "Joanna and I care very much about you, Em. We like to see you happy."

Emily smiled warmly, "You have made me feel very welcome here. Brentwood Manor feels like home to me, and I know Andrew feels the same way. We were frightened when we left England, not knowing what to expect. But you have both been wonderful."

"Do not forget to include Jonathon. He is, after all, your guardian. And he is the one who made Brentwood Manor your home," David said.

Emily shot Joanna a glance. "Yes, Jonathon has been wonderful . . . to both of us."

Joanna rose. "Well, is anyone in the mood for a game of whist?"

*

Phillip arrived punctually the next afternoon. After hopping down from his carriage, he bounded up the steps to the front door. He awaited Emily in the parlor, and then greeted her with a warm smile and an approving look when she entered. Emily wore a powder blue dress embroidered with pale yellow flowers, yellow lace at the neckline and at the elbow-length sleeves. Phillip helped her with her blue velvet cape, and then they walked out into the sunshine. Making her way carefully down the steps, Emily waited for Phillip to assist her into the coach.

The carriage rolled off and Emily settled back into the seat. The sun was bright, the air crisp and bracing, and Emily breathed it deeply. The carriage rolled over a muted carpet of newly fallen leaves. The sharp smells of fall, dead leaves and fresh earth, were invigorating and Emily felt refreshed.

"Comfortable?" Phillip asked.

"Mmm," Emily murmured.

They rode in silence for a while. Occasionally Phillip would point out an interesting spot or a lovely view. He watched Emily out of the corner of his eye, enrapt with her beauty, sensing her coolness.

"Emily, what was the voyage from England like?" he asked.

"Long." Emily laughed. He waited for her to continue. "Well, sad, I suppose. Yes, I was very sad to leave London, and I was grieving for my father. There was a terrible storm, and Andrew was almost killed. Jonathon saved his life."

"Jonathon's quite a man."

"Yes, he is."

"I wonder that he never married," Phillip said looking at Emily. She was silent.

"Why do you suppose that is?" Phillip persisted.

"I do not presume to know Jonathon's mind, Phillip. I am sure he has his reasons."

Phillip slowed the carriage down. "What was it like being together on the ship all that time?"

Emily looked at Phillip angrily. "Just what are you suggesting, Phillip?"

He looked out at the trees, then at Emily. "I am sorry, Emily, I did not mean to suggest anything. It is just that . . . Well, I wondered how you feel about him. He is a very handsome, rugged man, one I am sure women fall in love with easily." The carriage had stopped. The forest sounds filled the silence between them.

"Perhaps you had better take me back, Phillip."

"Wait, Emily. Please let me explain." He took her hands in his. "Emily, I have come to see you almost every day. When I leave you, my soul aches to return to you. I see your face and hear your voice waking and sleeping. I long to reach out and hold you in my arms; crush you to me. The feel of your hand against my lips thrills me through my whole being, and I am driven to the brink when I think what the touch of your lips would do to me. Emily, I want you to be my wife."

In spite of her anticipating this, Emily sat rigid in shock. Phillip took her in his arms and gently kissed her lips. She felt him shaking as he released her, and she looked into his blue-gray eyes that were half shocked at his own boldness and half-delighted at finally having kissed her. Although his kiss was tender, it did not send shivers of delight through her as Jonathon's mere look did.

"Phillip—" she began.

"No, Emily, do not answer yet. Think about it carefully. I still have to wait for Jonathon to return and ask for your hand properly."

Emily's head reeled as she thought of the possibilities in that encounter.

*

Shortly after Phillip and Emily had left, another carriage arrived at Brentwood Manor and out spilled Andrew and Jonathon.

"We are home!" Jonathon called.

Joanna ran from the house and Dulcie ran out another door to fetch David. Jonathon grinned at his sister and swept her into his arms, but kept one eye on the door, the whole time awaiting another.

"What a lovely greeting, Jonathon!" she laughed. "Did you miss me so much?" After she hugged Andrew, the three walked into the house together.

"Where is Emily?" Jonathon asked nonchalantly.

"She went for a carriage ride with Phillip," Joanna answered pouring wine into four goblets. Jonathon's face fell, but he recovered quickly. David entered and greeted them both heartily. They toasted a successful voyage and Jonathon filled them in on events while he was away. As his eyes frequently wandered to the front windows, Joanna hid a smile in her wine glass. A half-hour passed, Jonathon pacing the room. David rose to return to work, and Joanna put the glasses on a tray and carried them out. Andrew left to see to his unpacking, and Jonathon continued to pace.

Alone in the room, Jonathon leaned his forearm against the marble mantle and stared at the fire for a long time. The exuberance he had felt upon arriving was replaced with disappointment. Where the devil was she? His arms ached to hold her, to feel her warmth, to smell the sweet scent of jasmine that she always wore. To feel that silken skin beneath his hands and the passion that stirred in her small, slender body. He shook his head to change his train of thought. Keep that up and he would take her right in the foyer. Throughout the trip from Massachusetts his mind had been full of the possibilities their reunion presented. The carriage ride from the port had been almost unbearable. And she was out riding with Phillip.

After what seemed an eternity he heard horses' hooves and hastened to the window. Phillip was drawing the carriage up to the house and beside him sat Emily. Jonathon watched as Phillip hopped down and went around to help Emily alight. They spoke briefly and Phillip bent and kissed Emily's cheek tenderly. She gave him a small smile, and he helped her make her way carefully up the steps. Once at the top, they were out of Jonathon's view. He wondered if Phillip were kissing her again, perhaps more passionately than before. He wondered how Emily would respond to Phillip's kiss, and his disappointment at Emily's absence upon his return slowly turned to anger. He stood lost in thought until he heard the front door close and Emily's footsteps in the hall. Turning slowly, he faced her as she entered the room.

"Jonathon!" It was a question as much as a statement, for her initial impulse upon seeing him was to run to his arms. The look on his face stopped her.

"Good day, Emily."

She glanced at the window, then at him.

"When did you arrive?" she asked.

"Shortly after you left with Phillip."

Emily winced. She had been waiting for this moment for weeks, but it was not as she had imagined it so many times. Instead of taking her in his arms, Jonathon stood rigidly, looking at her strangely, a frown on his face.

"Well, did you have a pleasant ride?" he asked flatly.

"It was nice to get out for a bit, yes," Emily replied removing her cape and turning to a chair to lay it on. "Jonathon . . ." she said turning back to him, "I . . ." She stopped, his cold, flinty stare freezing her approach, suspicion clouding his face. "I need to lie down for a while," she said and left the room.

*

Emily lay across her bed, one arm flung over her tear-stained face, confused and angry. Rather than Jonathon's arrival helping solve her problems, it seemed to complicate things even more. At least she had been assured a few days earlier that she was not with child; that was one less complication, although she felt strangely disappointed.

Her head whirled with the events of the day. All her high hopes had been crushed; her eagerly anticipated ride turned into a nightmare. How could she refuse Phillip's proposal without hurting him deeply? Jonathon obviously had seen them arrive, but *what* had he seen? Phillip's kiss had been brotherly. Could Jonathon be jealous?

Or, could Mrs. Dennings have been right? Had their times together been mere play for Jonathon before he moved on to his next conquest? As he had done to Deidre? Emily felt sick. She buried her face in her pillow giving vent to her broken heart. Finally, she lay in silence, drained and tired. Although the afternoon sun was low on the horizon, she did not rise to light the lamp. She stared at the canopy over her bed and tried to sort out her mind and come to some sensible solutions. Her heart stopped at a tap on her door.

"Who is it?" she called.

"Andrew."

"Come in, Drew," she answered, sitting up. He poked his head in and glanced around at the darkness. Emily lit the lamp beside her bed and laughed at her brother's rumpled clothes and tousled hair. Yawning, he padded across the floor in his stockinged feet and gave her a hug.

"I started unpacking and sat down on the bed. The next thing I knew, it was dark outside! Jonathon is quite the taskmaster!"

"It keeps you out of mischief." Emily smiled and kissed his cheek. They visited awhile, talking of his voyage. Andrew was almost as good a storyteller as his father had been, and his animated tale kept Emily entertained until Dulcie came to announce supper.

Emily looked down at herself. She was as rumpled as Andrew. They looked at each other and laughed.

"I shall be back in ten minutes to escort you," Andrew challenged.

"I shall be ready!"

Splashing some water in the basin, Emily washed her face. She pinched some color into her cheeks and took a comb to her golden-streaked hair. Hurriedly, she changed into a fresh dress and checked her appearance in the mirror. With a minute to spare before Andrew arrived, she thought about seeing Jonathon again at supper, and her heart began to hammer.

The candles lent a golden glow to the dining room reflecting off the crystal and china. David, Joanna, and Jonathon were seated and speaking excitedly when Andrew and Emily entered. She caught Jonathon's eye, but could not read what was there. He and David rose as Andrew seated her.

Emily's heart pounded so hard she was certain everyone at the table could hear it. She picked at her food, hardly eating anything since her stomach was full of butterflies. She looked up and caught Jonathon staring at her, a bemused look on his face. Then he turned to answer David's question.

The men talked about the voyage and the plantation throughout the meal. Joanna offered comments occasionally, but for the most part, the women were quiet. It was torture for Emily to sit so near Jonathon and neither talk to him nor understand what he was thinking. The meal dragged on until Joanna finally excused herself and Emily while the men lingered over brandy and cigars. As the women rose and left, Jonathon's eyes never left Emily's back.

Picking up some embroidery, Joanna sat in the chair across from Emily. She looked at the younger girl who was staring into the fire. Dulcie entered with a tea tray and set it down on a table beside Joanna.

"How was your ride with Phillip today?" Joanna asked, pouring the tea.

Emily accepted the cup from Joanna and sighed.

"He asked me to marry him," Emily answered dully. "He was waiting for Jonathon to return so he could ask for my hand."

"Oh, dear!" Joanna stopped stirring her tea.

They sat in silence for a while, each lost in her thoughts. Joanna finished her tea and picked up the baby gown she was working on.

"Things did not go well with Jonathon today?"

"No," Emily replied.

Joanna pursed her lips and nodded once slowly. She began to prattle on about local gossip, aware that Emily needed some senseless noise and time to think.

The men joined them, and David pulled a footstool over to Joanna's chair. Jonathon pulled on a fresh cigar while he stoked the fire. He walked over to the window and stared, unseeing, into the night. Andrew talked Emily into a game of cards, and as he sat at the table he called, "Come on, Jonathon, play a while. Let me win back some of my money."

"Andrew, were you gambling?" Emily gasped.

"We must do something to while away the lonely hours at sea and in strange ports," Jonathon answered her. Emily's heart raced and she realized that his words were intended to send her a message: his time away had been spent innocently in the company of his men. Slowly, she looked up into his eyes, soft and brown. She had memorized every detail of them.

He sat at her right, and they began the game. Emily felt exhilarated at his nearness, yet frustrated that she could not reach out and take his hand. It was a wonderful-terrible evening, and she was glad when it ended for she pondered—half hoping, half dreading—the possibility that Jonathon would come to her room later.

*

Emily sat before the mirror brushing her hair. She had donned a filmy, cream-colored nightgown that flattered her shapely figure. Her heart raced and her ears strained for the sound of Jonathon's footsteps at her door. She realized as she viewed her image that she would not refuse him if he came to her. All her brave resolutions and promises to herself had melted away at the sight of him today.

Slowly, she approached her bed and climbed between the cool, smooth sheets. She extinguished the lamp and watched the flames in the fireplace. Every nerve and muscle in her body was tensed and waiting, hoping for the door to open. As happens in the stillness of the night, all her fears and doubts snaked through her mind, magnified by the dark, and the quiet, and the solitude. She lay like that for what seemed like an eternity and finally admitted that he was not coming. She tossed and turned trying to ignore the thoughts in her head that said: *Mrs. Dennings was right. Deidre was right. You are a fool.* Exhausted, her pillow crushed against her ears to drown out those insistent voices, she fell into a restless sleep as dawn streaked the eastern sky.

*

"Good morning, missy," Dulcie trilled as she opened the drapes.

Emily emitted a moan as she peered from beneath the pillow.

"You will miss breakfast if you do not hurry," Dulcie admonished. "Come on, I shall help you."

Washing and dressing quickly, Emily was soon down in the dining room. The sideboard was still full of plates offering ham, eggs, corn bread, and sweet rolls, but everyone else had eaten and gone on about the business of the day. Emily poured some coffee and reached for a slice of ham. She nibbled thoughtfully and sipped her coffee. Her appetite meager, she left in search of the others. Joanna had gone off to visit the neighbors. Andrew had gone off with David and Jonathon to see about one of the tobacco fields in the southern portion of the plantation. They were not expected for dinner.

Emily wandered aimlessly through the house and, then, donning her cape, went into the garden. The day was overcast and cool, and the damp air signaled a pending shower. She walked the grounds for a bit and then went inside, returning to her room and curling up on the bed with a book. The lack of sleep from the previous night caused her to yawn again and again. Soon, the book slipped from her hands, and she slept deeply.

*

Emily slept until after teatime; the sun was low in the sky. She felt refreshed, though still a little groggy. There was a rap on her door and Dulcie entered.

"Captain Brentwood would like to see you in his study, Miss Emily."

Emily looked at her in surprise.

"Tell him I shall be there in a moment, please, Dulcie."

As the door closed, she hurried to the mirror. She brushed her hair and pulled it back in combs. She patted her face with a cool, damp cloth and then, satisfied with the results, went downstairs.

Emily found herself trembling, so she clasped her hands in front of her in an attempt to quell their shaking. She knocked on the study door and heard his deep voice, the voice she longed to hear more than any other, bid her enter. Taking a deep breath, she did so.

The fire crackled and spit, but did not seem to warm the icy stillness of the room. Drizzle spattered against the windows and ran down the panes in weeping rivulets. A slash of pale white across the horizon was the last evidence of the setting sun. Ticking ominously, the grandfather clock seemed to hold the couple to a set cue.

Jonathon stood behind his desk, his back to Emily. He was looking out the window with his hands clasped behind his back, a cigar in his mouth. Reaching up, he removed the cigar, but did not turn around.

"You slept soundly," he stated.

"Yes, I was quite tired," she replied, trying to see his face.

"Phillip was here."

She did not speak. Her mind raced. What did they say to each other? Did Jonathon, in a fit of jealous rage, order him from the house? Or did he, unmoved and uncaring, smirk at the innocent young man's request? The silence fell between them like distant thunder.

"He said that the two of you want me to give you my blessing." Jonathon turned, eyes blazing. "Are you so fickle, Emily, that if I cannot warm your bed, you will find another who will?"

"How dare you . . ." she sputtered.

"I thought you were the innocent virgin—well, I was right about the latter, but perhaps once that was taken care of you felt free to, shall we say, dabble?"

"Why, you hypocritical bastard!" she seethed. "I suppose you were celibate all this time too? No frolicking with the seaport whores for Captain Brentwood. Your reputation for faithfulness precedes you. Just ask Deidre Manning—she can give a full account of the wandering captain," Emily stormed.

"Well, Phillip seemed entirely pleased with himself. Puffed up like a cock-rooster thanks to your charms, Emily." He glared at her. "You seem to be quite generous with them."

"Just what did Phillip say to you?"

"That you were so moved by his proposal, you were speechless. But that it was sealed with a kiss. A kiss my eye!"

Emily stood stock still in amazement. How could Phillip have jumped to that conclusion? What was worse, how could Jonathon believe this of her? She shot him a scathing look.

"A kiss was all, Captain. Phillip is a *gentleman!*" turning in a whirl of skirts, she fled to her room.

Jonathon slammed his fist on the desk and cursed.

*

Pacing in her room, Emily muttered angrily. She stopped and jabbed at the fire, then slammed the poker into the stand. Angry tears flowed down her cheeks, and she brushed at them with the back of her hands. She stopped at the window and pressed her forehead against its coolness. Rage lessened to frustration, and her shoulders shook with despairing sobs.

After a while, she pulled herself together and freshened up for supper. She would not hide in her room—she had done nothing wrong. Squaring her shoulders, she went downstairs. She met David and Joanna walking arm in arm into the dining room. At the sight of Emily, they stopped in their tracks. Her red eyes held such sadness they were shocked. Joanna went to her.

"Emily, dear, what is wrong?" she asked.

"A slight misunderstanding," Emily tried to laugh, shrugging her shoulders. "Please, Joanna, I cannot talk about it right now." She pressed past them and sat down.

She was the first at the table, and then Joanna and David sat down. Andrew was spending a few days at his best friend, Calvin's. Finally, Jonathon stalked in scowling, a drink in his hand. Joanna looked from him to Emily as David began the grace.

When he finished, David raised an eyebrow at Joanna. She shrugged slightly and began to eat. The two of them might have been alone for their attempts at drawing Jonathon and Emily into the conversation proved useless. The meal passed in stilted conversation and awkward silences. Finally, all excused themselves to different parts of the house: Jonathon to his study, Emily to her room, David and Joanna to theirs.

*

Emily changed into her nightgown and gave her hair a quick brushing. Feeling tired and drained, she climbed into bed. As she pulled the blankets over herself, there was a knock on her door. Her heart pounded.

"Come in," she called.

Joanna entered, and Emily's heart sank. Sitting beside her on the bed, Joanna took Emily's hand.

"What is it, Emily?" she asked gently.

"I do not think I can talk about it."

"I know Phillip was here this afternoon. Did he ask Jonathon for your hand?"

Tears sprang to the girl's eyes then ran unchecked down her face.

"He led Jonathon to believe that I had already accepted and in my fervor, kissed him passionately. Jonathon practically accused me of lying with Phillip while he was away." She buried her face in her hands; the hurt was almost unbearable.

Joanna wrapped her arms around the sobbing girl. "My brother's a fool!"

"We said terrible, hurtful things to each other," Emily cried. "How could he believe this of me? Why did Phillip think I had accepted his proposal?"

Joanna stroked her hair and patted her back.

"Emily, it will all work out," Joanna said, wishing she felt more confident that it would. She stayed until Emily settled down, talking softly, soothing Emily's fraught nerves. Finally, seeing exhaustion taking over, Joanna left and Emily fell asleep.

*

When Emily awoke the next morning, her head ached and her eyes burned. The bright sun streaming in the window did not help. Rising slowly to ease the throbbing in her head, she bathed and dressed. Making her way down to breakfast, she paused at the front door. Impulsively, she opened it and stepped out to take some deep breaths of fresh air. The air filled her lungs and her head began to clear. The sun still stung her burning eyes, but she felt better. She hurried inside to join the others.

David and Joanna still lingered over their breakfast. Jonathon's place had been cleared away already, and Emily felt a mixture of relief and disappointment.

"Jonathon had to go into Williamsburg for a few days," Joanna explained, reading Emily's thoughts. "How are you feeling?"

"Tired."

David rose to seat her and patted her shoulder, smiling into her eyes. Emily covered his hand with hers and squeezed it gently in thanks.

They talked of trivial matters and tried to keep the conversation light for Emily's sake. There was to be a public time, a social gathering including theatre and a ball, in Williamsburg the following week, and the House of Burgesses would be in session. David suggested they accompany him and spend a couple of nights.

"Oh, David, how wonderful!" Joanna cried. Rising, she went over to kiss him and boldly sat on his lap. David grinned and hugged her, then coughing, blushed and lifted her to her feet.

"Joanna—" he said.

The women laughed and, blustering, David rose and excused himself. Then he laughed, returned and gave Joanna a long kiss, winked at Emily, and left for the fields.

"You are so fortunate, Joanna," Emily sighed.

"I know. And I thank the Lord every day. Things will work out for you as well, Emily." Joanna reached over and gently held the girl's hand.

Emily did not answer. She just tried to swallow the lump in her throat.

*

Phillip arrived that afternoon, as Emily suspected he would. Instead of feeling the friendly warmth his visits brought, resentment welled up within her. It was made worse by the fact that he came in the carriage again rather than on horseback. Emily awaited him in the parlor, and when he entered and took her hand to kiss it, it was all she could do not to shrink away from him.

"Shall we take a ride, Emily?" he asked excitedly.

"No, Phillip, not today.

He looked crestfallen. He sat beside her on the settee, and she rose to ring for Dulcie. She then sat in a chair across from him. A look of bewilderment crossed his face and then disappointment when Joanna entered with a tea tray—with three teacups.

Setting the tray down, she stole a glance at Emily who smiled in gratitude. Then Joanna sat beside a confused Phillip and began to pour.

They passed a congenial time chatting, and Emily almost giggled in relief several times. She was too drained and too tired to handle Phillip today. She suspected Joanna had an alternative reason for appearing, though she did not know what it was.

Finally, sensing that Joanna was a permanent fixture for the afternoon, Phillip rose to leave. Noting that Emily remained in her seat, he quickly donned his cloak and left.

"I suspect Phillip is a little disappointed with this afternoon's visit," Joanna remarked.

"More than a little. Thank you, Joanna. After the scene with Jonathon last night, I could not have taken another one with Phillip today."

"What will you tell him?"

"I do not know. But I cannot marry him, not when I. . ." she stopped. "The affection I feel for Phillip has been shaken by his presumption and premature action," she said stiffly.

Joanna looked at her. "Remember why he acted that way, Emily." Then to soften the rebuke she added, "Love does strange things to people."

*

Everyone had gathered in the parlor, Joanna working on more baby clothes, David reading beside her. Andrew and Emily were playing cards when she heard Jonathon's horse in the drive. To Emily, it seemed like forever before he entered the room. He called a greeting to everyone and, meeting Emily's eyes, nodded slightly. Emily's eyes followed his every movement, admiring his tall, lean figure dressed in a brown longcoat and tan breeches. He looked drawn and tired as he walked to the fireplace to warm his hands. David poured him a drink, and they chatted about his trip.

Emily felt his eyes on her several times, and finally she had the nerve to look up and meet his gaze. Their eyes locked for a moment, and Emily's heart raced. Then Andrew reminded her again of her turn, and she looked down at her cards. She felt flushed and her palms were sweaty. Unable to concentrate, she lost the game, and she and Andrew joined the others in conversation.

They began to plan their trip into Williamsburg. Everyone was excited at the prospect, for a play was planned at the theater, and a ball would follow at the Governor's Palace.

David turned to Joanna. "Not too much excitement for you, my dear," he scolded gently.

"I shall be careful, David. Let me have some fun, too!" she pouted and laughed.

"What is going on here?" Jonathon demanded. Then, for the first time looking closely at what Joanna was sewing, the light dawned and he rose and embraced his sister.

"Joanna!" He laughed and turning, he pumped David's arm. He was beaming at them both. "How wonderful!" He grinned from one to the other. Sitting back down, he grinned at them again, then struck with a thought, his grin faded to astonishment and he looked over at Emily. His eyes searched hers; she lowered them and blushed.

The others had continued talking and missed the silent exchange. Jonathon was quiet for the rest of the evening.

*

Emily stirred in her sleep. Slowly coming awake, she was aware of Jonathon before she opened her eyes. He was standing next to her bed gazing down at her. She raised her eyes to his silently. A moment passed.

"Did you come to fling more accusations?" she asked bitterly.

"No."

She sat up and pulled the blanket around herself. "As you can see, I am alone!" she hurled at him.

He looked down at his hands. The silence surrounded them like a mist. Slowly, he sat on the bed.

"Did you come to ease your lust then? Do you think I am that wanton?" she demanded.

"Well, I am not the one who is going to marry someone else, am I?" he whispered hoarsely. "And just who will be the father of your firstborn?"

Emily slapped his face.

"Not you!" she seethed. "If that is what concerns you, Jonathon, put your mind at ease. I do not carry your child. Now, may I get some rest?"

She flopped back on the pillows and rolled over with her back to him. She heard the door close, and her body was racked with sobs.

*

Emily was in her room and, with Joanna's help, was deciding what to pack for Williamsburg. They chatted excitedly, holding up gowns, matching ribbons and shoes, and picking out toiletries. Dulcie entered and informed Emily that Phillip was downstairs. The excitement drained from her face, and she looked at Joanna.

"Do you want me to come along?" Joanna asked.

"No, it is time I tell him," Emily replied.

Phillip rose when Emily entered the parlor carrying her cloak.

"Let us take a stroll, Phillip," she suggested.

He helped her with her cloak and, after adjusting it, placed his hands on her shoulders. Emily moved away, slipping on her gloves. Phillip offered her his arm, and they walked together out into the garden. The day was mild, the sun warm on Emily's face. They walked in silence for a bit, and Emily sat down on a stone bench. Sitting beside her, Phillip took her hand and looked into her eyes. Emily noted that, despite the intensity of his gaze, it had none of the effect that a similar gaze from Jonathon would elicit.

"I spoke to Jonathon," he said.

"He told me."

"He wanted me to think about this for a few days. But I can wait no longer; I intend to press him for an answer today. I want us to be together, Emily," he said as he slipped an arm around her and drew her to him. Emily pushed away.

"Phillip, please. I have something to say."

He looked at her, waiting for her to continue.

"I do not know what I have done to mislead you. I am truly sorry if I have done so. You are a dear friend, Phillip, but—"

"But you have changed your mind," he finished for her.

"There was never anything to change. I tried to tell you so right away, but you stopped me. Then, taking my silence as consent, you went to Jonathon. Phillip, I cannot marry you. I am so sorry to hurt you like this." Tears glistened in Emily's eyes.

"I. . . I do not know what to say."

They sat in awkward silence. Finally, Phillip stood. "I am sorry for the embarrassment, Emily. I hope you will forgive me."

"There is nothing to forgive, Phillip. I am honored that you asked me," she replied earnestly.

He looked down at her. "Since I have no further need to be here, I shall take my leave."

"You are always welcome here, Phillip."

He bowed over her hand, turned, and left.

Emily sat lost in thought as the afternoon shadows gathered. She pitied Phillip; she knew what it was to burn inside with love for someone who did not return it.

Chapter 7

Emily and Joanna were snug in the carriage with lap furs tucked about them. David, Andrew, and Jonathon were riding a little ahead of them. It was a cold day; frost had been on the ground that morning. The horses' breath steamed in the air as they snorted and stamped their hooves. But their excitement about this trip to Williamsburg kept the travelers from feeling the chill.

Everyone looked forward to these public times when society gathered from all the plantations to celebrate with races, fairs, balls, and plays. A ball would be held at the palace of Lord John Murray Dunmore, Governor of the Virginia Colony.

Emily's spirits were higher than they had been in days. Joanna's excitement had been contagious, and she had looked forward to this trip, too. As the coach rocked along the road, they chatted gaily, imagining who would be at the ball, discussing the latest fashions. The day sped by, and they reached the townhome of the Cosgroves, where they would be staying during their trip, just in time for supper.

James and Martha Cosgrove were gracious hosts, and they greeted the group warmly. That evening they dined on roasted pork, candied yams, spinach toast, and buttered onions. Just when everyone agreed they couldn't eat another bite, the apple pie, redolent with cloves, was placed before them, and all somehow found room for a slice. The trip had been draining, so they all retired early after only one lively game of whist. Martha walked Emily to her room talking all the way. Emily nodded and murmured "uh-huhs" politely, noticing that Jonathon's room was right next to hers. He reached his door ahead of them and, turning, said good-night and bowed slightly. His eyes held Emily's briefly before he entered the room and closed the door.

Martha turned to Emily. "What Jonathon needs is a wife."

Emily, taken aback, looked at the older woman and laughed.

"Well, my dear, we old married women cannot bear to see a handsome, virile man like that run around without benefit of a soft shoulder to lay his head upon at night—the *same* soft shoulder!" She laughed again. "Do I shock you? James tells me I am much too bold. But honesty is a good thing; do you not agree, Emily?"

"By all means, Mrs. Cosgrove."

"Bah—call me Martha, child. I am not that old!" she chortled down the hall.

Emily was thoughtful as she prepared for bed. Martha's words ran through her mind. "Honesty is a good thing." If she had been honest with Phillip from the start, she would not be in this predicament. And if she had been honest with Jonathon at the outset and told him she had never accepted Phillip's proposal . . . But he had said such awful things, she could not even think straight. Well, at least she had finally been truthful with Phillip, as painful as it had been for them both.

*

The next day was a whirl of events. They attended the fair and walked among the booths sampling foods and viewing the crafts, especially the homespun clothing that was so popular due to the protest of imported British goods. Many of the women planned to wear gowns made in the colonies to the ball that night to bring the protest right under Lord Dunmore's roof.

After the fair, they attended the horse races. Following an active afternoon, it was time to return to the Cosgroves' to prepare for the ball. Emily and Joanna waited in the carriage while the men collected their winnings. The atmosphere was festive, and many of the men lurched and stumbled as a result of their early celebration.

The two women were having such an amusing time watching and commenting on the scene that they did not notice a tipsy gentleman approach their carriage. Clumsily tipping his hat, he leaned in toward them.

"Af'ernoon, ladies," he hiccupped. "'Scuse me. May I take you two lovely. . .*hic*. . .ladies for a ride?" He began to climb in beside Emily.

She held up her parasol, jabbing him in the chest.

"No, thank you, sir," she said firmly.

"Oh, a spirited vixen," he snorted, trying hopelessly to focus on her. He slapped her parasol away and lunged into the seat next to her. Before he made contact with the cushion, he was lifted up and thrown out of the carriage. Landing on his back, he looked up through bleary eyes to find Jonathon glaring down at him. Rage filled Jonathon's eyes; his jaw twitched with anger.

"I suggest that the next time you see these ladies you head as far in the opposite direction as your legs will carry you. Do I make myself clear?"

The man sprawled out on the road blinked and nodded. Pulling himself up and away from Jonathon, he scrambled to his feet and hurried down the road.

Jonathon turned to the women, a concerned look on his face. "Are you two all right?"

They nodded, both a little shaken, and Jonathon climbed in beside Emily. His nearness was almost too much for her to bear, and she clutched her hands together to hide their trembling. David and Andrew joined them, David beside Joanna, and Andrew on the other side of Emily. With Andrew beside her, Emily had to move closer to Jonathon; the sensation of his arm against hers was like fire. She looked out Andrew's side of the carriage and spoke little. All she could think about was lying in Jonathon's arms as one of his limbs pressed impersonally against her at the moment.

The rest of the day was spent getting ready for the play and the ball to be held that night. After napping, Emily rose to bathe and dress. She dabbed jasmine cologne liberally, and then donned her fine silky chemise and underclothes. A maid came in to dress her hair. Sweeping it high, she twined ivory colored ribbons and pearls into it. Then she helped Emily slip into her gown of ivory silk covered with tiny seed pearls. Small, pale blue flowers were embroidered along the bodice that plunged low to reveal the creamy white fullness of her breasts. Ivory lace bordered the neckline and billowed at the elbow-length sleeves. Seed pearls and flowers covered the skirt, except for the lacy petticoat revealed in front. Emily wore a pearl necklace and drop earrings that had belonged to her mother. She stepped before the mirror and gasped. She did not recognize herself. Her blue-violet eyes sparkled, and the excitement lent a rosy hue to her cheeks. Her hair gleamed silken, and her dress accented her shapely figure.

Andrew knocked, entered, and, seeing his sister, halted and let out a low whistle. "Emily, you are beautiful!"

"You cut quite a handsome figure yourself," she laughed looking admiringly at him. He stood a head taller than she and his lean body was complemented by a royal blue longcoat over a powder blue vest and breeches. His shirt had a ruffled front with lace at the sleeves. Pointing one high, leather boot, he struck a dignified pose.

"Do you think I shall catch the young ladies' attention?" he asked with mock seriousness.

"You will win their hearts. Do be kind, sir," she laughed and reached for his arm as the two descended the stairs together.

Joining the others in the parlor for a drink, Emily was instantly aware of the men's reaction to her appearance. Admiring glances preceded the compliments, and she especially noticed the gleam of approval in Jonathon's eyes. She glowed with warmth and sat beside Joanna and Martha.

"You look beautiful, my dear," Martha said sincerely. The décolletage of her deep burgundy gown was even more daring than Emily's, and she wore a patch at the top of the fullness of her left breast.

"You are lovely, Em," Joanna agreed.

"Joanna, you look radiant," Emily answered, for she did. Joanna's skin seemed to glow set off by an emerald gown trimmed in snow-white lace. "And Martha, you look exquisite."

Finally there was confusion and laughter as they hurried to get their wraps and leave for the play. In the din, Jonathon took Emily's cape and, placing it across her shoulders, he stood closely behind her and whispered, "I am sure your fiancé will appreciate your revealing beauty tonight."

Emily's heart sank. Of course, Jonathon still did not know of her conversation with Phillip. If nothing else happened tonight, she would get this straightened out between them.

So upset was Emily over Jonathon's words that she was impervious to the excitement of the evening. The audience, a kaleidoscope of color, would normally have entranced her as fashionably dressed people mingled and greeted one another. Men sported breeches and coats of linen or silk with lace or silk jabots at the neck. Women wore gowns of silk or brocade with petticoats that cascaded in layers of lace. Oblivious, Emily gazed at the audience. She tried to focus during the performance, but feeling eyes upon her, looked across at the box opposite to find Deidre Manning grinning slyly. Emily realized that it was not she that Deidre was looking at, and without moving her head, followed the woman's gaze to Jonathon, who was smiling back. Having conveyed a message, the two returned their attention to the play.

All the gaiety washed from her, Emily wanted to return to the townhouse, strip off this ridiculous costume that belied her mood, and . . . scream.

After the play, everyone took the short carriage ride to the Governor's Palace. Brightly lit candelabra sparkled over the festive guests. Laughter and conversation mingled, rising and falling in myriad tempos. Music floated gaily from the ballroom, which was brightly lit by three magnificent crystal chandeliers. Rich blue wallpaper trimmed with gilt leather covered the walls. Tables laden with food and drink stood in the Supper Room, which was decorated in the Chinese style so popular at the time.

Andrew led Emily through the first dance, and then Calvin asked for the honor before the orchestra took an intermission and they all had some refreshment. Emily spotted Phillip in the crowd. Joanna spoke to her then and, turning to answer, she lost sight of him. They slowly made their way back to the ballroom, and Phillip was beside her.

"You look beautiful this evening, Emily," he said.

"Thank you, Phillip. And you look very handsome."

The music began and he bowed to her. As they walked to the floor, she caught sight of Jonathon, a deep frown on his face. Phillip took her hand and they began to dance. They talked of inconsequential things as they twirled about the floor. Emily caught sight of Jonathon talking to Deidre, and as it happened, they ended the dance right in front of those two. Innocently, Phillip brought Emily over to Jonathon and presented him her hand.

"Thank you, Emily," he bowed and kissed her hand then hurried off.

Jonathon gave Emily a puzzled look as Deidre slipped her arm through his and held it tightly against her bosom, pushing her already overflowing breasts dangerously close to tumbling out.

"Jonathon, you did promise me a dance," Deidre purred.

"I was hoping you would honor me next, Deidre." Randy appeared out of nowhere, and before she could protest, he was leading her onto the floor.

Having no other alternative, Jonathon bowed to Emily and led her out, too. Emily trembled at the feel of his strong arm about her. They danced silently for a while, Emily staring at his chest.

"What a strange way for a fiancé to treat his beloved," Jonathon finally said.

"He is not my fiancé."

"You broke the engagement?" Jonathon's eyebrows shot up.

"There never was any engagement!" Emily snapped.

Jonathon looked more confused.

"I vowed to myself that we would get this all straightened out this evening. Shall we do it here and now?"

Jonathon danced deftly to the edge of the room. Then he led Emily out into the main hall. He ordered their wraps, and they stepped out onto the grounds. They walked through the gardens a bit before sitting on a marble bench. Emily turned to face him.

"Phillip proposed to me in the carriage the day that you returned. I suspected it was coming; yet still I was unprepared. I was speechless for a moment and when I finally started to speak, he bade me wait and consider for a time. He said he would have to await your return to ask you anyway. He then kissed me." She looked at him squarely. "*He* then kissed *me*," she repeated. "He thought it was quite passionate, but then he has never kissed you."

Jonathon threw his head back and laughed, perhaps too loudly because of the lightness of his heart.

"Finding you had returned, he must have taken my silence as consent. I never intended to marry him, Jonathon."

"Why did you not tell me so immediately?" he blurted out.

"Because you were too busy flinging accusations that I had to answer immediately. You were like a crazed man, and I was astounded that you could believe those things of me."

"Em, I was crazed. All the while we sailed, my thoughts were only of you. Every other time I have sailed, the sea was like potent ambrosia. I felt serene and happy, long voyage or short, for she was all I needed. But this time was different. I shook my fist at the heavens and cursed the winds for their feebleness. I lay at night aching for the feel of you in my arms, for your skin against mine. Emily, the sea was not enough anymore. Do you not realize how I felt? My heart was singing as we drove up to the house, for soon you would be in my arms. Then disappointment upon disappointment, you were not there when I arrived. In fact, you were out riding with Phillip. When I saw you return, I was confused. He was so tender, and you did not rebuff him. I did not know your heart and wondered if it was his now. The next day he arrived to announce your engagement and ask my blessing. I was a crazed man, Emily. I realized while I was at sea, and it was brought painfully home to me during Phillip's visit, that—I love you. More than the sea. More than the land. I love you."

Emily smiled through the tears that streamed down her face. "Oh, Jonathon, I love you so."

They were in each other's arms; their lips met in a long, lingering kiss. Emily pressed Jonathon close to her while he nuzzled into her neck.

"I have longed to hold you like this," he murmured against her throat.

"I know," she whispered.

He lifted his head and kissed her again, their tongues searching, probing. His hand slipped beneath her cape and caressed her breast, teasing along the line of her bodice. Emily tingled with delight. They held each other a long time.

"We had better return to the ball," Emily whispered.

"We could just leave."

"No, we must return." Emily laughed, and Jonathon took his handkerchief to wipe the last few tears from her face. Tiny tendrils had escaped her coiffure, and he unsuccessfully attempted to brush them back.

"You look ravishing tonight, Em. I was insane with jealously when you first came down."

"No need, Captain. I am yours."

He kissed her softly, sending shivers through her whole body. Then they rose and returned to the palace. The glittering lights were too bright for their eyes so, before returning to the ballroom, they stopped for refreshments. A few people mingled about in the Supper

Room, and Jonathon nodded greetings but never left Emily's side. Then, setting down their glasses, they returned to the crowd.

The music began and Jonathon took Emily into his arms. They glided and swirled gracefully, speaking softly, laughing gently, and looking into each other's eyes.

Nearby, Joanna commented to David as they danced, "I think things are rapidly improving."

David glanced over at them. "I believe you are right, Joanna." They grinned at each other and David winked.

They were not the only ones to notice the handsome couple gliding effortlessly, almost as one, across the floor. Voices murmured throughout the ballroom for, in all these years, no one had seen Jonathon look so smitten. Deidre was fuming, and Phillip began to understand.

Jonathon reluctantly handed Emily over to other gentlemen who requested dances, confining his requests to grey-haired matrons who tittered with delight at his attention. Until Deidre approached him.

"Well, you look positively besotted over your *ward*, this evening Jonathon," she snarled as she was upon him. She slipped her arm through his and pressed into it, gazing askance at him. Her scolding tone changed to a purr. "From the look you gave me at the theater, I was anticipating a long and interesting evening."

"The look I gave you was simply a cordial smile, Deidre," he replied, his eyes never leaving Emily.

"That is not how it looked to me."

Pulling his eyes from the dance floor, he looked down at the woman next to him. "Interpretation was never your strong suit."

She rubbed against him. "And just what is my strong suit, Jonathon? Perhaps over a drink we could find out?" she smiled up at him.

"I think not, Deidre," he said removing his arm. "We explored that avenue once before, and that pathway is finished." He turned looking for Emily. Her partner was just escorting her to him.

Jonathon took her hand when she approached.

"Good evening, Deidre. You look lovely this evening," Emily greeted her.

"You look all grown up tonight, Emily my dear," Deidre said wickedly.

"I know I shall never mature as gracefully as you have, Deidre, but one can hope," Emily smiled sweetly.

Deidre glared from one to the other then turned on her heel, grabbed a surprised man behind her, and stalked toward the dance floor.

Jonathon laughed. "I believe she has met her match. You can be quite impish, Emily."

"Why thank you, Captain," she curtsied when she said it. "Do you suppose we could sit somewhere? My leg has held up quite admirably, but I fear it needs some rest."

They sat near the wall and Emily was introduced to many new people, some of whom raised an eyebrow slightly when Jonathon introduced her as his 'ward' with a devilish grin on his face.

As Jonathon helped Emily with her cape, he again stood close behind her and whispered in her ear, "I have a most perfect view of your soft and tempting bosom, Madame. I fear I wrinkle your cape with my clutching hands in an effort to keep from reaching around and grasping you in a most ungentlemanly manner." His breath was soft against her hair; Emily felt a blush creep all the way up from the spot he was perusing. She felt his hands drape her cloak around her and linger briefly at her shoulders. She turned to look at him and caught a devilish twinkle in his eye.

"I could have stood there forever."

"Jonathon!" she said, trying to still the familiar excitement his words brought.

He offered his arm and led her to the carriage. The others were seated, and he and Emily climbed in beside Andrew. Emily folded her hands in her lap; Jonathon took one of them and, tucking it through his arm, smiled down at her.

*

They all chatted gaily on the way back to the Cosgroves'. Andrew was quite tipsy since he and Calvin had been sneaking champagne all night. He grinned crookedly at Emily when she scolded him, but did not look properly ashamed. The others laughed.

The Cosgroves had already returned and were waiting for them with a nightcap for a traditional exchange of stories from the exciting evening. Gossip, jokes, and funny incidents were recalled merrily until yawning became more and more frequent, and all headed to their rooms. Jonathon paused by his door and waited for everyone else to disappear from the hall. Then he stepped down to Emily's door and opening it gently; he slipped inside.

Emily gasped in surprise. She was bent forward removing her dress. The view made Jonathon gulp.

"Oh, Emily, you are beautiful."

"Jonathon, you must leave at once!" she demanded. "We are guests here."

"I do not intend to stay, Em. I just wanted to kiss you good night." He stepped toward her and lifted her dress off the floor and flung it across a chair. Then he wrapped his arms around her and pulled her close, kissing her hungrily. He ran one hand up and down her silken arm, down her side and hips. Emily moaned soft and low as he cupped her breast and lowered his lips to it.

"Jonathon, please . . .not here," she whispered.

He gently kissed her again and turned to leave.

"I cannot wait to get home," he grinned.

*

Emily and Joanna were again tucked into lap furs as they jostled along the road. The air was crisp and cold and there had been a scattering of snowflakes early that morning. Both women were tired from the previous night's festivities so they rode in silence for a while.

"You and Jonathon seem to have worked things out," Joanna finally said.

Emily smiled. "He noticed a definite lack of passion on both Phillip's and my part."

"Emily, you have some decisions to make now."

"What do you mean?"

"Will your relationship . . . uh, continue as before?"

"I fear I would be unable, no perhaps unwilling to stop it."

"Has Jonathon discussed marriage?"

"No," Emily whispered.

"Are you willing to be his mistress then?"

"I love him, Joanna."

"He is my brother, Emily. I love him, too. But sometimes I fear he wears blinders. He will never even think of marriage unless you make him do so. And the way to do that is to . . . well is to not . . . "

"I understand what you are saying, Joanna. But I do not want to bribe him into marriage. Yes, I want to be married, but not if I am the only one who wants it," she said. "In my mind I vow I shall tell him 'no.' But when he is near I lose all my reserve and melt. He has only to say my name softly, to reach out and touch me, and my defenses are useless."

"Emily, you must consider the consequences. You were lucky in the past. But do not tempt fate."

"I know you are right, Joanna," Emily sighed.

*

The weary group arrived at Brentwood Manor for supper. Andrew was still feeling the effects of his first hangover, so he ate little and retired early. David insisted that Joanna get her rest, so they did the same. Jonathon and Emily were in the parlor. With a devilish grin, Jonathon extinguished all the lamps until the room was bathed in the soft glow of the firelight. Pouring them each some wine, he sat beside Emily on the settee and placed an arm behind her. Emily's heart pounded and she was sure he could hear it. She smiled up at him.

"What is it?" he asked.

"Can you hear my heart?" she asked.

"No, mine is beating too wildly." He laughed softly and reached up to brush a wisp of hair off her face. Then his fingers lightly ran down along her neck. She shivered.

"Are you cold?" he asked.

"Not a bit."

He pulled her close, and she leaned her head against his shoulder. His hand ran up and down her arm.

"Emily."

"Yes, Jonathon."

"Please forgive me for doubting you. When I thought I had lost you to Phillip, I could not think rationally."

Emily looked up at him. "I was afraid that I was just another . . . conquest." Tears filled her eyes at the memory of that pain.

He held her close and kissed the top of her head. "Why do I hurt you so?" They sat together in silence for a long while, sipping wine, enjoying their nearness. Then Jonathon reached down and tilted her face up to his. He kissed her gently at first, brushing her lips, her cheek, her forehead. Then his mouth sought hers and moved over it, demanding, searching almost fiercely. Emily's arm went up around his neck and they clasped each other tightly. Jonathon's hand roamed her back, over her hips and breasts, savoring the softness of her. Slipping one arm beneath her knees, he lifted her and stood heading for the stairs.

"Jonathon, what are you doing?" she whispered as he took the steps two at a time.

"Bringing you where you belong."

"*Shhh!* You will wake the whole house."

"I do not care. It is my house."

Emily gasped when, instead of turning towards her room, he turned towards his own.

"Jonathon . . ."

He opened the door, strode across the room, and plopped her on the bed. In one movement he kicked the door closed and undid his shirt, a wicked gleam in his eye.

Emily began to protest, but he covered her mouth with his and did not let up until her complaints turned to compliance. She responded with the passion he remembered so vividly. He slowly unfastened her dress while still kissing her, and slipped it off her shoulders. He kissed their creamy whiteness while he unlaced her stays.

"How do you women stand those things?" Jonathon murmured in her ear.

"We do so to appear attractive to you men," she replied firmly.

"If you dressed to please us, madam, you would do away with clothes entirely," he grinned at her.

"And would not the Governor's Ball have been an interesting sight. All of you dandies turned out in your finery and we ladies strutting through the minuet in our nakedness."

"Mmmm. An interesting picture to ponder. But another time when I do not have something eternally more interesting to attend," he bent down toward her. Emily held him back.

"Jonathon I must go to my room."

"Do you not like mine?" he asked.

"I mean alone." She struggled to sit up but was caught in her half-shed clothing. Finally she succeeded. "Jonathon, I think we are being rash and not thinking about what may result from this encounter."

"You mean a child? I have thought about that. I was quite disappointed to discover you had not conceived when you told me so, so delicately."

"Your question was not too delicate either as I recall," Emily said trying to arrange her corset. Jonathon tugged it away and nibbled at the peak of one breast. "Jonathon, we are discussing something!"

"Oh yes. Well, I suggest we keep trying until we get it right."

"Jonathon! You have the child to consider, too. I can bear being your mistress, but an innocent child—"

"Mistress!" he shouted. "What the devil are you talking about?"

"Shhh. Well, look at us, Jonathon. Here we are ready to make love again. That is what they call a woman a man takes to his bed."

"You would willingly become my mistress?" he asked in disbelief. "You would live under this roof with me, sharing my love as my mistress?"

"I know it seems wrong, Jonathon, but my love for you is not. I have never felt this deeply about anyone before. I love you more than life itself. But when I think of a child suffering because of my love for you—"

"You do not think I would make a good father?"

"You would make a wonderful father, Jonathon, but a child needs—"

"Emily," he stopped her again. "There is another word for a woman that a man takes to his bed. She is called a wife."

At first it did not register, then Emily realized what he had said. She stared at him, her mouth agape.

"Well, I guess I must be proper about it." He knelt before her. "Miss Wentworth, would you do me the honor of becoming my wife?"

Emily leaped forward and wrapped her arms around him, cradling his head in her breasts.

"Mmmm," he smiled. "Does this mean yes?" He lifted her onto the bed and they celebrated their betrothal.

"Jonathon," Emily said sleepily, her head resting on his chest. "I must go to my room now."

"No, love. Stay." He held her tighter.

Exhausted from the last few hectic days and soothed by their lovemaking, they drifted off to sleep entwined in each other's arms, Emily's leg draped over Jonathon's.

And that is how Dulcie found them in the morning.

"Lord a' mercy!" she cried out on entering the room.

Opening one eye, Jonathon peered at her.

"Quiet, Dulcie, you will wake Emily."

The maid just shook her head, backing out of the room. When she was gone, Emily opened her eyes.

"Oh, no," she moaned. "How do I gracefully get back to my room?"

"First, I suggest you get dressed, although I much prefer you like this." His hands teased her beneath the blankets.

"Jonathon!" she laughed trying to stop him.

"Then, fully dressed, you open the door and hold your head high," he laughed. "We shall announce our engagement at breakfast."

Emily need not have worried, for she met no one as she made her way down the hall. Quickly washing and dressing, she hastened down to breakfast. Everyone was there but Jonathon, who appeared presently carrying a tray of champagne-filled glasses. He set the tray on the table and distributed the glasses. Andrew moaned when he saw the beverage and turned pale.

"Is this some sort of punishment?" he asked.

"No, a celebration!" Jonathon exclaimed and stood behind Emily's chair.

Raising his glass, he said, "To Emily, my ward, soon to be my wife."

Amid oohs, aahs and congratulations, the others raised their glasses and drank the celebratory champagne. Except Andrew, who sipped his.

Jonathon bent and kissed Emily tenderly and the others came over to embrace them. Andrew had tears in his eyes.

"This is the happiest moment I have had in a long time," he grinned. Then he set his glass down and looked at it ruefully.

Jonathon clapped him on the back and laughed. Just then Dulcie entered and, seeing her, Jonathon offered her his glass.

"Will you drink to our engagement, Dulcie?" He laughed.

"I should say so!" she looked at him scandalized, then drank down the champagne and gave Emily a broad smile. "God's blessings on you," she said and left the room singing.

*

Their wedding banns were posted at the church, and the date was set for the week after Christmas. Jonathon left for another voyage north and was gone two weeks. Emily busied herself with preparations for the wedding, and again she and Joanna sat down with a long invitation list. This time many of the names were familiar, and she thought fondly of the friends she had made in Virginia. When they came to Deidre Manning's name they stopped cold and looked at each other.

"She could make things unpleasant," Joanna said.

"We must invite her. She has been a friend of your family's for years."

"What if she creates a disruption?"

"Do not worry. I can manage Deidre," Emily answered firmly.

"I think you are out of your depth, Emily. But you are also right. We must invite her."

*

Jonathon returned one evening shortly before Christmas. Emily ran to the front door and flung it open when she heard his horse. He bounded up the steps and she was in his arms. Lifting her off the ground, he twirled her around. They laughed and then smothered their laughter with a long-awaited kiss. A cough from Andrew brought them apart, and they joined the others for supper.

"Jonathon, I hear discontent is building in the northern colonies," David said.

"That is so, David. The First Continental Congress has adjourned. They are demanding the right of assembly, petition, and trial by peers. They have rejected Parliament's right to levy internal taxes and will accept only regulation of external commerce."

"This bodes ill," David mused.

"Thirteen colonies scrapping like puppies in a tussle. But their mutual mistrust—even hatred—of the British is binding them into a common cause," Jonathon answered.

Emily, disturbed as she listened, tried to understand the turmoil that gripped this land. When they moved into the parlor to relax and chat, conversation turned to the upcoming wedding. Emily became animated as she and Joanna related the plans. Jonathon sat beside Emily and watched in delight as her eyes lit with excitement as she spoke.

Soon they prepared to retire, and Jonathon held Emily's hand to keep her beside him. When the others had left he leaned back, stretched out his legs, and pulled her close.

"I have missed you so, Em," he said softly.

"I have missed you, too," she sighed.

He ran his fingers lightly along her throat. Emily looked up at him, her eyes glowing with love, and slowly his head lowered and their lips met, softly at first, then fervently as their passion mounted. Emily pulled away and sat up.

"Jonathon, I have to ask a favor," she said.

"Anything, my love," he leaned forward and nuzzled into her neck.

"You are making it very difficult," she murmured, her eyes closed, her heart racing wildly.

"Mmmm."

"Jonathon, my favor is this. I would ask you not to come to my room again before the wedding."

His nuzzling stopped and slowly he rose up to look at her. "This does not mean you will come to mine, does it?" he asked.

She shook her head.

"Nor does it mean that you want me to take you here in the parlor?" he asked in mock seriousness, working the last of the fasteners on the back of her dress. So intent was Emily on stating her case that she had not noticed, and he was quite skillful. He gently held the dress for a moment.

"Of course not!"

"Then I have no alternative but to leave you alone," he replied and released the back of her dress. The bodice gaped suddenly revealing much of her shapely breasts—golden in the firelight.

"Oh!" she gasped and grabbed at the dress. "You devil!" she laughed. With an attempt at modesty, she pressed the garment to her bosom, only causing it to push up and swell more. Jonathon moaned in dismay and averted his eyes.

"Woman, you should not deny me your charms and then display them so shamelessly."

Emily was attempting to refasten her gown, and she threw him a scornful look.

"Your talents are quite refined, Captain."

He smiled wickedly. "And yours are quite apparent." Then he held her against him once more. "Now tell me the reason for this sudden attack of propriety."

Emily nestled in his arms and played with a button on his vest. "Well, it is difficult to put into words, Jonathon. Actually, I thought you would be quite upset when I proposed this," she looked at him curiously.

"I must confess, I have had similar thoughts, love. We have guests arriving tomorrow for the holidays. I am afraid we are in for a period of enforced separation," he gently kissed her hand. "I would never want anyone to think ill of you, Emily, and others just might not understand." He brushed her hair back and kissed her temple and nuzzling her ear whispered, "But there is tonight."

Emily sighed and took his hand.

*

Jonathon sat on the bed and again undid Emily's dress as she held up her thick, tawny hair. Kissing her back as he worked the fastenings, he mumbled, "I do not know why you bothered to do these up again." She slipped the gown off of her shoulders and faced him, continuing to undress.

Jonathon watched admiringly, and when she stood before him naked, he pulled her close, cradling her between his legs. His tongue traced warm wet circles around her taut nipple and then he nibbled it gently. Emily trembled and her hands caressed the smooth skin of his back and shoulders. He lay back on the bed bringing her down on top of him, and their mouths locked in a demanding kiss that spoke of their long separation. Their lovemaking was urgent, and they clung together in the reeling, intoxicating climax.

As they lay entwined in the peaceful afterglow, they watched the shadows from the fire flicker in dancing rhythm on the ceiling. The flames crackled and spit in the silence that enfolded them. Emily's head rested in that perfect hollow of Jonathon's shoulder and his arm encircled her. Her leg was thrown across his thigh and her fingers rubbed gently across his chest.

"Will you stay tonight?" she asked quietly.

"No, love. Morning will find me in my bed." He kissed the top of her head, burying his nose in the sweet smell of her hair. "Soon I will never have to leave your bed. . . our bed."

*

James and Martha Cosgrove arrived the next day while Jonathon and Emily were hanging sprigs of holly and mistletoe. The manor was festively decorated with greens and candles, and soon an enormous fir would be cut and hauled in along with the yule log to complete the Christmas atmosphere. David's sister, Carolyn Hanover, her husband, Thomas, and two children would arrive soon and the house would resound with the gaiety and liveliness children bring to the holidays.

Joanna's pregnancy was becoming obvious and her morning sickness had abated. She glowed with happiness at the first movements of her child. Emily insisted she not overdo in holiday preparations and limited Joanna's involvement to a supervisory position only. Their merry laughter rang throughout the house.

The Cosgroves and the Hanovers were delighted at the news of Jonathon and Emily's engagement. Martha plucked at Jonathon's sleeve and remarked, "It took you long enough to discover the prize that was beneath your nose all along."

They toasted the beaming couple and settled before the fire in the parlor. Joanna played the pianoforte as they sang Christmas carols and drank wassail punch. Standing beside the pianoforte, Jonathon slipped his hand into Emily's and smiled down at her. His deep baritone blended perfectly with her clear, sweet soprano voice. Emily felt that familiar fire as their eyes locked, and she wished that he held her in his arms. He gave her hand an understanding squeeze.

*

Christmas Eve was overcast and the wind whipped around the brick manor. The smell of crisp wood fires blended with delightful aromas of Christmas dinner wafting temptingly from the kitchen house. But anyone who ventured near the outbuilding—and everyone did—was duly chased out by Dora.

"I can't get nothin' done with all these folks in an' out, sniffin', tastin' and pokin'," she exclaimed chasing a chuckling Andrew into the garden.

The tall pine tree in the parlor was decorated with candles and strung with berries, fruits, and homemade ornaments. The yule log waited beside the hearth for its ceremonial placement in the fireplace, a signal at Brentwood Manor for the exchange of gifts.

Richard, seven, and Jenny, four, David's nephew and niece, could hardly contain their excitement, and Andrew teased them and played games outdoors to keep them occupied. They adored him and begged for stories and treats from "Uncle Andrew."

On Christmas morning, everyone piled into carriages and headed for church services. Emily felt tears stinging her eyes as she sang the final hymn and realized how fully God had blessed her life. Leaving the church on Jonathon's arm, she caught sight of Deidre climbing into her carriage. The woman looked over at Emily and hatred filled her eyes as her nostrils flared. She spoke to her driver and the carriage rolled away. Emily wondered if Joanna had been right—was she unable to handle Deidre?

The Yule log was spitting and crackling as everyone gathered around. Confusion reigned as people called out names, accepted gifts, expressed their thanks, and marveled over the perfect choice, the perfect color. Richard and Jenny squealed with delight while their sticky fingers clutched their new treasures.

Jonathon pulled Emily to a quiet corner and took a small package from his pocket. His eyes held anticipation as he handed it to her.

Emily unwrapped the gift and caught her breath. A large ruby sat in the midst of a circle of diamonds on the gold ring. She slipped it on her finger.

"Oh, Jonathon, it is the most beautiful ring I have ever seen," she whispered.

"It was my mother's and my grandmother's before her. Joanna was afraid I would never give it to someone. Do you like it?" He smiled.

Emily was still looking at the dazzling ring. She raised her eyes to his, tears shining in the candlelight. "I love it. And I love you more than life itself." She rose on tiptoes and gently kissed his cheek. "Now I have something for you." Going to the tree she knelt and found a small package hidden beneath some others. She carried it over and handed it to him. Unwrapping it, Jonathon held up a gold brandy flask. He burst out laughing and clasped her to him. The others looked over at the two inquisitively.

"It would need a great deal of explanation," Jonathon said simply.

Christmas dinner was a feast of turkey, yams sweetened in syrup, and steaming warm breads that melted fresh creamy butter into sweet puddles. Emily sat on Jonathon's right and his nearness was sweet pain. She longed to climb into his lap and press against him, to feel his strong, lean hands caress her and bring her to that unbearable brink before they moved together in rhythmic unity. These thoughts left her staring at her plate, and when she raised her eyes they met steamy brown ones that apparently traveled the same path. Jonathon reached beneath the table to grasp her hand. Neither of them did justice to Dora's feast.

Chapter 8

The brilliant winter sun splashed across the manor house unimpeded by barren trees. It cut a dazzling shaft into the room and spilled across the polished hardwood floor.

Emily walked to the window and was bathed in the glow, her hair afire with golden highlights. She watched the carriage approach the door and stop. Deidre alit, her black velvet cape parted slightly to reveal the scarlet red of her dress. Her jaw was set, her eyes sparked. She looked like a woman determined to do battle. A desperate woman.

Emily drew away from the window and sat on the bed as Dulcie entered.

"Time to put on your dress, Miss Emily," she called out. Emily stood up trying to still her trembling. She had listened to guests arriving all morning as she bathed, dressed and patiently sat while Dulcie fixed her hair. She had caught the sound of Jonathon's deep voice in the hallway laughing with David, and her heart raced.

She looked over at her wedding dress that lay across her bed. The sun shimmered off the rich gold brocade overskirt that was embroidered with tiny dogwood blossoms. Rows of pleated satin formed the bodice, with a teasing row of lace across the top of it, cut low and designed to enhance Emily's décolletage. The sleeves ended at the elbow with cascades of lace that matched the lace trim on the bodice. This would be the first gown she would wear as Jonathon's wife. She raised her arms as Dulcie carefully lifted the soft, white satin gown over her head. The maid deftly fastened the stays up Emily's back and placed a veil on her head that cascaded against the satin train.

Andrew knocked and entered. He had been away at William and Mary College for three months, and Emily was struck by the difference in him. He certainly had grown taller, and his boyish good looks were changing to perilously handsome features. She was so proud of her younger brother and so happy that he was here with her on this day of joy.

"You look beautiful, Em," he said planting a kiss on her cheek. "Are you ready?"

Emily nodded and took a deep breath. She slipped her arm through her brother's, and they headed to the stairs.

At the signal, the pianist began to play, and they slowly descended. David and Joanna waited at the bottom of the stairs and preceded them into the ballroom past the guests. Jonathon's tall, handsome frame blocked the view of the minister until he turned and awaited Emily's approach. Jonathon's eyes locked with hers; a thrill went through Emily and she gave him a dazzling smile.

Emily's heart raced and she barely comprehended the minister's words. But she knew their importance—she and Jonathon were bound in a sacred and holy union in the eyes of God. Love and joy overwhelmed her. Her soft, gentle voice was a contrast to Jonathon's strong tones as they spoke their vows.

At the end of the ceremony, Jonathon took Emily into his arms and kissed his wife long and full. Some of the guests shifted in embarrassment, some laughed encouragement, and one glared, reddened with anger.

Toast followed toast to the handsome, beaming couple. The pair stayed close to each other, fingers entwined or Jonathon's hand resting on the small of Emily's back. They danced smoothly and their eyes never left each other. Jonathon bent his head low to whisper to Emily, making her blush and laugh. They seemed unaware of anything or anyone around them.

Jonathon left Emily to get them both some food. Deidre approached her, and Emily's heart began to pound. The older woman wore a blazing scarlet dress that was cut so low Emily caught her breath. Her hair was swept up into an intricate pattern of curls and jewels; her cheeks were pink with emotion. She looked beautiful except for the hardness of her eyes and the thin line in which she set her lips.

"So, you have done it," she hissed standing close to the girl. "Apparently I did not stay beneath his roof long enough to achieve the ultimate victory, but you arranged it all so . . . innocently. Well, he will tire of you and your Tory sympathies. And he will tire of bedding a mere child. When Jonathon is ready for a *woman*," she spat the word, "I shall be waiting for him. I do not think I shall have to wait long."

Emily's stomach was tied in a knot; she hid her hands in her voluminous skirts to conceal their trembling. She coolly looked at the woman from head to toe.

"Deidre, my dear, you cannot afford to wait long."

Deidre clenched her fist and longed to strike the girl. Just then Jonathon returned.

"Giving us your blessing, Deidre?" he smirked. Deidre softened her face as she turned to look at him. She gave him a dazzling smile and lowered her eyes.

"Why that is exactly what I am doing, Jonathon darling," she smiled demurely. Emily stared in amazement at how instantly she was able to transform. "May I kiss the happy groom?"

Not bothering to look at Emily for an answer, Deidre placed her hands on Jonathon's shoulders and kissed his lips. He was startled as she thrust her tongue into his mouth and pressed her breasts against him. She pulled away and said in a low voice, "Remember that when you tire of this farce." Then she turned on her heel and marched through the hushed crowd that parted before her and murmured behind her.

Jonathon regained his composure and slipped his arm around Emily's waist. He looked at the shocked and puzzled faces surrounding them.

"Friends," he called, "there is much more food and drink to be sampled," and signaling the musicians, he led Emily to the dance floor. As if awakened from a trance the guests returned to the celebration and began to talk and make merry.

*

Some of the women escorted Emily upstairs and helped her prepare for her wedding night. Her bath was perfumed with jasmine and her hair brushed to a gleaming honey gold. She put on a gossamer gown and tied the belt to her equally diaphanous robe. Then they left her to await her husband.

Jonathon arrived bearing a tray with a bottle of champagne and a single glass. Emily stood up when he entered and he stopped in his tracks at the sight of her beauty. He kicked the door closed behind him and set the tray down on the mahogany nightstand, his eyes never leaving her.

Emily warmed under his perusal; that familiar shiver ran through her. She smiled at him, suddenly feeling shy and awkward. Jonathon came to her and untied the belt and slipped the robe from her shoulders. It fell to the floor in a gauzy heap. He gazed down at her womanly form enhanced by the gossamer folds.

"You are so beautiful," he whispered hoarsely. "And, I love you so."

"I love you, too, Jonathon," she answered.

He walked over to the stand and poured champagne in the glass. "To you, Mrs. Brentwood." He took a sip.

Emily gasped. "That is right, I am Mrs. Brentwood now. Oh what a beautiful sound. Mrs. Jonathon Brentwood." She took the glass from him. "To you, my husband," and she sipped also. Jonathon took the glass from her hand and set it on the tray. He held her against himself and stroked her hair. Emily gently rubbed his shoulders, so broad her hands seemed tiny. She nuzzled into his chest. Jonathon wrapped her in his arms and kissed her, his lips slowly tasting hers, drinking in their sweetness. His tongue slipped into her mouth, and their hunger for one another mounted. He picked Emily up and laid her on the bed, slipping the gown from her shoulders. Once again he found himself stunned by her beauty. He gazed at her lovely face full of love for him, at her slender, white throat and her full, pink-tipped breasts. He gently caressed her skin, running his fingers along her neck and shoulders.

Smiling impishly, Emily untied his jabot and began to unbutton his shirt. She ran her fingers through the mat of hair on his chest and slid her hands into his shirt and around his back. Gently tugging the shirt from his breeches, she traced his waistline and teased below it. She pulled his shirt off and tossed it on the floor. Then she slid her hands down and assisted him out of his breeches. As he stood up beside the bed she stroked his legs, his thighs, and explored his hardened manliness.

Jonathon moaned softly, surprised by her newly gained expertise. He joined her on the bed and hungrily kissed her mouth, her throat, her breasts, tracing a trail to her velvety softness. They explored and teased and tasted one another until their passion erupted as they strained to become one.

Their passion spent, they lay in contented silence for a time. Jonathon brushed the rounded curve of her breast then intertwined his fingers with hers and brought them to his mouth. He kissed each of her fingers in turn and raised his eyes to hers.

"My sweet Em," he whispered. "I thought I loved the sea and my land, but I had never known the meaning of the word love until you came into my life. For love is complete and total giving—I cannot believe you love me so. And I love you, Em. I am yours forever. With the ship's wheel in my hand and a crew in my command, I never felt so fulfilled as I do in your arms. With Brentwood soil moist beneath my feet and the manor and everything in it, I have never felt so rich as I do when you speak your love for me. I love you, my wife."

Emily ran a finger along his jaw and traced his lips. Her eyes glistened with joyful tears. "You make love to me with your words,

Jonathon. I burn with desire at their sound and stir inside for your touch. I love you with all my heart."

Jonathon lowered his lips to hers in a kiss that enflamed their passion. They clung to each other in an embrace that spoke their love and the desire to hold this moment forever. And they celebrated their union as husband and wife in the swelling passion of lovers.

*

Spring was in Emily's heart long before the first bud appeared to announce the season. She barely noticed the heady smells from the garden and the brilliant pinks, violets, and yellows that burst among the fresh, bright greens of the trees and the grasses. For, to Emily, they had been there all along. Life was so wonderful, it seemed dreamlike to her. The days were full of tending to the manor, keeping Joanna's company in the last days of her pregnancy, or riding with Jonathon to see the fields of tobacco or the newly planted wheat fields. The lilac-scented nights found them lying in each other's arms, moonlight spilling over their naked forms.

These were Emily's favorite times, when she nestled against Jonathon, her head on his shoulder. Exhausted and exhilarated from their lovemaking, they would talk softly in the darkness, their love deepening with their knowledge of each other. Emily would brush her fingers through the soft hair on his chest, sometimes tugging it playfully. Jonathon ran his fingertips over her silken skin, his head full of her sweet smell of jasmine. Sometimes his hands would tease her nipples taut and explore and caress until she was writhing with desire. Then he would rise above her and together they would climb to that ultimate ecstasy.

*

Everyone was anxiously awaiting the birth of David and Joanna's child. It had been a tense time for all as each tried not to be overly concerned about her, and all prayed that she would carry the child to full term. Dr. Anderson ordered complete bed rest for Joanna for the final month of her pregnancy. It was difficult for her because she was usually quite active. But for the sake of the baby she complied and kept a cheerful outlook, often boosting the others' spirits.

It was a morning in April, a perfect spring day with the sun casting brilliant light across a land gone wild with color. A gentle breeze tossed the chintz curtain back in an endless game of tag; Joanna lay against sheets full of the smell of outdoors. Emily did not notice the wince the first time for she was concentrating on the blue flowers she was embroidering on the border of the baby's gown. Sensing something amiss she glanced up to see Joanna set her lips and grip her abdomen.

"Joanna? Is it time?" Emily asked going over to her.

Joanna let her breath out slowly. "I think you had better call Dulcie," she replied.

Emily hurried downstairs and found Dulcie. "Miss Joanna is in labor. Have Dora prepare water and sheets, and send one of the boys for David. I think we had best send for Dr. Anderson. Miss Joanna has had too many difficulties."

"Yes, Miss Emily," Dulcie called as she hurried off.

Emily returned to Joanna's room and sat beside the bed. She took her sister-in-law's hand in hers and smiled reassuringly.

"How do you feel?" Emily asked.

"Frightened but excited at the same time. Oh, Emily, I do hope this child lives," she cried, and then squeezed Emily's hand as another contraction began.

Emily and Dulcie assisted Joanna throughout the morning and Dr. Anderson arrived shortly after noon. Joanna's labor continued into the afternoon, but all seemed to be going well.

Jonathon kept David supplied with brandy and cigars while the two paced the length and breadth of the parlor. Often one would surreptitiously pause by the door to the hall, straining to hear any sound. Jonathon tried to keep a conversation going but David babbled incoherently, so the two yielded that game. The afternoon dragged on. The evening cast long shadows on the floor and a cool breeze came from the open window as the men sprawled out in chairs. David arose to begin his endless pacing ritual and suddenly halted in his tracks. Jonathon looked up as the wailing sound of a baby's cry carried down from upstairs.

"Ha!" David bellowed unable to conjure up a coherent word. "Ha!" And he ran from the room and took the stairs two at a time. Dulcie heard the racket and met him at the bedroom door, a finger pressed to her lips and wailing bursting from behind her. David stopped and nodded.

He entered and went to Joanna who lay spent but beaming against the pillows. He gathered her to him and a sob escaped as he buried his face in her hair.

"We have a son, David. And he sounds quite healthy."

David looked over to where Emily was just finishing wrapping the baby in a blanket. She gently cradled the bundle in her arms and brought him to his father. David looked down in awe at the reddened face that had ceased its crying. He held a tiny fist between his thumb and forefinger and looked up at Joanna.

"Thank you," he whispered, his eyes glistening. "I love you."

"And I love you," she said softly.

The baby began to cry again and Joanna took him to her and loosened her gown. Holding him to her she began to nurse him and he hungrily sucked and rested a fist against her breast.

Jonathon came in and congratulated them both, then hugged Emily to him and kissed her forehead.

They named the baby William, and Dr. Anderson pronounced him a fine, healthy boy.

*

A sunny morning two days after William's birth, Randy rode up to the manor at breakneck speed. Before his mount halted, he leapt from its back and ran up the steps.

"Jonathon!" he called bursting in the front door. Jonathon came from his study and stopped in bewilderment.

"What is it Randy?"

"Jonathon, open rebellion has begun!" Randy gasped, trying to get his breath. "There has been a battle—in the Massachusetts Bay Colony. We met the British at Lexington and Concord!" They walked back to Jonathon's study, and Randy sank into a chair as Emily hurried in.

"What is it?" she asked.

"We met the British in battle . . ." he turned to Jonathon, ". . . and we did damned well." Emily's face paled and her hand went to her mouth. "Gage discovered we had military stores at Concord and sent in troops to destroy them. But the militia awaited them—they drove the Redcoats back to Boston. We lost about 100 men; they lost over 200!"

Jonathon's face was grave as he listened.

"The committee needs you to sail again, Jonathon. Do you think you can make New York in a week?"

Jonathon looked up at Randy and caught the look on Emily's face instead. He sprang to her side and, placing an arm around her waist, led her to a chair.

"Your exuberance has disturbed my wife." He cast a frown at Randy.

Randy reddened as he mumbled an apology. Pale and shaken, Emily's face showed confusion and fear.

"I do not understand," she whispered.

Jonathon poured a glass of wine. Emily sipped it and color began to return to her face. She looked from Randy to Jonathon. "I do not understand," she repeated.

"Em, they were going to destroy our arms. Render us helpless against them."

"Them—us? Why do we have arms? Are we not part of the British Empire? What is happening?" she cried.

Jonathon looked at Randy, who rose. "They need you to sail in three days, Jonathon. And it could be . . ." he glanced at Emily, ". . . difficult."

Jonathon lowered his brows in anger. "I shall stop over later, Randy," he said evenly.

When Randy left, Jonathon took his chair and held Emily's hand. She raised her eyes to his.

"Jonathon." She did not know what to say.

"Confrontation has been coming for a long time, Em. As I think back on it, confrontation was inevitable. Maybe this will be the end of it. Maybe King George will finally intercede and make Parliament stop its oppressive legislation. They are breaking us, Em. We cannot continue to sell them our goods at a low price and buy theirs at a high one. Some plantations are so far in debt it will be sons and grandsons who rescue them. Maybe they will finally understand that we will not stand for it anymore."

"What will Virginia do—and the other colonies?"

Jonathon stared at the deep red liquid in her glass for a moment. "I honestly do not know," he answered slowly.

*

Jonathon left for Randy's and was gone through supper. Emily picked at her food but barely ate a thing. She tended William while David and Joanna took an evening stroll in the fragrant garden, and when they returned, she went to bed. She heard Jonathon return shortly before midnight, and as she rose to don a robe, she heard David pass her door. She followed him to the study.

Jonathon sat grim-faced, a brandy on the desk before him. He looked up as David and Emily entered and was silent as David poured himself some brandy and Emily a glass of wine. They sat down and looked expectantly at him.

The windows were opened to a rain-scented breeze, and crickets chirped against the blackness. Jonathon lifted his glass and gently sloshed the liquid around its sides before he drank. Then he set his glass down and placed his hands behind his head and rested his left foot on his right knee. Emily felt a knot tighten in her stomach for she knew his display of nonchalance could have a dire meaning.

"Lexington and Concord are not the only news of the day. Lord Dunmore, our good friend and governor, confiscated all the gunpowder stored in the arsenal at Williamsburg, ordering it loaded onto a British schooner. We almost followed Massachusetts into armed conflict, but Patrick Henry appeased the militia by convincing Dunmore to agree to pay for it."

"My God," David said as he exhaled.

"I must set sail for New York in two days. I should return in less than a fortnight, if all goes well."

"Jonathon, please do not go!" Emily cried.

"I must, Em." He downed his drink and rose. "We had best get some sleep."

*

Emily's head rested on Jonathon's shoulder. Although she could not see his face, she sensed that his eyes were open and he was in deep thought.

"Jonathon?"

"Yes, love?"

"I am frightened."

He pulled her closer. "Anyone with any sense would be."

"Are you?"

"Yes."

"But there is more, is there not? Besides fear?"

"Yes," he paused. "I feel excited. This is our chance to make our voices heard, to stand up for what we believe—to become masters of our own destiny."

"Has it really been that bad?"

He was silent a long time.

"Yes," he answered.

"I love England. It is my home."

"It was your home, Em—"

"Jonathon, I cannot break ties to my homeland just like that."

"You may have to."

Emily rose up on one elbow, her tawny hair tumbling about her shoulders. Her eyes blazed.

"You cannot really mean that!" she exclaimed.

Jonathon lifted a tress that rested on her breast and let it curl around his finger. Then he gently laid it back in place. His eyes looked into her with tenderness, and he brushed a tendril from her face.

"I pray we settle it peacefully."

*

Jonathon was gone for almost three weeks, and Emily was hardly able to eat or sleep. She helped Joanna with Will, as he had quickly been nicknamed, but her thoughts were always on Jonathon. She was in the garden when she heard his footsteps and instantly she was in his arms. Laughing and crying, she clung to him as if her very life depended on it. Finally, he laughed, picked her up and carried her back to her seat.

"What news? How are you? Oh, I was so worried," she sputtered.

He laughed again and kissed her.

"We ran into a little problem in New York and could not leave quite as planned. Nothing dangerous," he reassured her. "The northern colonies are rallying around Massachusetts and vowing to fight to the death. The Continental Congress meets soon, and perhaps they will resolve all of this."

*

News arrived in spurts from the north. Emily was on edge most of the time, hating to hear people speak of her homeland in such derogatory ways. She could not understand their mistrust—which was fast growing into hatred—for all around her life at Brentwood Manor had seemed so good. What were these people upset about? Many times in gatherings she would rise to defend Great Britain, and that usually put an end to the discussion. At least in her presence.

Randy and Deidre rode over one afternoon and found everyone gathered on the veranda. They gratefully accepted a cool drink, but Randy did not sit down. He shifted from one foot to the other, seeming almost ill at ease, not joining in the conversation. Finally, he spoke.

"Jonathon and David, could I speak to you in the study?"
"Whatever you have to say can be said here, Randy," Jonathon stated.

Randy shot Emily a furtive glance. "I would rather speak to you in private."

An embarrassed silence fell. Emily rose.

"I understand. A Tory's sympathies are not welcome," she said sharply.

"Emily. . ." Jonathon began.

"Well, it is true. All of our friends are uncomfortable around me. Sentences are left unfinished; conversations are carried on out of my earshot. I can see it in their eyes," she cried.

"Let her go," Deidre smirked. "Then we can freely discuss—"

"Be quiet, Deidre," Jonathon said in a low voice. "When you visit Brentwood Manor, you will be respectful to my wife!"

The muscles in Deidre's jaw twitched as she smarted at that remark. She arched one eyebrow.

"I was merely thinking of the girl's comfort," she said, sounding wounded.

Jonathon snorted. He turned to Randy. "What news?"

"Tobacco is rotting in the ports, trade has virtually ceased. The *Cerberus* arrived carrying Howe, Clinton, and Burgoyne aboard and reinforcements for Gage."

Emily recognized the names of the three British military leaders, and the realization of possible war struck her hard. Her head reeled and her heart ached at her divided loyalties. She looked over at Jonathon who was concentrating on Randy's words as he continued to describe the situation. Jonathon's mouth was set in a grim line; his eyes were grave. Excitement flickered in Randy's eyes as he spoke.

"What of the Continental Congress?" David asked.

"They have shifted from the trade embargoes to investigating the best way to raise a continental militia!" Randy exclaimed. "The committee needs you again, Jonathon. This time it will take longer. They would like you to sail as soon as possible. Communication is vital if we are to beat the damned British—"

"Damned are we?" Emily rose, her eyes blazing. "You will not curse the British in my home!" she yelled.

Jonathon rose and faced her. "It is my home . . ." she spun and fled from the veranda not hearing him finish, ". . . too."

Jonathon turned to Randy.

"Can you not be a bit more sensitive?" he cried out and then strode into the house.

David glanced at Deidre who merely smiled and rearranged her skirts.

*

Emily stormed to their room and stopped. If this was *his* house, then this was *his* room. She turned and ran to the room she had occupied before their marriage. She flung herself across the bed and cried, confusion and anger overwhelming her. Then she rolled onto her back and stared at the ceiling.

Not finding her in their room, Jonathon returned to the veranda. Randy and Deidre were leaving, and as they mounted their horses, Randy turned to Jonathon.

"I am sorry, Jonathon. I did not mean to hurt Emily. But this is war against Britain, and we all had better decide where we stand."

Jonathon squinted in the sunlight as he watched them ride out of sight. The full impact of Randy's words hit him hard. What would Emily decide?

*

Jonathon became worried when Emily did not appear for supper. He had returned to their room several times to look for her and checked the stables to see if her horse was gone. Seeing Shadow in her stall, he then dashed through the gardens to the dining room where Joanna and David still sat.

"I cannot find her anywhere," he fought the panic in his voice.

They rose to help him search, and as the four of them reached the hall, a sleepy Emily was descending the stairs.

"Em, my God, I have been worried!" Jonathon said as he met her halfway down. He reached for her but stopped at the look in her eyes.

"I fell asleep."

"I have been to the room—you were not there," he said, perplexed.

"I was in my room," she answered.

"Your room!" he demanded.

David and Joanna withdrew quietly to the dining room. Jonathon stood two steps below Emily so that he looked her eye-to-eye, but she would not meet his gaze. She stared at his vest.

"Since this is *your* house, I did not feel welcome in *your* room, so I went to *my* own."

"Emily—" Jonathon felt his anger rising.

"Shall I call you Captain Brentwood again?" she asked coolly.

"You are my wife!" he bellowed.

"You take great pride in your possessions, do you not?" she asked. Then, brushing past him, she walked down the stairs to the dining room. Jonathon gripped the railing until his fingers hurt. Then he descended the stairs and slammed out the door.

*

Jonathon set sail on an errand for the Committees of Correspondence two days later with nothing resolved between him and Emily. She had moved her things into her old room and remained politely cool toward him. She did not resume calling him Captain Brentwood; she did not call him anything. She did allow Jonathon to kiss her cheek before he left.

As Emily watched him walk to his horse, she fought the urge to run and wrap her arms around him. But, though her heart ached, her pride kept her solidly in place on the steps as she blinked back the tears. Jonathon swung up onto Neptune and looked at her.

"Good-bye, Emily," he said in a tight voice.

Emily's throat ached, and she knew if she tried to speak, she would be unable to stop the sobs that fought for release. So she lifted a hand and waved, trying not to notice the pain in Jonathon's eyes. He kicked Neptune into a gallop and did not look back as tears began to run down Emily's face.

The life and vitality seemed drained out of her, and if it were not for the enjoyable distraction of helping Joanna tend Will, Emily was sure she would go mad. They sat in the garden together one fine June morning as Will slept peacefully in Joanna's arms.

"Emily, this must be so difficult for you," she said sympathetically.

"I feel torn, and I do not know what to do. I love Jonathon very much, but I love England. Perhaps I feel somewhat like he did—torn between the land and the sea," she replied.

"But you changed all of that, Emily. He came to love you above all else."

Emily looked at Joanna thoughtfully.

"It seems he loves *his* home very much. Enough to humiliate me in front of our friends."

"Emily, stop it. He defended you. You did not hear it all—"

"Joanna, please, do not speak of it. I am so confused. If Jonathon does love me above this patriotic furor, he must prove it to me!" she exclaimed.

"So you will play games with him? Make him dance to your tune? Is a puppet what you want, Emily? I gave you much more credit than that. It is obvious to everyone but you how much Jonathon loves you. And that is because you refuse to see it. Your pride is wounded, and now Jonathon must pay the price. Do you love him so little?"

Joanna's words stung with their accuracy, but Emily did not care. She rose angrily.

"How can you understand? You are surrounded with lifelong friends who believe as you do. You live in a home you grew up in with your family all around you. You do not know the isolation I feel and the anger and humiliation as everyone degrades the only home I ever knew. My lifelong friends—they are the ones who will do battle against yours. And I am forced to take sides. The man I love seems to be on the other side. Tell me, Joanna, how would you feel?"

Joanna was at a loss for words as she heard the anguish pour out of the girl. She remained silent as Emily slowly walked toward the manor. For a brief moment, Joanna imagined the loneliness that entering that red brick house would bring if it belonged to others. She shivered in the sunlight, and through tear-filled eyes, bent and kissed William's forehead.

*

Emily was like a walking ghost; she appeared to be in a stupor at times. At other times, a frown crossed her features as she struggled with her inner turmoil. She was most animated when she played with Will, but even then, she seemed distracted, not noticing the smiles he was beginning to bestow. She would sit by the river and watch the water flow lazily by, searching its depths for answers.

Jonathon was gone for an agonizing two months, and all the while Emily struggled with a decision she felt she must make. When his horse approached, it was with a mixture of relief and dread that she awaited him. She did not know what to say to him, and the hurt she had felt was still deep. He seemed to place Brentwood Manor, Virginia, and this rebellion far above her, and she felt betrayed. And she felt so alone.

She watched him ride up the drive, tall and lean, bronzed from the sun and wind of the voyage, incredibly handsome. His horse trotted at a fair pace, yet to Emily it seemed that he came no closer as he rode, as if he were trapped in a single spot on the lane unable to move past it. Her heart pounded in her chest and the familiar warmth that Jonathon's presence had always elicited spread through her. Yet the hurt she had felt all this time battled for control. Her emotions roiled in a battle of love and pain that had been her existence these two months. She wanted to fly to him and feel his arms wrap around her in his familiar embrace, yet the thought of his rejecting her rooted her where she stood. Finally, he neared the porch, slowed Neptune to a walk, and stopped before her.

"Good day, Em."

Soft and low, just the sound of his voice sent a tremor of desire through her. She was afraid to speak; afraid she would be reduced to sobs in front of him. How she had longed to see him all this time; she could not—would not—lose control of her emotions in front of him.

"Good day. I am glad you are safely returned."

He studied her. "Are you?" He dismounted and a stable boy came to take his horse.

"I wish you no harm," she replied defensively. Joanna came out then and, going to her brother, gave him a welcoming embrace.

"Welcome home, Jonathon," she said. Emily silently watched the woman do and say what she should have done and said. She felt awkward, almost like an intruder. Feeling the tears filling her eyes, she turned and went inside so the others would not see her pain.

Jonathon watched Emily walk away, misreading her action for anger, or worse, indifference. He looked down at Joanna for help, but his sister merely shrugged. They headed indoors.

They had supper after sunset when the oppressive August heat had abated somewhat. To avoid contributing any more heat to the room, as few candles as possible flickered at the table casting long shadows on the papered walls. David and Jonathon carried on most of the conversation throughout the meal, discussing the progressing conflict.

"The Continental Congress has adopted the Olive Branch Petition, professing their loyalty to the king and a desire for a peaceful reconciliation. Perhaps this will all be resolved soon," Jonathon said.

Emily looked up at him quickly. He caught her eye and gave a slight smile.

"We cannot give in, Jonathon!" David exclaimed. "Not after working so hard to make our voices heard. We cannot afford to soften."

"No, we will not soften," Jonathon reassured him. "Our grievances are stated quite clearly in the petition. King George must intervene with Parliament and put a stop to their oppression."

Emily's heart sank. The conflict continued, and who knew how long the communication to England and back would take? Or what the king's answer would be.

"I must sail again soon. It looks as if I shall be at sea almost continuously for a while, sailing out of Yorktown." He turned to Emily, his eyes soft. "Emily, I would like you to move to Williamsburg. I have spoken with the Cosgroves, and they would like to have you as their guest. You might find them kindred spirits for they are loyalists also," Jonathon smiled gently. "And I would be able to see you more often."

Emily's heart quickened at the tenderness in his voice. "Yes, Jonathon. I shall go."

*

Emily sat before the mirror in her room and brushed her hair, the golden highlights dancing in the glow from the candles. It had been awkward saying good night to Jonathon and then coming to this room. But she did not know what else to do. She had left him in the parlor with David, deep in discussion. He had not invited her back to their room; there had been no opportunity for him to do so with the others present. And she was not sure whether she would have accepted that invitation. Her pain had brought her to a difficult decision, and returning to Jonathon's bed would make that decision even more difficult.

She looked into the mirror on her dressing table feeling an aching emptiness. The soft, fragrant breeze billowed the curtains on either side of her bed, and she closed her eyes, inhaling deeply the heady scent of summer. She exhaled long and slow, her breath ruffling the lace of the nightgown that lay low across her breasts. Setting down her hairbrush, she rose and walked toward the bed. A light rap sounded on the door.

"Emily, may I come in?" Jonathon called softly.

A thrill ran through her at the sound of his voice, and she felt flushed all over. She looked around for her robe and quickly put it on. It was filmy and scant; one that Jonathon had bought her for enticement rather than modesty, but perfect for a hot summer night. She realized this too late, for she had already called, "Come in."

Jonathon closed the door softly behind him. He stepped toward Emily and silently inhaled her beauty. Gently he raised his hand, lifted a curl from her shoulder, and placed it behind her back. Then he ran his finger lightly along her cheek, her jaw, her throat. Emily trembled beneath his touch and felt that familiar longing spread throughout her body. She closed her eyes and heard the rush of excitement pounding in her head. Suddenly his hand was gone, and she opened her eyes. Her knees shook, and she felt as if she would collapse. He turned toward the fireplace and leaned against it looking at the figurine on the mantel.

"I would like an explanation," he stated.

"I would like an apology," she countered.

"An apology?" he blurted out. "What in blazes have I done? It seems to me that I am the one who has been wronged."

"You humiliated me in front of everyone! It is *your* home, you said. Shortly before that you had assured me it was *my* home, too. In fact, you asked me to make a choice between Brentwood Manor and England. And then when I call it *my* home, you contradict me and say differently. Well, forgive me for assuming too much, Captain—" her voice had risen with her anger and hurt.

Jonathon gripped her arm tightly. "Do not *ever* call me that again!" His eyes bored into hers, angry sparks seemed to fly from them. "You are my wife, and you will act like my wife from now on. I have had enough of this silly childishness."

Emily bristled. "Well, Deidre was right. You did tire of this *child*. Now you can return to her arms and *experience*. And she will listen to your patriotic drivel and cheer your cause with equal fervor."

"I came here tonight to try to straighten out this mess, but I can see I shall get nowhere with you. I came to ask you to come back to our bed." He approached her slowly, his eyes a mixture of rage and desire. "I want you so badly, I could hardly bear to look at you all through supper for fear I would take you then and there." His fingers lightly caressed her shoulders and ran up and down her arms. "I thought we could settle this and bring back the magic that we shared." His voice was soft and low, his breath brushing her hair. "I wondered for two months why you treated me so. I still do not understand, even with your explanation." He placed a finger beneath her chin and lifted her face to his.

Emily's heart beat wildly, and the flame he had enkindled raged through her like wildfire. Her lips ached for the touch of his, her body cried out for the feel of his against her. Her taut nipples pushed against the sheer fabric of her gown.

"But I see now that I shall get nowhere with you until you decide to grow up."

Abruptly, he released her and walked to the door. Emily grabbed for a bedpost to steady herself. He turned at the door and said over his shoulder, "Be ready to leave for Williamsburg the day after tomorrow."

And he was gone. Moments later Emily heard hoofbeats travel down the drive. She sighed; Deidre had won.

*

Emily glanced around the room one last time to see if she had forgotten anything. She had lain awake the night before last listening for Jonathon's return. But the sun rose and still she waited. She took coffee alone, purposefully waiting until David and Joanna had eaten. Then she wandered through the gardens absent-mindedly touching the blossoms that surrounded her with vivid color, not seeing their beauty, not noting their fragrance.

Dinner was strained, for no one seemed to know what to say to Emily, and their attempts at conversation with each other were feeble at best. David rose with ill-concealed relief to return to the fields. Joanna sat a little longer, but finally left to tend to William. Then Emily sat alone at the large table in the large dining room that suddenly felt cold and strange to her. Her joy at finding a new home and family was so distant at this moment that she thought she must have dreamed it. She rose and dragged herself to her room, loneliness engulfing her.

She sat in her room and stared out at the brilliant sunshine spilling across the emerald green lawns. It all blurred as tears filled her eyes and ran unchecked down her cheeks.

She sat there still when Dulcie came in to pack her things. The tears had dried, but the loneliness lingered. Emily went through the motions of making decisions regarding what clothing and toiletries to bring, but once or twice Dulcie looked at her curiously and, when Emily turned away, substituted the appropriate articles. The activity at least gave Emily something to do as the afternoon dragged on, and she was grateful for the distraction.

Supper was a little more relaxed as conversation turned to the Cosgroves and their last visit with them. Jonathon still had not returned, and Emily began to wonder if, indeed, she was to go to Williamsburg after all. She joined David and Joanna in the parlor after the meal and watched Will in his mother's arms. She had hoped to conceive a child by now and felt envious of Joanna. She realized how much she loved little Will and how much she would miss him.

"May I hold him, Joanna?" Emily asked.

"Of course, Emily," she said. She rose and brought the baby to her. As Joanna laid Will in Emily's arms, she smiled into the girl's eyes in understanding.

Emily cradled the baby against herself and, as she looked down at him, her eyes brimmed with tears. She tried to blink them back, but they caught on her lashes and spilled down her cheeks. Joanna sat beside her and draped an arm around her shoulders.

"I seem to keep losing the ones I love most," Emily whispered.

Joanna hugged her. "We love you, too, Emily. And so does Jonathon . . . very much. And I think you know that."

"I know that at a time when I needed him most, he seemed distant," she stated firmly.

"Did you stop to think, Emily, that he might need you, too?" Joanna answered softly.

Joanna's words continued to echo in Emily's ears long into the night as she lay awake once more listening for Jonathon's return. Finally, exhausted, she fell into a deep sleep and did not hear hoofbeats as they pounded up the moon-speckled drive.

*

The next morning, not knowing what else to do, Emily arose and prepared for the trip. She was checking her appearance in the mirror before going down to breakfast when a knock sounded on the door. Two of Dulcie's sons came in to carry down her luggage.

Emily was surprised to see Jonathon awaiting her at the breakfast table. He looked drawn and tired, and circles darkened beneath his eyes. Once again Joanna's words came to her.

"Are you ready, Emily?" he asked.

"Yes."

She waited for him to say more, prayed that he would say more, but he returned to his breakfast. Emily's heart pulsed furiously. She knew she should say something, anything, but the words that welled up, caught in her throat. She turned to the sideboard and poured coffee while she felt his eyes on her every move. When she turned to sit down she saw him avert his eyes and look back at his own plate. They sat in strained silence, each waiting for the other to speak. Finally, David and Joanna entered and conversation about the plantation ensued. When breakfast was over, they walked to the front steps. Jonathon gave David some last minute instructions as Joanna embraced Emily.

"Take care, Emily. We will miss you, but we hope that soon you will be able to return to us. Remember what I said."

Emily took Will from her and kissed the baby's head. "I shall remember." She hugged the baby and handed him back to his mother. The women hugged and cried together until David finally came over and turned Emily toward him.

"Good-bye, Emily," he said tenderly. He hugged her gently.

They looked at each other, all of them knowing that there was so much more to say, but not knowing how to say it without causing more pain. David helped Emily into the carriage and Jonathon climbed in across from her. They waved and called good-bye as the carriage trundled down the drive, then they settled back into the silence.

Emily glanced at Jonathon, and then gazed out at the passing countryside. Jonathon started to speak, then stubbornly folded his arms and settled back against the seat, his mind filled with instructions and plans he had been making over the last two days as he readied to sail again. He had gone to Randy's the night he stormed out of Emily's room; he had gotten little sleep or even rest since.

The flight of Lord Dunmore to the British warship *Fowey* at Yorktown had brought the patriots and loyalists of Virginia to open conflict. Jonathon had wrestled with the thought of bringing Emily to Williamsburg, fearing for her safety. But it would be no better at Brentwood Manor, for mistrust and hatred were spreading rapidly, and at least he would be nearby if she were in Williamsburg. Jonathon did not expect to see his beloved Brentwood Manor until this conflict was resolved. If things became dangerous for Emily in Williamsburg, he could bring her aboard the *Destiny* and, somehow, return her safely to England.

His thoughts became a jumble of the serious conversations, heated arguments, and intense planning that had been his life for the past few days. Slowly his eyelids became heavier and heavier, and sleep finally overtook him.

Noting his deep, even breathing, Emily glanced across at Jonathon. His head lay forward on his chest and swayed with the motion of the coach. Emily took her silk shawl and folded it into a small pillow. Propping it against the sidewall of the coach by the top of the seat, she gently nudged a groggy Jonathon until his head rested comfortably against it. He stretched his legs out across the coach and fell into a deep sleep.

Nearing Williamsburg, Emily became anxious. Granted, their last visit to the Cosgroves' had been most pleasant, but the circumstances had been quite different. Jonathon said they were loyalists, so perhaps they would welcome her sympathetic company. She certainly would welcome theirs.

"Jonathon," she called softly. "Jonathon."

He was still sleeping soundly, so she carefully rose and crossed to his seat. Swaying with the movement of the carriage, she looked down at his face. How she longed to bend and kiss him awake and be wrapped in his strong arms. She slowly reached out her hand and brushed a lock of hair from his brow. Instantly he jerked up, grabbed his pistol and pointed it at her. She had fallen back into her seat and stared at him with wide, terrified eyes.

"Will you kill me, too?" she whispered, trying to still her trembling.

Fully awake, finally, Jonathon slowly put away his pistol.

"I am sorry, Emily. I was dreaming."

"Has it been that bad?" she asked.

Jonathon gazed out the window for a moment.

"People should do whatever possible to avoid war," he said quietly.

They rode in silence through the countryside surrounding Williamsburg.

Chapter 9

The Cosgroves were as warm and welcoming as the first time Jonathon and Emily had stayed as houseguests. Martha fussed over Emily and kept glancing at her trim figure in disappointment. She did not say anything, but Emily was disconcerted by it and realized that if things continued as they were between her and Jonathon, she would have this shapely figure for a long time.

They had a glass of wine before supper and then sat down to a delicious meal of broiled sturgeon, potato balls, and macaroons with cream. Emily began to relax as she realized that conversation would not turn to politics. Even Jonathon seemed more at ease than he had been since his return. He was attentive to Emily, and she responded in kind, remembering his warning as the coach pulled up to the house. "Now remember, Emily, these people know nothing of our—marital difficulties. They are lifelong friends, and I do not want to bring them into this or make them suffer as a result of it. They share your loyalist sympathies, so it is the most comfortable place I can find for you at the moment. Please respect my wishes and act the loving wife."

Emily was thankful to Jonathon for understanding her need for sympathetic company in these difficult times. She looked across the table at him and smiled. He attempted to hide a look of surprise and smiled back. After dining they played cards, but Martha noticed Jonathon discreetly stifling his yawns and suggested retiring early.

As before, Martha showed them to their room, only this time there was only one room for the two of them. Emily began to protest, but Jonathon silenced her with a look. They bade Martha good night, went into their room, and closed the door.

"Jonathon," Emily hissed between clenched teeth, "you did not tell me about this!"

Jonathon began to undress nonchalantly. "What did you

expect? I told you they were expecting a newly married couple. Of course they would provide only one room."

"You could have said you snore too loudly—"

"Or that you do," he replied lazily.

"Or something," she snapped.

"So that performance at supper was only for the sake of our hosts?" he asked.

"That is what you asked for, a sweet and loving wife. And that is what I shall be when they are present." She looked at the four-poster bed, its crisp sheets folded back invitingly. "Oh, this will never work out."

"Oh, I see endless possibilities," Jonathon murmured.

"You are impossible," Emily said turning to look at him. He stood before her naked, grinning from ear to ear. "Oh!" she stamped her foot and turned around.

"Are you coming to bed?" Jonathon asked climbing between the sheets.

Emily began to unfasten her gown as she blew all the candles out except a single one by the bed. Standing in the farthest, darkest corner of the room, she slipped out of her clothes and into her nightgown.

"Do not try to hide that beautiful figure from me, Em, for I have every curve, every detail etched in my mind."

"Stop it, Jonathon," she scolded.

Carefully climbing into bed, she lay on her side as close to the edge as she could. Jonathon chuckled in the darkness.

Emily lay awake a long time and listened to his even breathing. When she was sure he was asleep, she finally began to relax and allow her eyes to close and sleep to overtake her.

*

In the early morning hours when the birds were just beginning to stir and the sun glowed just beneath the eastern horizon, Emily came awake slowly. She felt warm, safe and secure, as she snuggled into the warmth of Jonathon. Slowly rising to consciousness, she realized she lay against him, her head on his shoulder, his arm wrapped around her. Not wanting to wake him lest he discover her nearness, she gently began to move away. His arm tightened around her.

"Do not leave, Em. It feels so good to have you here again."

"How long have I been like this?" she asked.

"Most of the night."

They lay in silence for a while watching the eastern sky lighten to a rosy pink. Jonathon's hand slowly caressed Emily's arm. Finally he spoke.

"It was never my intent to humiliate you, Em. I still do not understand how I did, but it matters not if I understand, only that you were hurt. I am sorry. Will you forgive me?"

Emily rose up on one elbow and looked down at him. "I am sorry, too, for acting like a child. Please forgive me?"

He looked up at her lovely face, her hair cascading like a curtain to his chest. He saw her tears brimming, and when she blinked, one escaped to run quietly down her cheek. He reached up and brushed it away.

"How we can hurt each other when we love each other so much," he whispered, as if to himself.

Emily nodded.

He drew her down against him and their lips met softly. Jonathon wrapped his arms around her, and Emily's arms encircled his neck as he eased her back on the pillows. His mouth moved over hers slowly and his hand reached down to untie her gown. As it opened he slipped it off her shoulders and caressed her silken back. He raised his head and looked into her shining blue eyes. She smiled at him and, sitting up, slipped off her gown. Climbing back under the covers, Emily snuggled against him and pressed her hips against his. He kissed her again, his tongue probing deeply the sweetness of her mouth. She responded eagerly and pulled him closer. His hand slipped to her full, rounded breasts, cupping them, teasing the nipples, and softly tracing their curves. Then his mouth followed down her throat, across her shoulders, down to her velvety soft skin. Emily shivered in delight as his tongue aroused and warmed her with its fire. Her hands rubbed gently through the soft hair on his chest and slowly ran down to tantalize and excite him. Jonathon moved back up to kiss her and she felt the firm manliness of him. He moaned with delight, and their hands explored and touched bringing them both to the edge.

Jonathon rose above her and gently entered her. Emily trembled as she felt him throb within her. They moved together in a rhythm of longing and delight. Finally, Jonathon began to thrust within her and Emily cried out in ecstasy. She pulled him closer, and her breath sounded in his ear. She clung to him as he nuzzled into her and closed her eyes against the waves of unbearable pleasure. At last they lay spent in each other's arms. The sun spilled across them in a soft, rosy glow.

Jonathon rolled onto his back and cradled Emily in his arm. She ran a finger across his lips, over his chin, down his throat and rested it on his chest.

"I love you, Jonathon," she whispered. "I am sorry that I hurt you."

"These are terrible times, Em. Many people are hurting those they love." He smoothed her hair. "I love you so, Em." He held her closer. They lay in the afterglow of passion that only true forgiveness and healing brings. They lay together for a long time.

*

Their stay at the Cosgroves' was enjoyable, and Martha was pleased to note their eagerness to retire in the evenings. James thought she was exaggerating, but she said with a twinkle in her eye, "A woman knows these things." As he watched them exchange glances one evening, he had to admit that she was right.

They played cards well into the night, and as they were about to retire, they heard a knock at the front door. They were all surprised, for the hour was late. Their servant ushered in Mr. Gates.

"Mr. Gates, how wonderful to see you," Emily exclaimed as he bent over her hand.

"Good evening, Mrs. Brentwood."

Jonathon introduced him to the Cosgroves and seemed to note Gates's agitation. James poured wine for everyone, and they sat down.

"I am afraid I have bad news, Captain," Mr. Gates began. "The King has declared the colonies to be in a state of rebellion. He has ordered suppression of the resistance."

The room was hushed as each one attempted to digest this news. Emily clutched Jonathon's hand. No one spoke for a full minute, the silence broken only by the ominous ticking of the parlor clock. Mr. Gates cleared his throat.

"Shall we sail as scheduled, sir?"

"I will make inquiries tomorrow, Gates. I shall be out to the ship by afternoon."

Mr. Gates rose. "Aye, sir. I am sorry to bring such terrible news to you." He bowed and left.

*

Emily had been quiet after Mr. Gates left, and she was quiet still as she brushed her hair before the mirror. The pink gown she wore fell in delicate folds around her, enhancing her curves and gracefully floating around her as she moved. Jonathon stood behind her and bent to place a kiss on the back of her neck.

"Jonathon," she said. The tone of her voice made him stop. He looked up at her reflection in the mirror and saw the confusion and anger in her eyes.

"Yes, love?"

"Will you continue to sail for the colonies?"

"Yes, love."

She turned around in the chair and looked up at him. "Please do not," she pleaded.

"I must, Em."

"Then you will fight against the King, against England?" she asked.

"Yes," he answered softly.

"Jonathon, please—"

"Emily, do you not understand what we have endured here? Parliament does not even consider us Britons anymore."

"Nor do you!" she cried.

Jonathon was stunned as the realization hit him. "No, I suppose I do not."

"Jonathon, what if it were reversed? What if you were forced to leave your lifelong home and sail across an ocean to England? And once there, what if everyone around you spoke of Virginia in the most derogatory ways and of Virginians as the enemy? What would you do? England is my home—"

"No, Emily, not anymore!" he shouted.

"Always, until a year ago, Jonathon. It was all I ever knew. I want to go back."

Silence fell between them. Jonathon turned away and walked to the window. He leaned a forearm against the frame and stared out at the blackness.

"Please, Jonathon. I asked if you would continue to sail for the colonies, and you said you must. To you it is patriotism; to me it is treason. Just as you must sail, I must return to England. I must," she finished

"You think I am a traitor?" he demanded.

"Yes!" she sobbed.

Jonathon's eyes blazed into hers. "Then allow me to remove myself from your company." He grabbed his coat and slammed his tricorn on his head.

"I sail tomorrow. I do not know when I shall return," he stated as he opened the door. He turned to look at her then slammed the door behind himself.

Emily sank down to the bed and stared ahead at nothing, drained and angry. Life had been tumultuous over the last year and she did not know how much more she could bear. She climbed into the empty bed, strangely cold in the August night, and longed for the warmth of Jonathon's arms. Jonathon's treasonous arms.

*

The next day Emily received a curt note in Jonathon's neat handwriting:

Emily,
Set sail today. Will return in a fortnight.
Jonathon

On reading it, she crumpled the note into a ball and threw it into the cold hearth as she swallowed down the lump in her throat.

She and Jonathon were to visit Andrew today at William and Mary College. They had seen him quite often since arriving in Williamsburg, and Emily realized how much she had missed him at Brentwood Manor. She decided to ask Martha to accompany her there, for she could not bear to stay in the house all day long. She went to find her friend.

Martha saw at once that something was amiss with Emily.

"What is it, dear?" she asked.

"I just received word that Jonathon is sailing today. He will be gone a fortnight," she replied.

Martha would have accepted that as the entire answer if she had not heard Jonathon slam out the door last night and seen Emily's tired and drawn face this morning.

"It must be terribly difficult for you both," she said gently, urging Emily to confide in her.

"Yes, it is."

Martha was disappointed that the girl said no more.

"Martha, would you accompany me to visit Andrew today?" she asked.

"Oh, that sounds lovely. Let me fetch my bonnet."

The air crackled with tense excitement as they drove along Duke of Gloucester Street to the school. People were reading posters about the King's declaration and talking animatedly in groups and pairs in front of the shops. Murmurs and cautious looks filled the streets as mistrust lodged deep within people's hearts and began to take root, dividing the loyalties of lifelong friends.

Emily was oblivious to the atmosphere, for her mind was filled with confusion and anger. She would return to England as soon as possible for she could not remain in these seditious colonies.

The carriage halted before the stately Wren Building where Andrew had been waiting for them as previously arranged. He hurried over to help the ladies alight.

"Have you heard the news of the King's declaration?" he asked excitedly.

"Yes, Andrew, and we have much to discuss," Emily replied.

They strolled to a bench beneath a shady oak tree and sat down.

"I have decided that we will return to England," Emily stated. Andrew and Martha looked at her in surprise.

"What does Jonathon say to that?" Andrew asked.

"Jonathon and I are on opposite sides in this issue, Drew. I believe he will agree to take us there. I have already told him of my desire to return, and you, naturally, will too."

"I will not."

Emily stared at her brother in stunned silence. She began to speak as if to a child.

"Andrew, you do understand what is occurring, do you not? The King has said that the colonies are in a state of rebellion. That their actions are treasonous."

"Emily, do not treat me like a child. I understand perfectly what is going on. The colonies want their independence. I believe they should have it. Britain has not been fair at all in her treatment of Virginia, nor of any of the other colonies. Many of my friends here are carrying a heavy burden of debt to London creditors; some were forced to discontinue their studies for lack of funds. Some are in danger of losing their lands and homes. Britain has strangled trade and dealt in mercantilism. These are a proud people, Em. This is an exciting time, and I intend to be part of it."

"Then you will fight for the colonies?" she gasped.

"I shall fight for no one. I shall observe, I shall learn. But I shall cheer for them, yes."

"Andrew, I cannot believe this of you."

He took his sister's hand in his.

"This is a troubling time, Em, but an exciting one. If you feel you must return to England, so be it. But Jonathon and I must do what we believe, also."

*

Emily was shaken by her visit with Andrew. It was inconceivable that he could support a cause that was, to her, so wrong. She took comfort in the sympathy that James and Martha Cosgrove showed her. They agreed with her assessment of the situation and had decided to join her on her voyage to England.

Leaving the colonies couldn't happen soon enough for Emily. Tension mounted throughout the fall. Although Virginia did not see the battles that were waging in the northern colonies, Lord Dunmore was increasingly infuriating the local patriots. He ordered printing presses to be confiscated and in October ordered the seizure of all ships off Hampton and the burning of the town. The militia drove the British off, but tempers were flaring and loyalists and patriots were squaring off to fight.

Emily was preoccupied with concern for Jonathon. He was

to have returned from his trip a month ago and she had heard nothing from him. The news of the attack on Hampton frightened her, and she feared for his safety.

She was preoccupied with something else, too. It was becoming difficult to keep her breakfast down, and she was exhausted by afternoon. She had also missed menstruation and was certain that at last she had conceived. The fear and confusion that possessed her were not enough to overshadow elation that, logically, she found strange, but could not deny.

James and Martha had lost their effervescent sparkle. James looked drawn and thin. A constant look of concern touched his face, and he seemed to glance out the window as if to check the street many times. Martha tried to hide her worry behind false gaiety, but Emily saw through it, though it endeared the woman to her even more.

The atmosphere was one of waiting. In the evening, as they sat in the drawing room reading and embroidering, it seemed as if all ears were stretched to listen. The clock ticked off the minutes in the ominous silence. Each time a rider passed the house, Emily's fingers would pause as she stared, unseeing, at the work in her hand. James and Martha would exchange sympathetic looks when the horse passed and Emily's shoulders sagged as she continued sewing.

The war continued to rage in the northern colonies and Canada, and news spread quickly to the southern colonies. Fights broke out in the streets as insults flew and honor was upheld. Troops from British ships were pillaging the towns and villages up and down the coast causing many loyalists to change their sympathies. And through it all one question swirled in Emily's head— *Where was Jonathon?*

Early in November Lord Dunmore, now on a warship off Norfolk, ordered Virginia placed under martial law. Two weeks later his troops met a militia marching toward Norfolk to aid its defense. Armed conflict had come to Virginia.

Another agonizing evening of waiting settled around Emily and the Cosgroves. The air seemed heavy and oppressive, and James in particular seemed on edge. Emily's nausea was easing, but she still fought fatigue. Her back ached as she leaned over her work, and a yawn overtook her once more.

"Emily, dear, why not get some rest?" Martha said gently. The strain of the past few months was evident in Emily's thin face with its dark circles under her eyes.

"I think I will—" she stopped in mid-sentence and listened.

James jumped up from his chair and ran to the window. The sound of raised voices grew louder, and he turned to the women in alarm. "I had heard this was happening elsewhere, but I never thought to see it here. They are coming to burn our house."

Filled with panic, Emily fought back a cry of fright.

Martha rose and went to the window where she saw a crowd of men, some bearing torches, approaching the house.

"No," she wailed. "They cannot!" She grabbed the lapels of James's longcoat. "James, we must do something. They will kill us all."

James dashed to the gun cabinet and removed two fine pistols. Then he rang for a servant.

"You two must flee through the back of the house. I shall hold them off for as long as I am able."

The servant arrived, his eyes wide with fear.

"Gather the others and go wherever you know you will be safe," James instructed.

Emily rose, her legs trembling with fear. "James," she said, "do you have other arms? I can shoot fairly well."

He looked at Emily tenderly. "Thank you, dear, but you and Martha must leave immediately. I insist."

"I will not leave you, James!" Martha cried.

"Nor I," Emily agreed.

The crowd had arrived in front of the house and was shouting at the gate. Firelight from their torches illuminated the blackness of the windows, and angry voices yelled insults and threats.

James seized another set of pistols, handing one to each woman. He kissed Martha's forehead and started for the front door

"You two stay here. I recognize some of these people; perhaps I can talk some sense to them."

He opened the door and the voices died down. "Friends, please. Violence between us will not further our cause—"

"Your cause is different from ours!" a voice rang out.

James looked around the crowd as they jostled and vied for position. He saw several familiar faces, some he even had considered friends. He appealed to one of them.

"Ben, we have been friends for years. Granted, we have divided loyalties right now, but—"

"Loyalist! Tory!" another voice shouted. Then from somewhere in the crowd a large egg was hurled toward James's head. He ducked in time to avoid being hit, but he was shaken. He straightened and held up a hand.

"Please, violence will not help—"

"Tell that to your redcoats," someone yelled.

Martha and Emily rushed to James urging him inside when a voice rang out, "Burn the Tory's house down!"

At this James drew a pistol and the crowd quieted.

"Leave my house!" he roared.

Voices rose and as one the crowd began to move forward. Emily raised her pistol and fired once above their heads, knocking off the hat of one of the torchbearers. Again, as one, the crowd stopped.

"They cannot hold us all back!" a voice shouted, and again they advanced.

This time James fired at the ground between them but they surged forward, coming up the walk and flowing across the neat front yard. One torchbearer lowered his fire to the yew hedge while others swarmed to the other side of the house. Just then horses' hooves thundered up the road, and a powerful rifle discharged into the night air.

"Stop!" Jonathon's baritone rang out, and the crowd turned to stare. Riding along with Jonathon was Mr. Gates, and behind them were three other crewmen.

"It is Brentwood!" Emily heard a man nearby say. Suddenly people scattered in all directions as Jonathon jumped from his horse, his face glowering. He grabbed one man and brought him face to face.

"Get water; all of you get water now!" he roared at him.

Pushing the man away, he ran to the well. Mr. Gates and the three crewmen followed, and a bucket brigade, including the man Jonathon had caught, was formed. They doused the yew hedge and that wall of the house that had caught fire. Emily and Martha dashed back in the front door to see one of the curtains ablaze. Martha ran forward, grasped the material, and ripped it from the windows. Throwing the drapes on the floor, she began stomping out the blaze. Jonathon saw her through the window and, breaking the glass, handed a bucket of water inside to Emily, who grasped the heavy, sloshing bucket and drenched Martha and the draperies. Then she tore upstairs to check the rooms on that wall of the house. Everything appearing all right, she rushed back to Martha.

The woman sat on the floor surveying the damaged room, and her eyes filled with tears. Emily brought a quilt from the corner chest and wrapped it around Martha's shivering shoulders. The voices of the men floated clearly through the broken pane. The fire had been contained, and the damage was limited to the yew hedge and the east wall of the house.

Drawing Martha to her feet, Emily led her upstairs and eased the shaking woman onto her bed. She took out a warm nightgown and assisted Martha into it. The woman seemed in shock, staring straight ahead as she shivered in her gown. Emily folded back the bedclothes and urged Martha to lie down.

"I shall make us some tea, Martha dear," she said gently. Then she hesitated, not sure if she should leave her alone. She rang for a servant remembering as she did so that no one would respond. She looked down at Martha and concern welled up within her. Martha stared at the ceiling, still shivering, her eyes dry. Emily sat beside her and took her hand. It was icy cold.

"Martha, will you be all right if I leave for a short time?"

Martha nodded, but still Emily hesitated. At that moment James entered the room, rushed to his wife, and drew her into his arms. Emily rose and slipped from the room.

She hurried down the stairs and went out to the kitchen house. The fire on the hearth was still warm, so she put the kettle on to boil and started to prepare a tray of food for the men. Her knees began to shake again as she had time to think of what had happened—and what might have happened. She tried to still her trembling and concentrate on preparing food for the others, but finally, exhausted and frightened, she collapsed into a chair and sobbed into her hands.

*

The water boiling over and hissing on the hearth brought her back, and she rose to finish her preparations. She readied a tray for the men and a small tray for Martha. That one she carried up first.

She found Martha much as she had left her, James beside her, a look of concern creasing his brow. He looked up gratefully as Emily entered with the tray and as she left, he was coaxing Martha to sip some tea.

Emily returned to the kitchen house and brought the tray of cold meats, cheese, and bread in for the men. She found them in the drawing room nailing boards across the broken window. Jonathon saw her enter as he turned to get another nail. Handing the hammer to Mr. Gates, he approached her.

"Is this how your fellow patriots treat their neighbors?" she cried. All the anger and fear that had welled up within her burst forth.

"Emily—"

"Where have you been, Jonathon?" The fear for his safety that had gnawed at her for months flooded over her again, even as he stood before her.

"Emily, I had to sail—"

"For the blasted colonies!" she cried.

The other men in the room shifted uncomfortably. Emily looked over at them as if seeing them for the first time. She tried to settle her anger; she took a deep breath and fought for control. After a moment, she spoke.

"Forgive me, gentlemen. This has been a most distressing evening. Thank you for your most welcome assistance. Here, I have brought some food. I am afraid it is cold—the servants were told to leave when the disturbance began. I hope everything is suitable . . . " Her voice trailed off. She felt as if she were in a dream, as if it were not even herself speaking.

"Everything looks delicious, Mrs. Brentwood," Mr. Gates spoke as he approached her and took her arm. "Here, please sit down and join us."

He looked meaningfully at Jonathon as he led Emily to the settee. Jonathon looked puzzled and still angry. Mr. Gates poured out brandy for everyone, including Emily, and they began to eat. Mr. Gates went upstairs to check on Martha and came down to report that she was resting comfortably. He kept a close watch on Emily as the men continued to eat. She stared at the food before her but did not touch it. Finally, he crossed the room and sat beside her.

"Here, missy, drink this," he said in the gentle voice he had used aboard the *Destiny* when Andrew had been injured. Emily looked at him, about to decline, but he pushed it into her hand

and smiled. Relenting, she took a sip. The warmth seeped through her, and after a time she began to relax. The murmur of the men's voices lulled her, and she leaned back and closed her eyes, but did not sleep. She listened as they spoke. James joined them when Martha had finally fallen asleep.

"These people have had enough. Ben Coates lost his entire plantation to British creditors. His family has owned that land since the late 1600s, and now he cannot afford even the family home," Jonathon said quietly.

"Matthew Brookside lost everything when his mill was burned. His youngest was killed in the fire," James responded.

Emily's heart ached as she listened to the stories of the destruction of people's lives being whispered in the half-light of the room. But the blame fell on both sides, for both loyalists and patriots were destroying and being destroyed.

Her strength had drained completely, and she could not stop shivering though the evening was warm.

Her eyelids felt too heavy to open and her limbs too heavy to move.

"Come, Missy, I shall help you to your room," Mr. Gates said softly. Slowly Emily's eyes opened and focused on his kind face. Why was it not Jonathon who stood there looking so concerned? His voice still rose and fell across the room, deep in conversation with James. He seemed unaware of Emily's state of exhaustion.

With Mr. Gates's assistance, she rose and started toward the stairs. She stumbled, and he supported her with a strong arm. What Emily did not see was worried brown eyes following her every move and how Jonathon began to rise when she stumbled.

When Gates returned to the drawing room, Jonathon was bidding good-night to James who was retiring to his room, and to the other men who were returning to the *Destiny*. When they had gone, he turned to Gates.

"Is she all right?" he asked anxiously.

"You should have gone to her," Gates replied. He spoke as a friend now, his deference for his captain set aside out of view of others.

"She wanted me nowhere near her," Jonathon said bitterly. "It will never change. She will come to resent me more and more. But I cannot give up the cause. I will not."

"Life does not offer easy paths. But love can make them smoother."

"I do not believe she even loves me anymore," Jonathon said quietly.

"You do not give your wife enough credit. She is a brave, loving, dedicated woman."

Jonathon looked at the man for a moment, and then patted him on the shoulder.

"You are a true friend, Gates," he said warmly.

"Aye, Captain," Gates smiled.

*

Muffled sounds coaxed Emily to consciousness, but exhaustion kept pulling her back into a deep, heavy sleep. When she finally, slowly came awake, the morning sun was high in the cold, clear, late–November sky. The events of the previous night seemed like a bad dream, but the acrid smell of burned wood still lingered to attest to the reality of it all.

Emily wanted to close her eyes and make it all go away, but she remembered how Martha had looked as she lay on the bed. And she remembered that Jonathon had safely returned. She rose and readied herself for the day.

The house was quiet as she crossed the hall to Martha's door and gently knocked. Opening the door slightly, she saw Martha sleeping soundly. Reassured, she hurried downstairs and stopped in the doorway to the dining room. Jonathon sat alone at the table. He looked haggard as he rose to greet her. Neither of them spoke for a moment. Relief for his safety and excitement at his presence washed over Emily. She took in his deep-set eyes, dark circles beneath them. His face looked thinner, proof of the strain and hardship he had been under. Although a rush of concern swept over her, Emily stood her ground. Finally, she spoke.

"Jonathon."

His name sounded like a prayer to her. How many times had she whispered it in the dark? How many nights had she begged God for his safe return? All of this was wrapped in his name as she spoke it.

"Are you well?" she asked. The question seemed hollow. She wanted to go to him; to hold him, support him, but her pride held her in check.

"Yes, Emily, I am well. And you?"

His voice flowed over her like a refreshing stream—its sound a healing balm. But the restraint it held was clear. Neither of them would relent.

"Well. I am well, thank you," she replied.

They had remained rooted in place, frozen figures masking true questions with safe ones. Suddenly they came to life, as if aware of the idiocy of this moment.

Emily looked at the sparse sideboard. Jonathon moved to her chair to hold it for her. Their discomfort was that of a newly courting couple.

"Breakfast is wanting, I am afraid," Jonathon said ruefully. "The servants have not returned, and I am a bit unused to kitchen duty."

Emily looked at the cold ham, cheese, fruit, and coffee. She looked at Jonathon in amusement.

"You did this?" she smiled. "Quite impressive for a sea captain."

Jonathon visibly relaxed at the lightness of her words. He bowed solemnly as he held her chair and swept his arm forward in a gallant gesture.

"May I wait upon you, m'lady?" he asked in mock formality

"If you would be so kind, sir," Emily returned in kind.

Their eyes locked with a smile that they understood as the groundwork for some painful and difficult decisions that would follow. But this moment was for adjustment and reacquaintance, and their silent, mutual agreement was to meet on lighter terms.

Jonathon piled a pewter plate with hearty fare and poured strong, black coffee and set it before her. Emily's exhaustion and excitement left her fair game for what little morning sickness remained. Her head swam as she eyed the overflowing plate. The smell of the coffee intensified it. But this was not the time to reveal news of such consequence, so she fought the nausea down and reached for some bread.

Jonathon returned to his chair. He caught a long look at Emily before she glanced up. He ached to take her in his arms. He was concerned about the circles beneath her eyes and the exhaustion he sensed within her.

"Em, I am preparing to take you to London," he said finally. "James and Martha will accompany us. Andrew wishes to remain here. I believe he is old enough to make that choice."

"You seem to allow Andrew to mature much faster than I," she replied. She regretted the remark instantly. She saw a flicker of anger in his eyes and relented.

"Jonathon, this has been difficult for all of us. I appreciate your generosity in taking us to England. Will it not be dangerous for you, though?" she asked.

"Getting out of Yorktown may be difficult, but so far I have had no trouble. We must stop at Norfolk en route, and that is a concern. It is a Tory stronghold, so my ship will not be welcome. But James will acquire papers from Dunmore that should ease the situation. It will be a brief stop. I cannot sail with you all the way to London. I have a friend who will meet us and deliver you safely," he explained.

The impact of what this meant hit Emily full force. An ocean would separate her and Jonathon—perhaps forever. Tears stung her eyes, and her throat ached. She could not bear to think of the danger Jonathon would face throughout this conflict.

"Jonathon—" she began but her throat hurt too much to continue.

Jonathon saw the tears streaming down her face, heard the pain in her voice. He wanted to go to her but was still uncertain of her feelings for him. She had called him a traitor, and the sting of that word still held. He understood her anger, torn loyalties, and confusion. But his convictions held, too, and he could not relinquish them. He was torn also, for his beloved Emily hurt, and yet she did not seem to want his comfort.

"Emily, what can I do for you?" he asked gently.

"Jonathon, I am so frightened," she sobbed.

He rose and slowly went around the table to where she sat. Tentatively he placed a hand on her shoulder and patted it. He felt awkward and, for the first time in his life, at a loss for how to treat a woman.

He knelt beside her, one arm across the back of her chair, as she continued weeping. The strain of the last few months was apparent in her face. Gently, Jonathon reached up and held her face in his hands. He brushed the tears from her cheeks.

"Em, I am sorry that you hurt so badly."

She raised her eyes to his, they glistened, but she smiled through the tears.

"Jonathon, I am so glad you are here," she cried and threw her arms around his neck. His arms wrapped around her eagerly, and she dissolved into tears of relief, confusion, and fear. They held each other close, able to comfort, able to support, but unable to compromise.

Emily's sobs began to subside. Her face was still buried in Jonathon's shoulder. His hands caressed her back and ran through her hair. He whispered reassurances softly and pressed his lips against her temple. Emily wished they could remain like this forever—just lock out the world with its wars and suffering and insulate themselves in this moment. She knew better.

Reluctantly she pulled away, noting every detail of his face, his eyes, his hair, committing each to memory for a time soon when she would not see them. *Perhaps forever.*

Jonathon smiled softly at her and brushed a lock of hair from her eyes.

"My sweet Em," he whispered.

It forced an answering smile from Emily. She touched his lips and brushed his hair back.

"Jonathon, I am so frightened for you. It will be very dangerous for you to transport us. How will you—"

"I shall have no trouble in Yorktown, Em. My ship is familiar there, and my friends are many. James will obtain the necessary papers for me to sail into Norfolk. There could be trouble there, but his influence should ease our arrival. From there we shall head out to open sea. I shall be unable to put in at London; I have a friend who will assist me and take you safely to your home."

The last word caught in his throat and fell on the air like a dead weight. It sounded discordant to Emily and she stiffened.

"Jonathon—" she cried.

"I thought I could make you love Virginia as I do, Em. I was wrong to try to force you. I wanted to share what makes me happy with you so it would bring you happiness, too. But it does not make you happy. I have taken you away from what does, and I am sorry," he said.

"Jonathon, my love, I have never known such happiness in my life as you have brought me. I am proud to be your wife, proud to be mistress of Brentwood Manor. Virginia is everything you promised and more, and I have begun to love it as my own. I cannot lie to you and say I support the patriots' cause—I do not.

But I love you, Jonathon. I cannot be an ocean apart from you; I want to stay here with you. Perhaps there will yet be resolution—some kind of merging of patriot demands with British loyalty. And our child can be one of the first born in this new era."

Emily had not quite meant to break the news like that, but she had become so absorbed in the excitement of the moment that she blurted it out.

"Emily, there is not much hope right now of—" Jonathon stopped in mid-sentence. He blinked a couple of times as her words sunk in. He looked into her eyes. "Our . . . our . . . child?" he stammered. "Emily?"

She nodded, breaking into a wide grin.

"Our child!" he shouted gleefully.

"*Shhh*, Jonathon. Martha is resting," Emily scolded. But he scooped her up in his arms and twirled her around three times.

"Oh, sir, how cruel you are!" she gasped. "My breakfast will have no chance to stay put if you continue."

Jonathon stopped and laughed. "Forgive me, Em, but you have made me the happiest man in the world." He danced lightly and set her down on her chair. He threw his head back and laughed again.

"A child, our child! Oh, Em." Tears glistened in his eyes, and he leaned forward and tenderly kissed her.

"I would like to pursue that, but perhaps the dining room is not the place," he whispered.

"I believe in celebrating life's important events, sir. Perhaps we should retire upstairs and discuss possible ways of doing so," Emily suggested, a devilish twinkle in her eye.

And so the impending birth of the newest Brentwood was fittingly celebrated.

Chapter 10

The brisk November wind whistled around the house and rattled the windowpanes. But the sun streamed in across the bed where Emily lay nestled against Jonathon. They lay half dozing; rousing only to touch and reassure themselves it was not a dream. Months of separation resulted in lovemaking that was passionate, almost fierce, in its demand to fill up the emptiness, the loneliness of that span of time spent apart.

Now they lay drowsing, but never asleep, never unaware of the other. Emily's head rested on Jonathon's shoulder, her leg thrown over his. Her fingers slowly worked through the hair on his chest while he soaked in the silkiness of her skin. Every so often he traced the curve of her belly, just a little fuller than usual. Each time he smiled, once he almost laughed aloud. He was full of questions: *How did she feel? When did she know? When was their child's birth expected? When would he be able to feel it move?* Emily laughed joyfully at his excited curiosity and answered each question with equal happiness.

Jonathon rolled Emily onto her back and kissed her long and full.

"Excuse me a minute, love," he said playfully. "I must speak with someone."

He kissed her neck, her shoulders, and her breasts and reached her belly. He covered it with kisses and then addressed it.

"Good day in there. I am your father. Yes, I am a tall, strapping man, quite handsome, most virile. I thought we should get to know one another. Are you well? Have you any idea how beautiful your mother is? She is a bit scrappy at times."

Emily tapped him on the head and cried, "Well!"

" . . . But she gets over it. You must be unusually comely to be born of two such handsome people. I suspect you will be quite spoiled. You must have your mother's good looks and my sweet temperament—"

"Oh, Jonathon," Emily ruffled his hair, "How you exaggerate!" Jonathon moved back up and faced her.

"No, Em, you really are beautiful," he teased.

She grabbed a pillow and swatted him.

"Oh-ho, so you want a duel!" he laughed.

He grabbed another and lightly fought back. Their game was interrupted by a knock on the door.

"Jonathon, excuse me. Mr. Gates is here," James called.

"Duty calls, my love," he whispered. He pressed his face in her hair, close to her ear.

"I love you, Em," he said. "I love you so." She caught him in her arms and pulled him close.

"I love you, too, Jonathon. I suspect these days will be difficult ones for us. We must face painful decisions and different loyalties. But one thing is sure. I do love you."

Their kiss was long and lingering, full of things unspoken, a promise of further understanding.

"I had best go or Mr. Gates will feel terribly affronted and dreadfully jealous."

Emily released him reluctantly. They rose and dressed quickly and went down to greet Mr. Gates.

*

Gates was delighted to see the metamorphosis that had occurred since the previous night. Both Emily and Jonathon glowed; they entered the room with their hands lightly clasped.

"You are both looking well," he said brightly.

"Yes, well, hmmm," Jonathon blustered. "It is amazing what a little nap will do."

"Indeed," Mr. Gates grinned.

"Well, what news, Gates?" Jonathon asked.

"Let me check on Mrs. Cosgrove, Jonathon, then I shall better be able to tell when we can set sail."

Martha was more alert today, but Gates suggested she rest for a week or two while they readied the ship and loaded supplies. That would mean setting sail in the midst of the holidays. All agreed it must be so. It seemed the holidays would be marred in any event by the division between the patriots and the Tories.

The remainder of the afternoon and early evening was spent in planning their voyage. The servants had returned by afternoon, and supper was a welcome meal, heartily enjoyed by all. Mr. Gates checked on Martha before he left and said he would be by again on the next day.

James and Jonathon continued discussion of the voyage after Mr. Gates left. As they talked, Emily neglected her embroidery and stared into the fire. Finally she spoke.

"Jonathon."

Both men looked up, startled at her voice.

"I will not sail to London," she declared.

"What?" they exclaimed in unison.

"James and Martha must go; however, I will remain here."

"Emily, it is no longer safe for you here," Jonathon answered.

"I shall return to Brentwood Manor. It will be safer there—and I promise to be less vocal about my sympathies," she argued.

Both men vigorously protested, nodding in agreement at each other, talking over one another's reasons.

Emily rose and walked to Jonathon' chair. Kneeling beside him, she looked up into his eyes.

"Jonathon, this morning you said your friend would take me home to London. It is no longer my home. My home is with you. I will stay here in Virginia. I cannot bear to be parted from you— so far away, so long a time. I am your wife; I will stay by your side. I can never embrace your beliefs, my love, but I want to stay with you. And our child must be born at Brentwood Manor."

James started and looked at each in turn. The looks on their faces said it all. Of course there would be a child.

"It is precisely because of the child that you must leave," Jonathon said softly. "We must ensure his safety."

"Please, Jonathon—"

"No, Emily. It must be this way. But I promise you, as soon as I am able and it is safe, I will return for you and bring you home. Your home, our home. I cannot keep alert if I am worried about you, love. Please do as I ask."

Emily was prepared to fight him on this, but what Jonathon said made sense. He must concentrate on his mission and be alert to any danger. His safety was paramount to her.

"I shall consider it," she said.

Jonathon knew better than to push.

*

David and Joanna decided to come to Williamsburg to celebrate an early Christmas with Jonathon and Emily. Jonathon was anxious for news of Brentwood Manor. He also hoped to enlist Joanna's help in convincing Emily to sail to London.

They had not spoken of it again since Emily had announced her refusal to go. But Jonathon knew how the situation in the colonies was deteriorating—especially in the North. Concepts previously unheard of were being bandied about—individual freedom, popular sovereignty, power emanating from the people. The writings of Jefferson were awakening this infant coalition to ideas never before imagined. The price was rebellion. Jonathon knew lives were being lost; he feared for Emily and their child.

These thoughts ran through his mind as Jonathon sat in James's study. Gates had reported that they could sail as soon as December 23. It was vital to stop in Norfolk to deliver supplies to the Sons of Liberty who were working there. This would be an incredibly dangerous stop because the city had maintained its Tory sympathies. Once they were away from Norfolk he would rest more easily.

*

Joanna, David, and little Will arrived in a carriage burdened with gifts and food from Brentwood Manor. Emily was the first out the door to greet them, followed by Jonathon who carried a shawl to wrap about her shoulders. The women embraced while the men shook hands and then pulled each other close for a bear hug. Emily reached for Will and gasped in surprise.

"Will, how you have grown!" she exclaimed.

The baby looked at her with wide, wondering eyes then back at his mother.

"Oh no, he does not remember me!" Emily cried.

Will shyly looked at her again. She began to sing a lullaby that she had often sung to him at the manor. He stared at her steadily then broke into a smile and bounced in her arms.

"That is my Will," Emily laughed and they hurried inside. James joined them for tea, and once again laughter and voices filled the house.

"Well, sit down everyone. We have news," Jonathon beamed.

"Jonathon, my love, let them get settled in," Emily laughed.

"No, they are settled in enough," he answered. Raising his teacup he announced. "A toast to the expected, newest member of the Brentwood family."

"Oh, Jonathon, Emily!" Joanna cried. "How wonderful!"

She went to Emily and threw her arms around her. David pumped Jonathon's hand.

"Are you well enough to travel, Emily?" Joanna asked.

"Oh, I feel wonderful," Emily reassured her. "However, I am not to travel after all."

"Emily—" Jonathon began.

"Jonathon, I told you this before," Emily stated firmly.

"Emily, you must go," David interrupted. "The situation is worsening here for people sympathetic to the crown. The patriots are becoming more feverish in their cause. It is outright war in the northern colonies. It will take little time for that fervor to spread to Virginia."

Jonathon nodded in agreement. "That episode here last month was just a taste of what may happen," he added.

*

The Cosgrove home was transformed from its somber tone to one of a festive, holiday atmosphere. The excitement seemed healing for Martha. Emily and Joanna spent afternoons chatting with her in her room, and in a few days she roused enough to join them for dinner. Each day she seemed to gain strength, and Jonathon was relieved, as he had not been certain that Martha could endure the voyage to London.

Andrew joined them in the evenings for cards, and it was a happy company, although the specter of separation and danger hung over them.

One night as they played cards, plans were being discussed for the imminent voyage. Emily's heart sank as it always did at this subject. How could she leave Jonathon? She feared for his safety, his life. She was frightened that if she were not here something terrible would happen to him. She knew it was a silly notion, but she could not free herself of that foreboding.

"Andrew, are you not traveling with them?" David was asking in surprise. The question roused Emily from her reverie.

"I shall stay here, David. I may be of some use in the future," he replied.

"Again, Jonathon, you allow Andrew more freedom than you allow me!" Emily exploded. "How is it that a mere boy can remain, but your wife cannot? Explain that to me, sir!"

"Emily—" Jonathon began in measured tones.

"Your reasons make no difference to me. I belong here with my husband. Our child should be born at the manor. I will not have it otherwise." She threw down her cards and folded her arms with an air of finality.

"Emily, please be sensible." Jonathon pleaded.

"Sensible! Show me the sense in any of this, Jonathon," she exclaimed. "Show me the sense in dividing families, in leaving your home. Show me the sense in war and killing." Tears spilled down her cheeks.

"I hate war and killing as you do, my love," he replied softly. "But we are being strangled by a slower death otherwise. Please, Emily." He took her hand in his.

She calmed at his words, his touch. The pent-up fear mixed with fatigue due to her pregnancy had been too much for her. She took a deep breath.

"Excuse me for that outburst," she looked at each of them, then down at her hands. Jonathon reached over and took her hand and entwined his fingers in hers. Then he pressed them to his lips.

"You are under a terrible strain right now, Emily," Joanna said softly. "Your first thoughts must be for your health and that of your child."

Emily nodded, fighting for control of her emotions.

"I am very tired. If you will please excuse me," she said, rising.

Murmurs of assent and understanding went around the table as Jonathon rose and followed her.

Entering their room, he found her standing at the window, her forehead pressed against the pane. He crossed the room and stood behind her, their reflection soft in the candle's glow.

He put his hands on her shoulders and kissed the back of her head. They stood in silence for a time. Jonathon breathed in the scent of her hair and exhaled deeply.

"Love," he whispered.

Emily trembled as she fought back her tears. She turned to him, and his arms wrapped around her, holding her close as she surrendered to his tenderness. Jonathon whispered consolingly and stroked her hair. Finally, she looked up at him, her tear-streaked face tender and full of love.

"Jonathon, I am so afraid for you."

"Emily, I truly would be in less danger if I knew you were safely away. I do not want to be parted from you, but I cannot concentrate on my work if I am distracted by fear for you."

Emily reached up and touched his face, tracing the line of his jaw.

"I shall go, Jonathon," she said finally.

He kissed her forehead. "I shall come for you the moment it is safe, love. I promise."

"I will live for that day," she whispered over the lump in her throat.

*

It was a mild December day as David, Jonathon, and Mr. Gates strode along the pier toward the *Destiny*. Hogsheads of tobacco—the lifeblood of many planters—lined the shore, rotting because of British trade policies.

As they approached the ship, a burly sailor called out to them from amid his cronies.

"Captain Brentwood, I see," he said. "The great sea captain of the Sons of Liberty."

Jonathon continued walking.

"Ho, sir. I am speaking to you," the sailor demanded.

Jonathon stopped and turned slowly.

"Well, I have got your attention. A lowly sailor like me," he jeered. "And what will our cargo be this time, I wonder?"

"If you have something of importance to say to me, please speak," Jonathon commanded.

"I am just interested in the goings-on of the Sons of Liberty. Just what is your business with them, Brentwood?"

"I believe you already know that," Jonathon replied.

"But I wonder if the Sons know," he sneered. "Do the Sons know which side you are on? Do you know, Brentwood?"

"State your business or move on."

The man approached him, hunched at the shoulders, fists doubled.

"Do the Sons know that you have Tory sympathies, too? You seem to be on both sides of the fence, Brentwood."

Gates saw the look in Jonathon's eyes and feared for the obnoxious sailor. But time was pressing, and they had to finish with the ship and return immediately to the Cosgroves'. Realizing this, too, Jonathon restrained himself; David visibly relaxed.

"If you question my loyalty, sir, I invite you to sail with me and inspect my cargo and my actions," Jonathon snapped, then turned from the man and continued toward the *Destiny*.

"Yes, Brentwood," he spat out the name. "You sail for the patriots by day and sleep with a Tory wench at night. Tell me, Brentwood, does she—"

But the question went unasked for Jonathon swung around and struck him in the jaw, then in the stomach, before he had time to react. The sailor lurched backwards, and Jonathon assisted him with a second blow to the face. He dropped with a heavy thud in the dirt.

The man staggered to his feet with a murderous look on his face. He doubled his fists and came at Jonathon. They circled one another throwing lethal punches. Although the sailor was a burly man, taller than Jonathon by an inch, Jonathon had speed and agility on his side. And the wrath of a man in love whose wife had been insulted.

The sailor's friends gathered around and cheered on their companion. David was worried about Jonathon, but Gates stood calmly by and watched, almost in amusement. He had seen Jonathon come out the victor with worse odds.

The men continued trading blows, and it was evident that the bigger man was tiring. Jonathon had the advantage now and was making the most of it. One last blow to the head, and the sailor was down in a pool of blood.

His friends gaped in amazement, and all but one quickly dispersed. The one who remained knelt by the unconscious man and tried to rouse him.

Jonathon wiped the blood that trickled into his eye and picked up his hat. Gates looked him over carefully.

"Captain, you have a propensity to start trouble wherever you go," he said. "You really should curb that."

"Gates, I shall do my best," he breathed heavily, still trying to catch his breath.

Gates cleaned up Jonathon's wounds on board the *Destiny* and found him a change of clothes.

"It is good that Emily will be away from this, Jonathon," David said.

"Aye," Gates agreed.

Jonathon nodded in mute agreement. His heart was heavy at the thought of Emily being so far away. But he was more convinced than ever that it was becoming increasingly dangerous for her to stay.

*

The women were shocked at Jonathon's appearance when the men returned that night. Emily jumped up and flew to him when she saw his injuries.

"Oh, Jonathon!" she cried in horror. In her impatience to see him, she accidentally brushed his tender face. He winced in pain. She held him close, pressing against his bruised ribs. He held her away.

"Love," he begged. "Please do not care so much. Your concern is terribly painful for me to bear."

Realizing what she had done, Emily gasped and pulled back.

"I am sorry, love." She reached out to touch him, and he winced in anticipation. Seeing his look of apprehension, she paused, started again and finally threw up her hands in frustration. "How does one comfort an injured man?" she cried.

"Perhaps from afar, for now, Mrs. Brentwood," Gates offered, stifling a grin.

"Oh, of course," she murmured.

Jonathon laughed and put one arm around her shoulders carefully. On tiptoe she tentatively kissed his cheek where there was no mark. Then sitting together on the settee, Emily barely took her worried eyes from her husband.

The men explained the incident at the pier, although they modified it, leaving out the insults to Emily. The women were not reassured by the explanation, and Emily found a deep foreboding overtake her. Again she wanted to refuse to sail to London. She desperately wanted to remain with Jonathon, as if her presence would somehow protect him. She was unaware that it was her presence that caused his injuries that afternoon.

*

Parting with David, Joanna, Will, and especially Andrew was difficult for Emily. Their holiday celebration had been a deliberate disregard of the strife in the land. Their gaiety was often forced, but their love for one another and the appreciation of their time together was real.

Emily held little Will one last time as Joanna and David bid Jonathon farewell. Turning to her, they both had tears in their eyes. They embraced her together; no words seemed enough to convey their sorrow at her leaving. Joanna looked into her eyes and smiled through her tears.

"Emily, this is not forever. Soon we shall be taking tea on the veranda at Brentwood Manor again."

Emily nodded; her throat ached. "Joanna, David, take care. I shall be back as soon as possible." The words sounded empty to her.

They climbed into the carriage and waved until they were out of sight. Jonathon stood with his arm around Emily's shoulders. Tears streamed down her face.

They went inside where servants were busy preparing the house to be closed up for the duration of the Cosgroves' stay in London. Although still weak, Martha was able to supervise the work with Emily's help. Needing to keep busy, Emily joined her.

They would board the *Destiny* the next day and set sail the day following. It all seemed unreal to Emily, and she had difficulty staying with her task. But time was pressing, and she forced herself to concentrate.

When Andrew came for supper that night, conversation was not animated as it had been during David and Joanna's visit. Emily wondered how long it would be before she would see her brother again. She could not eat, but kept staring at her brother as he and Jonathon talked about the voyage. He occasionally caught his sister's eye and smiled reassuringly. Emily realized that Andrew was not the young boy she had convinced herself he was. He was a strapping young man, as determined and strong-willed as she. The realization sent a mixture of melancholy and relief over her. It was hard to see him grow up, but she knew he would be all right here.

Andrew lingered after supper, finding it difficult to finally say good-bye to his sister and Jonathon. They chatted about light subjects as they sat before the fire in the drawing room. The Cosgroves retired fairly early, and then Jonathon excused himself to finish some work in the study, realizing that Andrew and Emily needed time alone.

"Emily, you have been my strength since Father's death. I shall miss you and anxiously await your return," he said.

"Andrew, I do not want to go. Why is Jonathon making me do this?" she cried.

"You know why, Em. It has to be this way right now. It is becoming more and more dangerous for you here."

"I could go back to the manor. I would be safe there—"

"No, Em," he said quietly. "I do not think you would be safe even there now."

She knew he was right. She sighed in resignation.

"Andrew, you will be careful; promise me?"

"Am I not always?" he asked feigning innocence, and they both laughed.

Finally Andrew had to leave, and he and Emily held each other and cried. Again Emily fought against the sobs that threatened to overtake her. Andrew patted her back gently and let his tears flow. Emily realized that her little brother was no longer a child, as he was the one being strong and comforting her. She was grateful for his strength at that moment, for she had little to offer. Jonathon returned to say good-bye and hugged the boy heartily.

"You will keep things in order until I return. Is that not so, Drew?"

"Aye, aye, sir," he saluted.

Emily watched him canter down the road and stood, still watching even after he had disappeared. Jonathon coaxed her inside out of the cold night air.

*

The next day dawned sunny and breezy for their departure. The carriage and wagon were loaded, and they set out for Yorktown. Emily was amazed at the appearance of the harbor. The hustle that had greeted her on her voyage from England was replaced by cargo silently waiting at the waterfront for ships that would never come to claim it. The merchant ships that crowded the port had been refitted to become vessels of war. They sat lower in the water, weighed down by their added cannon.

The sight of the *Destiny* brought the conflict home to her more than anything else had. The ship sat deep in the water; it, too, was heavy with cannon.

"Oh, Jonathon."

He turned and saw the dismay in her face.

"It had to be, Em," he replied.

He continued scanning the wharf for a burly sailor. He hoped they would be able to board without incident. Then to his right he saw him. He took Emily's arm and continued walking, his eyes never leaving the man's. Finally, the burly sailor broke his glare, spat on the ground and walked away.

They boarded the *Destiny* without any further trouble, and Jonathon sought out Gates.

"I want to set sail as soon as possible," he told the man. "I do not want to remain here any longer than necessary."

"Aye, Captain," Gates answered. "I think that is wise."

The crew was still loading the ship when night fell, and Jonathon paced the deck nervously. Emily was bewildered by his behavior.

"Jonathon, what is it?" she asked as she fell into step with him.

"I am anxious to be off, love," he replied.

"What else?"

He leaned against the rail and looked at her.

"Do you know that you are beautiful in the moonlight, Em?" he asked lightly.

"Jonathon, do not patronize me," she said sternly. "Why are you pacing back and forth like a trapped animal?"

He looked at his wife and knew that it would be foolish to lie. He turned and looked toward the pier.

"The gentleman I had an altercation with recently is most interested in the goings-on of my ship," he answered.

Emily's gaze followed his.

"Do you think there will be trouble? Do you think he will try to hurt you again?" she asked anxiously.

"I honestly do not know, love. But if any trouble should break out, you are to go directly below deck," he said firmly.

"Aye, Captain," Emily said lightly.

Jonathon breathed a sigh of relief when everything was loaded and they could set sail. He had not planned to sail until morning; however, recalling the look in the sailor's eye, he decided to cast off and drop anchor just a short distance off shore for the night.

Emily stood at the rail and watched the glowing lights that were just visible on the shore. She would soon leave the Virginia that Jonathon had wanted her to love so much. The Virginia that she had come to love so much.

*

Jonathon's quarters had been redecorated to accommodate Emily's presence. A double bed replaced the bunk, a change that made it crowded but cozy for them. Jonathon and James had spent a good portion of the evening at Jonathon's desk poring over maps and documents in order to decide on a strategy for sailing into Norfolk.

The situation there was uneasy. Jonathon had to deliver supplies and communications to the patriots there, but Norfolk had strong Tory support. James had obtained documents that would allow Jonathon to pass unopposed through the town, but tempers were flaring all over, and no place was really safe there anymore.

Emily sat and tried to embroider by the light of a lantern, but her mind was too preoccupied. The men spoke softly at the desk, and the ship rocked gently, and soon she was nodding off. Noting her condition, James finally bade Jonathon good-night and took his leave. Jonathon saw Emily dozing in the chair and went over to her.

"Love," he said softly. He gently nudged her. "Will you deprive me of your warmth and spend the night so?"

Emily slowly opened her eyes. She sat up and yawned and stretched.

"I am sorry, Jonathon. Did James leave?"

"Yes, Em. And you look like a woman who needs some sleep." Emily nodded.

"Of course, I could be convinced of other activity if the speaker were persuasive enough," she said, smiling seductively.

"Well, let me compose a speech that will capture your heart and encourage you to agree to my idea," Jonathon said with a roguish gleam in his eyes. He scooped her up in his arms and carried her to the bed. Gently he laid her upon it and eased himself down beside her. He leaned on his elbow on the bed and looked down at her.

"Emily, you are my life," he said tenderly. He traced her cheek with his finger. His eyes looked into hers and spoke a love that was deep and true.

"Jonathon, I do not want to be parted from you."

"You will not be, Em. I will carry you in my heart. You will be with me every moment. I will never be without a thought of you in my mind. But I must know that you are safe."

He leaned down and kissed her eyelids. He moved back, and she opened her eyes and looked into his. They were warm and filled with a smoldering fire. She reached up and brushed a lock of hair from his eye. She ran her fingers through his thick dark hair and pulled him toward herself. Their lips met in a blazing kiss that made her squirm with desire. She pushed against him wanting to melt into one. His arms went around her, and he held her close.

Emily felt almost crazed with desire for Jonathon. Her mouth searched his hungrily as if she could not be satisfied. She pulled his hand to her breast needing to feel its heat against her skin. She worked the buttons on his shirt frantically, pulling it out of his breeches.

Jonathon pulled away and looked down at her, enjoying her enthusiasm. "Apparently my speech worked. Perhaps I missed my calling. I should have been an orator," he teased.

"Jonathon, this is not the time for more speeches," Emily sputtered. "I believe what I need now is action."

"Yes, love," he tried to say, but she smothered his reply with a kiss.

Emily eagerly assisted Jonathon out of his clothes and quickly doffed her own. They slipped between the sheets and their passion rose as they explored each other's body. Emily felt a more intense desire than she ever could remember, and Jonathon held her close as she reached the dizzying heights of her climax. She shuddered against him as wave after wave of pleasure engulfed her.

"Oh, Jonathon," she moaned.

"I love you, Em. You are so beautiful," he whispered as she clung to him.

"Hold, me, Jonathon," she begged. He wrapped her in his arms.

"I am here, love."

Emily snuggled into his embrace feeling that she could never get close enough. They lay together rocking with the rhythm of the ship. Their passion spent, they fell into a deep sleep wrapped in each other's arms.

*

They put out to sea in the morning, planning to take their time heading into Norfolk. It was almost Christmas, but no one on board felt in the holiday spirit. The sky had clouded over, and there was a brisk wind from the northeast. The crew was busy keeping the *Destiny* on course, and Jonathon was busy checking charts and maps.

Uncomfortable and anxious, Martha spent most of the time in her cabin. Deeply concerned about his wife, James was worried that she might not be able to make the long voyage. Emily spent time with Martha in her cabin each day, but regardless of the weather, Emily found it necessary to stroll the deck for a while, too. She felt restless, not wanting to go, but resigned to the journey if that was what must be.

Travel along the Virginia coast proved difficult and slow with the inclement weather. The ship was tossed about on the waves making it difficult for Emily to walk about at all. She hated being confined below deck, although being with Martha made it easier. When the winds died down, Emily was able to resume her walks.

She could not help but reflect on her last voyage aboard the *Destiny*. How different things had been then, how different she had been. But one thing was the same—she had not wanted to make that journey either. Both times she was sailing away from the land she loved, from her home. But both times she was with Jonathon and she trusted him. The trip to Virginia had resulted in happiness for her, for she had married Jonathon. She must believe that this trip, too, would end happily. Somehow things would turn out for the best. Perhaps the conflict would be resolved quickly, and she and Jonathon would be reunited in a short time.

These thoughts helped Emily get through this dreadful time. She had to remain optimistic and believe all would be well. If she did not, she was afraid she could not bear saying good-bye to Jonathon.

*

They finally reached Hampton Roads and turned the ship toward Norfolk. Emily sensed the tension in Jonathon. He checked and rechecked charts. He studied the documents James had given him for their safe passage into Norfolk. He peered out at the horizon in all directions looking, Emily supposed, for other ships. Friendly or unfriendly.

At last, one evening, they began to sail toward land. The crew seemed nervous and apprehensive, each man checking the shore and the horizon numerous times. The air was charged with unspoken tension. Emily could bear it no more; she searched out Jonathon and found him on the deck.

"What is it, Jonathon?" she asked. "Why do I sense this apprehension in everyone?"

Jonathon placed his hands on her shoulders. "It is becoming very dangerous to enter some of these ports, Em. We have heard that Dunmore is making mischief in Norfolk. We will all feel better when we have put that town behind us."

Emily looked into his warm, brown eyes. "It will be like this for you from now on, will it not? Like this and worse."

"I do not know, love. I have been careful so far, and I intend to continue to be careful. After all, I have a beautiful wife with very eager arms waiting for me, have I not? A man would be a fool to not be careful with the welcome I expect to receive when we are together again."

He pulled her close and held her for a long time. Silent tears traced a path down Emily's cheeks. She recognized that he was putting on a brave front and trying to sound lighthearted for her, and she knew she needed to be strong for him as well. He pressed a kiss on her forehead and looked into her eyes. He wiped her tears and smiled.

"Be my brave lady, Em. Keep praying, and God will protect us and bring us together again. I know that. Believe it, love."

He kissed her gently, and she left him to check on Martha. James was with her, and they chatted for a while, each trying to cheer the other.

They reached the port in Norfolk at night on December 31. The *Destiny* stayed a distance out while some crew members boarded a small row boat to check the situation on shore. All seeming to be quiet, they sailed in closer.

Jonathon ordered the sails trimmed, but insisted the crew be ready to sail at a moment's notice. There would be enough men on duty throughout the night to put out to sea if need be.

Jonathon and James prepared to go ashore accompanied by a few members of the crew. It was tempting to allow the crew ashore for some leave before the long voyage across the Atlantic, but Jonathon decided to get in and out as quickly as possible.

Jonathon took Emily off to the side. He looked deeply into her eyes then pulled her close.

"Em, there are so many things I want to tell you right now. Just know how much I love you. When I return tonight, I will show you how much, you will have no doubt," he said softly. He bent his head, and his lips found hers. He held her tightly and could not bear to let her go. When Mr. Gates coughed discreetly, Jonathon released her, his eyes holding hers for a moment. Then he turned to leave.

Jonathon, James, and a few crew members climbed into the rowboat, and the oars silently dipped in the water as they headed toward the shore. As Emily watched them, she felt heaviness throughout her body. She wanted to remain at that spot until she could see them rowing back to the ship.

The breeze picked up and the temperature fell. Emily had been standing there for over an hour when Mr. Gates approached her.

"Missy, they will be gone most of the night," he said gently. "Why not get some sleep? I promise I will call you when they are in sight."

Emily reluctantly agreed and went to her cabin. She lay in bed a long time before sleep finally overtook her. She awakened as dawn was just breaking in the southeast horizon. Something bothered her, but she was not fully enough awake to know what it was. Slowly she became aware of increased activity on deck. It seemed hurried and intense, and she suspected that Jonathon was returning. She rose quickly and bundled into her cape.

On deck, men were scrambling in all directions. Emily ran to the spot where she had kept vigil the night before. Peering into the darkness, she tried to spot the rowboat. As she watched, other shapes became visible; ships lined the entrance to the port. They began to load their cannon and fire on the town. The night air was shattered as the cannon exploded into a deafening roar. Flames shot up where the guns hit their mark. Emily watched in horror as homes, warehouses, shops all caught fire and began to burn. In the fiery red glow she spotted the rowboat with Jonathon and James in it.

The men in the small boat strained at the oars, pulling their hardest. Behind them came a similar vessel, more heavily manned and closing fast. Jonathon and James sat side-by-side working their oars in unison. It was a futile attempt, and soon the second boat was within firing range. A British soldier stood shakily in the skiff and fired, hitting one of the crew. The man slumped over and fell to the floor of the boat. Jonathon roared a command to pull harder and put more effort into his own task.

Emily stood frozen in place as she watched the scene before her. She suddenly realized that the *Destiny* was preparing to sail, and she panicked. The second vessel was closer to Jonathon's now, and two more soldiers began to fire on it. One by one Jonathon's men arched and fell when they were hit.

"Jonathon, hurry!" Emily screamed.

The *Destiny's* sails were raised and billowing.

"No!" Emily screamed. "Wait, please, wait!" she cried in horror.

The rowboat was almost overtaken. She saw Jonathon gesturing to the *Destiny* to go. Emily's heart wrenched as she grasped the situation. Her mind screamed in terror. Her eyes were locked on the boat that held her beloved Jonathon.

A shot rang out. Jonathon reeled to the left and grabbed at the oar. James caught him and kept him from falling overboard. Another shot rang out, and Emily saw the blood spurt from James' face. Her stomach turned over, and she thought she would retch. But her eyes were glued on Jonathon. He and one other crewman feebly worked the oars. He half stood, then stumbled and fell into the sea.

"Jonathon!" Emily screamed. "Jonathon!" The British skiff sailed up to the other boat. A final shot finished the last crewman, and he sprawled over his companions on the floor of the boat. Emily watched as the British soldiers pulled Jonathon's body aboard their skiff and started rowing back to shore. She felt rooted in place.

"Mr. Gates!" she screamed. "Gates!"

He had seen the whole incident, but had been readying the ship for its escape. Two other British ships were sailing toward them in an attempt to block their passage out into open water. Gates quickly reached the girl.

"Do something, please! Oh, God, do something!" she cried as she grabbed his lapels.

Gates's heart was torn. His friend was gone. He must follow his captain's orders and get the *Destiny* safely away.

In shock, Emily looked out at the British skiff that held Jonathon. Jonathon's body.

Her legs gave way, and all was darkness.

Chapter 11

Emily slowly rose to consciousness. The rocking motion of the ship had a soothing quality. Her eyes felt heavy; she could barely open her lids. Suddenly the image of Jonathon falling into the sea brought her fully awake. She sat up with a scream.

Mr. Gates came over to her bed swiftly and took her hand. The comprehension that Jonathon's death was real overwhelmed Emily, and she began to wail. Gates held her shuddering form as she sobbed forth her sorrow. Tears filled his eyes as he sought to deal with the loss of his dearest friend.

"No!" she sobbed. "Oh, dear God! No, no, no!"

Emily's body was wracked with anguish. Her throat ached, and she thought she would be sick. She grabbed Gates's jacket and crumpled the lapels in her fists. She shook her head back and forth not willing to believe the truth.

Gates murmured empty consolation to her not believing his own words. He stroked her hair and spoke gently, as if to a child.

"There, there, missy. We must be away. Jonathon would want you and his child to be as safe as possible," he said.

The sound of Jonathon's name tore Emily's heart in two.

"Oh, my God, no!" she sobbed.

Gates rose and went to a table where he had a flask of brandy. He brought it to her. Emily turned away; too many memories flooded in as she looked at the flask.

"Please, Missy," Gates coaxed. "You must think of your child now. You must calm down and rest."

"No, I do not want any! Please, Mr. Gates. Please find Jonathon," she begged.

"Jonathon is gone, missy. I am sorry," he said gently.

"No!" she screamed. "No!" Again she shook with desperate tears. Gates looked at her helplessly. All he could do was hold her.

Emily cried herself into an exhausted sleep. She awoke in

darkness and lay staring at the ceiling. She denied to herself that Jonathon was gone; she willed it to be untrue. It was all a bad dream. But the reality of the scene played over and over in her mind. She felt empty and hollow. Her body was cold and numb. Nothing mattered.

Emily remained in bed, unaware of how much time passed. All feeling was drained; all reason for living seemed gone. She wanted to die.

Gates came to her room the next morning. Concerned by her lethargy and the dull look in her eyes, he brought a tray of food for her, but it went untouched.

"Missy, I cannot begin to know your sorrow. But I am concerned for your child. You must keep up your strength for your child. Please eat something," he pleaded.

"I cannot," she said slowly.

"Please try, missy. Just some bread."

Emily reluctantly bit into a biscuit and began to chew it. She could not swallow it. Her throat was dry, and a lump was always there, threatening more sobs. She finally managed to get it down, then jumped up and ran to the basin retching violently.

"Oh, missy, are you all right?" Gates cried as he poured out some water. He led her back to the bed and helped her lie down. He soaked a cloth and gently washed her face. Then he poured fresh water in a cup and gave it to her.

"Try this. Drink it slowly," he urged.

Emily took the cup and sipped. She waited and then took another. The water stayed down. She lay back upon the pillows.

"Just try to sleep now, missy," Gates said softly.

Exhaustion overcame her, and Emily slept most of the day. That evening she was finally able to take a few bites of food, but she remained in the cabin.

She felt as if she were walking in a dream. Everything seemed so unreal; nothing seemed to matter. She dozed and awakened on and off throughout the night. When she awoke she did not open her eyes, as if that would keep away the awful sights she had witnessed. She pressed her fists into her closed eyes willing away the vision of Jonathon's body being hauled aboard the British skiff. But the vision persisted.

In the morning she took a little more food and sat with Gates for a while.

"How is Martha?" she finally asked. Emily judged she should be feeling guilty for having forgotten about Martha, but she did not feel anything.

"Mrs. Cosgrove is not well. The news of her husband's death was a terrible blow to her," Gates replied.

"You know that they are all . . . dead?" Emily could barely say the word.

"Yes. We recovered James and the others from the boat, and the British took Jonathon's . . . body." It was difficult for Gates to say, but he knew Emily needed to face the reality of the situation if she were to eventually recover from her grief.

Emily stared ahead. All of her strength went into blocking out the scenes of horror she had witnessed. She could not bear to think of them.

"Mrs. Brentwood," Gates said, calling her back from her daze. She started at his voice. "We have some decisions to make. I have orders to keep your safety as my first priority. We are out at sea now, but getting to London may be difficult."

"I am not going to London," Emily stated flatly.

Gates waited. Emily was surprised he did not argue with her.

"Please take me back to Yorktown. I want to return to Brentwood Manor."

Gates stared out the window for a few moments.

"I do not think Mrs. Cosgrove could make the trip to London. And I think there is as much peril in that voyage now as there is in returning you to your home. Aye, Missy, I shall get you back to Brentwood Manor," he agreed.

"Thank you, Mr. Gates," she said as her eyes filled with tears.

*

Emily's listlessness continued, but she knew she must check on Martha. She finally roused herself enough to go to the woman's cabin. What she found jarred her out of her state.

Martha lay on her bed with her eyes closed. Her face was as pale as the muslin pillow cover; her cheeks were sunken to a deathly hollowness. She opened her eyes when Emily entered.

"Rebecca, is that you? I asked you to bring in the flowers for the table. You know our guests will be here shortly. Hurry, girl, and get them now," she said, her glazed eyes on Emily.

"Martha, it is I, Emily," she said softly, frightened for the woman.

"Emily, how well you are looking," Martha said brightly. "Hurry, child, you must dress for the ball. All the finest young men will be there falling over one another to meet you."

Emily stared at the woman; she did not know what to say.

"I hope you wear that blue gown, it matches your eyes perfectly. You will be the belle of the ball, enchanting all the young men. But I wonder if you see how Jonathon looks at you—"

Emily's stomach lurched at the sound of his name.

"Martha, do you know where we are? Can you hear what I am saying?"

Martha's eyes went dark; she frowned as tears welled up in her eyes.

"James? Where is James, Emily? They tried to tell me he was killed, but he was not, was he? Tell me the truth, Emily. James is well, is he not? Why are they lying to me and telling me such awful things?" Martha asked.

"Martha, I am so sorry," Emily said as she sank into the chair beside the bed.

"No! Not you, too!" Martha screamed.

Emily reached for the woman's hand, but Martha struck out at her.

"Do not touch me! How dare you come here and tell me these lies!" the woman shrieked at her.

Emily was shaken. She stood, unable to decide what she should do. Just then Gates entered and went to Martha. He held a glass out to her.

"There, there, Martha. It is all right now," he said soothingly. "Here, drink this, you will feel better."

Martha eyed him suspiciously and looked at the cup. He nodded reassuringly at her. Slowly she reached for the cup and sipped its contents. She looked past him at Emily, her eyes brightened, and she smiled.

"There you are, Emily. See if you can find Rebecca, dear. She is supposed to bring in flowers for the table. Where can that girl be?" She lay back against the pillow. "You really must hurry and dress, my dear. The ball will be one of the best, I think, and that blue dress looks so lovely on you . . . ." Her voice trailed off as her eyes slowly closed.

Emily looked at Gates in fear.

"What is it? What has happened to her?" she asked.

"She never really recovered from the shock of the fire. I am afraid the shock of losing James was just too much for her. I do not know if she will ever recover," he replied sadly.

"Oh, my God," Emily whispered. She sank into a chair and gazed at the woman. How changed Martha was from the lively, jovial woman who had welcomed her so warmly.

"What can I do for her?" Emily asked numbly.

Gates was relieved. Emily would get through this horrible time. She was compassionate and courageous, even in her mourning, able to care for another.

"You are a strong woman, Mrs. Brentwood," he said softly.

Emily looked up at him in confusion.

"I do not feel strong, Mr. Gates. I feel tired," she said quietly. "And alone."

*

Emily spent the next days tending Martha. The woman would not eat anything despite Emily's urging. Just to encourage her, Emily would bring in a hearty tray and eat in front of her. It was only this ruse that made Emily eat anything herself. So her strength grew as she watched Martha's wane.

They finally reached Yorktown, but Gates did not pull into the port. He anchored a short distance out and sent several of his men to town on an errand.

"We shall stay here for a few days, Mrs. Brentwood," he explained, "until I know the situation on shore."

Emily would have thought he was being overcautious if she had not witnessed the scene at Norfolk. She was grateful for his caution . . . and for his presence.

The men returned the next day and had added one to their company. Emily gasped in surprise as she saw Randy in the returning boat. He climbed on deck and hurried to her; his eyes filled with sorrow.

"Emily," he said as he took her in his arms. "Emily, I am so sorry for you."

"And I for you, Randy," she answered. "I know you were lifelong friends."

They held each other and cried, drawing strength from each other and their love of Jonathon.

Finally Emily pulled back and looked up at him, puzzled.

"Randy, why are you here?"

"I was at the Swan Tavern when some of Jonathon's crew came in. They sought me out and told me what had happened. I also heard that Jonathon had some trouble at the harbor before he left. I have men on shore waiting if you need some help."

"Thank you, Randy. You are most kind," Emily said sincerely.

Gates approached them and greeted Randy. Reassured about the safety of putting into port, Gates ordered the *Destiny* to enter Yorktown. The two men went to supervise the unloading of the ship, and Emily returned to Martha. The woman was too weak to go above deck alone, so Emily assisted her.

"We are in Yorktown, Martha," Emily explained. "You are to come to Brentwood Manor with me."

"For the wedding, dear? I knew it would be so; I saw how Jonathon looked at you. I said to James—" She stopped and her face clouded. "James?" she said tearfully.

"Martha, you are to come to Brentwood Manor with me. I will need your help when it is time for the baby to be born."

Feebly, Martha walked to the deck with the girl.

Randy's friends awaited them at the pier and assisted the crew in unloading the ship. The women were made comfortable in a carriage, prepared to set off as soon as the necessary things were unloaded for their trip to Brentwood Manor.

Gates came over to Emily and took her hand.

"Good-bye, missy. You take care of yourself and your child," he said.

Tears burned in Emily's eyes; again she said good-bye to a dear friend.

"Mr. Gates, thank you for returning us safely. What will you do now?"

"I would like to continue sailing for the committees. It is your ship now, however, Mrs. Brentwood. You can order me to halt."

Emily was startled at the impact of this decision. To allow Gates to continue to sail was to work against the king. To make him stop would be to make Jonathon's death and everything he lived for worthless. She stared out at the sea.

"It is Jonathon's ship still, Mr. Gates. I believe he would want you to continue," she said quietly.

"Aye, Mrs. Brentwood," he replied respectfully.

*

Emily still felt as if she moved in a dream. Caring for Martha gave her something to think about, but the familiar sights brought back unbearable memories. They traveled straight to Brentwood Manor because unrest was building in the town. Night had fallen by the time they arrived. There were no lights on since they were not expected, so Randy went to the door.

David finally answered in his robe.

"Randy? What the—" he began.

"David, you had best come here," Randy answered. He led the man to the carriage.

"David, what is it?" Joanna called from the doorway. She followed the men.

David reached the carriage and looked in.

"Emily? Where is Jona—" he stopped as he realized the answer. He turned to Joanna. She reached him and looked up at his face, and then she looked in the carriage.

"Emily? Oh my God . . . Jonathon?"

"Joanna," Emily said through her tears.

Randy reached in and helped the girl out. The full impact of the situation hit, and Joanna began to sob. David went to his wife and helped her into the house. Randy turned to Emily.

"We must get Martha inside," he said. "Can you make it in all right?"

Emily nodded dumbly. Randy lifted Martha out of the carriage, and they hurried inside.

The sight of the house was more than Emily could bear. She walked into the hall and collapsed on the floor. David and Joanna ran to her, and David carried her into the drawing room. Joanna wrapped her in her arms, and the two women sobbed together.

"How? When?" Joanna asked.

"In Norfolk. He almost made it back to the ship. The British burned the town. Some British sailors followed Jonathon and James as they were returning to the *Destiny*, and the sailors overtook them. They killed them all. Oh, it was horrifying," Emily cried and buried her face in her hands. The retelling made her memory of the scene more vivid, and the pain was agonizing.

Randy held her as she gave way to more tears. She felt drained and spent. How many more tears could she cry?

David sat beside Joanna and held her through her sorrow.

"Why does everyone keep saying James is gone?" Martha asked in a singsong voice. "James will be back soon. He had to get some documents. James will be back soon."

Joanna and David looked at Emily.

"I think it would be good for Martha to rest," Emily said.

David grasped the bell pull, and in a moment Dulcie appeared.

"What a time a' night to be gettin' me up Master David," she scolded as she entered the room. "Why, Miss Emily . . . what happened? Why are you here? Where's Master Jonathon?" She stopped and took in the scene. She looked at Joanna.

"Dulcie, Jonathon's—"

"Don't say it, Miss Joanna. It's written on all your faces. Lord have mercy." The woman began to cry.

"Dulcie, Mrs. Cosgrove is in desperate need of some sleep. Could you see that a room is prepared quickly?" David asked gently.

"I jus' cleaned the room at the end of the south hall today, Master David. We can take her right on up." Dulcie wiped the tears flowing down her cheeks and started for the stairs. "My, my, my. Poor Master Jonathon. Lord have mercy."

Randy lifted Martha gently. "I shall take you to your room, Martha. Then you can rest."

"We must rest before the ball," she said merrily. "It will be a late night tonight." Her voice trailed off as Randy carried her out of the room.

Joanna turned to Emily. "Will she recover? She looks terribly thin."

"I have not been able to get her to eat a thing since it happened. She has little strength left; I am so worried about her," Emily replied.

"And I am worried about you, Emily," Joanna responded. "Have you been eating and getting some rest? Is the baby all right?"

"Yes, the baby is healthy, Joanna. But I had to come back here. I could not sail to London. Jonathon's child will be born in his home."

"I understand," Joanna replied reaching out and taking her hand.

Randy returned to the drawing room, and they talked quietly into the night. Silence overcame the group as each dealt with his or her own sorrow. A room was readied for Randy, and they all retired.

Emily entered her bedroom with apprehension. The room in which she and Jonathon had shared so many intimate moments opened before her. She looked at his dresser covered with his personal belongings. She touched each item while silent tears ran down her face and spilled on his brushes. She took a shirt from his drawer and buried her face in it. He had put it on the day they left for Williamsburg and then decided on a different one. It still held his scent. Slowly she walked over to their bed and lay down on the side Jonathon always slept on. She laid his shirt beneath her face, wrapped her arms around his pillow, and cried bitterly before falling into an exhausted sleep.

*

In January of 1776 Dunmore issued a document that encouraged slaves to flee the plantations and join the British cause. Many did so in the hope of finding freedom, but what they found were horrible conditions and, for many, death. With the loss of slaves, many plantations that were already suffering because of British trade policy were now ruined.

At Brentwood Manor the exodus was not felt as heavily because of the fair treatment slaves had received. This was a relief because David was required to be away from the manor for long stretches of time, partly due to trading in Williamsburg and partly due to the patriot cause. He could trust the running of the plantation to several loyal slaves. Joanna was glad of Emily's company even though it was a time of mourning.

Much of their time was spent ministering to Martha, who seemed to slip more deeply into the fantasy world that protected her from pain. Less and less often did she recognize her surroundings, and she became thinner and frailer each day.

Joanna finally sent for Dr. Anderson. He arrived in the afternoon and joined the women for tea. After offering his condolences, he listened as they explained Martha's condition. Finally, he went upstairs, examined the woman and spoke with her for some time. He returned to the drawing room where Joanna and Emily awaited him.

"I am sorry, ladies. I do not think there is anything I can do. The shock seems to have carried her beyond the brink," he said.

Emily's heart sank. "If we can get her to eat more, will that help?"

"Mrs. Cosgrove's problem is not her lack of food. It is possible that if she improved physically, it may help her mind. But I do not know if there is much hope of that," he answered. Then he looked at Emily. "It would be wise for me to examine you, too, while I am here, Mrs. Brentwood."

Emily looked at Joanna, who smiled gently.

"I must take care of you if you will not take care of yourself," she explained.

Emily complied and followed Dr. Anderson to her room. After examining her thoroughly, a look of concern showed in his eyes.

"You are a bit too thin, Mrs. Brentwood. If you want your baby to be healthy, you must provide him with more nourishment," he warned.

"Yes, doctor," Emily said meekly.

Dr. Anderson left with a promise to return the next week and check on Martha.

*

The days dragged for Emily. She had little motivation to do anything, and, except for tending Martha, nothing interested her. Every day she tried to think up a different scheme to get Martha to eat or drink something. Today, out of ideas, she went to the woman's room to bring her some tea. She knocked and entered the room, but since Martha was sleeping peacefully, she turned to leave. But something stopped her, and she walked over to the bed.

Martha lay against the pillow, her pale face fixed in a gentle smile. Emily took her hand; as she suspected, it was cold. She sank to her knees beside the bed and held the woman's hand against her face. Her tears were more for herself and her sorrow at the loss of her friend, for she knew Martha was happier now; she was with her James. Martha's voice echoed in her head: "*Why does everyone say James is gone? He will be back soon.*"

Emily wished she could do the same. Just drift away into the world where her beloved Jonathon waited for her. It would be so easy . . .

She heard Joanna enter and cross to the bed.

"Oh no," she cried, kneeling beside Emily and putting her arm around her. Emily turned to her.

"Martha is where she wants to be. I wish I could do the same. We should not weep for her," Emily said.

Joanna rose and looked down at her in anger. "How dare you say such a thing?" she cried. "Do you not care about the child you carry? Emily, you have much to live for."

"You can stand there and say that to me?" Emily shot back at her. "You, who have your husband beside you at night? You, who have a lifetime to live with the man you love? How can you know my anguish? Or Martha's?"

Joanna looked at Emily, the pain of her words evident on her face. "Am I supposed to apologize because I still have my husband? You have a part of Jonathon within you, yet you refuse to care about the baby, or take proper care of yourself. I cannot bring Jonathon back for you, but you can continue his legacy . . . if you choose to."

"I love this child I carry."

"Then behave so."

The women looked at each other. Emily's eyes brimmed with tears. She felt as if she had lost everyone she loved. Now she had even alienated Joanna.

"I am sorry, Joanna," she whispered. She turned back to the bed and looked down at Martha. No she did not want to follow her. She had a child to live for. *Jonathon's child.*

Emily felt Joanna's arm slip around her shoulders, and she turned to her. The women embraced and cried together, then knelt beside Martha's body and prayed. Finally, they rose, and Joanna rang for Dulcie.

*

Gray clouds hung heavy in the late January sky, and the wind whipped Emily's cape about her legs as she followed Martha's casket out to the church graveyard. The service had been brief, attended only by Randy, Joanna, David, and herself. The prayers had been comforting, and Emily wished that somehow Jonathon might have had some prayers offered over his body.

They entered the carriage, and rode home quietly as each was caught up in their own thoughts. The carriage slowed after a time and David looked out to see what caused the delay. Another carriage pulled up beside theirs, and Emily looked out to see Deidre.

"Emily, I had heard you were back," she said, her eyes held a strange look. "May I stop at the manor?"

"Certainly, Deidre," Joanna answered.

Tea was served when they returned to Brentwood Manor, and Deidre arrived shortly after them. Emily felt uncomfortable about this visit, but was not sure why. Perhaps it was because when anyone called to offer condolences, it evoked the pain so vividly. At least Deidre had the grace to make this call.

"So Jonathon is dead," Deidre blurted out as she entered the parlor. Emily recoiled at her bluntness. Joanna looked at David in concern.

"Deidre, we have just buried a friend. This has been a most trying time for us," David said.

"And do you know why Jonathon is dead?" she went on ignoring the warning tone in David's voice.

"Deidre!" Randy cautioned.

"Because of his blasted Tory wife!"

Emily blanched.

"Deidre, that is enough!" Randy exclaimed as he rose and moved toward her. She sidestepped him, crossing the room, and loomed over Emily who sat on the settee.

"If he had not been so concerned about getting you back to your loathsome, *beloved* England, he would still be alive," she shouted at Emily.

Emily sat frozen, agonized. The pain caused by Deidre's words was intolerable. The room swam in front of her, and her head filled with buzzing. Suddenly she felt flushed, and everything went white. Then black and silent.

Dr. Anderson had been summoned and came out to examine Emily. He announced that Emily and the baby were in no danger, but she needed rest for several days.

When she came to, Emily was lying on her bed; her head throbbed. Joanna was beside her.

"Are you all right, Em?" Joanna asked.

"It is my fault, is it not, Joanna?" Emily asked as tears streamed down her face. "If it were not for me, Jonathon would still be alive."

"*Shhh*, Emily. Do not even think such a thing. What Jonathon was doing required risks; he knew that. Sailing for the committees was dangerous work. He had to go to Norfolk. He would have gone whether he was taking you back to London or not. The patriot cause needed him there. He died for that, not because of you," she answered.

Emily felt reassured, but the pain Deidre's words had caused lingered.

*

She lay in bed with Jonathon's shirt against her face. She found comfort in it, and it helped her sleep. After the first day of being confined to bed, she became restless, and Joanna had to scold her to keep her down. She brought Emily some books from the library, which helped since reading diverted her thoughts from her intolerable grief.

The days passed uneventfully. Randy visited daily to check on Emily, and after a week, he agreed to take her downstairs for tea. It felt good to have a change of scenery, and Emily's spirits lifted. Each day she was allowed to be up a little longer, although Joanna bribed her by increasing the time according to how well she was eating. Emily realized how much weight she had lost when she tried on some of her older gowns. They hung on her in spite of her enlarging abdomen. She began to fear that Joanna was right; she had been neglecting her baby. She complied with Joanna's wishes and began to take better care of herself.

*

Life at the manor had changed since Emily had left with Jonathon the previous year. Some slaves did flee to the British side, leaving David shorthanded. Some rooms in the manor had been closed up in order to conserve fuel during the colder months. Food supplies were dwindling as Brentwood Manor began to feel the squeeze of Parliament's decrees. Life was not as luxurious as it had been, and everyone had a new appreciation of what food and supplies they did have. Some families were not so lucky.

Because of British trading policies, colonial planters were spending up to 75 percent of their profit on trade expenses over which they had no control. It was bad enough that freight commissions to British merchants, export taxes, and custom duties in Britain had to be paid, but the real blow was that the colonists could not ship directly to the European Continent. Most of their goods were re-exported from Britain.

The Brentwoods had been able to bypass some of those costs since Jonathon sailed his own ship and had established trade at a time when relations were better. Solid friendships and smooth talk had rendered a bigger profit for him. But now Brentwood tobacco, along with that of other colonial planters, was rotting on the wharf. British creditors eagerly lent money to Virginia planters, and by 1775 the colonists owed over 2 million pounds sterling to them. It would take some colonists several generations to repay the loans.

Fortunately, Brentwood Manor had not yet found it necessary to borrow, but the change in lifestyle was obvious. Emily was beginning to understand, not just the economic hardship that necessitated living more frugally, but also the frustrating, even enraging, predicament of being held down, dependent and powerless under the thumb of a far distant and indifferent power.

David had left on a trip to Yorktown to pick up supplies and sell goods, hoping to find a ship that would carry his tobacco to London. This was becoming impossible since Dunmore was impounding colonial ships off Virginia's coast. If he was successful, David planned to return in a week.

Will was keeping Joanna and Emily entertained as he became more mobile. He was their delight, and Emily anticipated the birth of her own child as she watched him. She wondered if her baby was a boy or girl. Would the baby look like Jonathon? She hoped so, and she placed her hands on her abdomen as if willing it to be so. Oh, how she missed him; how glad she was to have a part of him with her now.

The women were uneasy with David gone. The tense atmosphere of the cities and towns was seeping into the countryside, and hostility was building. Fear possessed the minds of each of the women. Fear for David, fear for themselves, fear for the future. What kind of world would their children grow up in? Would there be anything left for their offspring?

Sorrow also occupied their minds. Emily was just beginning to be able to sit for a while without breaking into tears over her loss of Jonathon. The worst times were at night when she climbed into their large, lonely bed and ached for his arms around her. She hugged his pillow close, laying her face against his shirt, and released her anguished tears into it until her head and sides ached. She moaned her agony to God, feeling wretched and desolate. She begged for freedom from this pain that exploded in her head and in her heart.

Mornings were unbearable, too, when she drifted on the edge of waking. For then she could feel Jonathon beside her, warm and strong. But as she snuggled closer, awareness grabbed her and roughly pulled her to consciousness. And emptiness. She cursed sleep for the wicked tricks it played on her, and she began her days as she ended them—weeping until she lay exhausted.

In the evenings as she and Joanna sat together, she tried to push these things from her mind, unwilling to allow her sister-in-law to witness her tears. The tenderness others showed at her sorrow only made it worse. And in a strange way she hoarded those tears, for they were her intimacy with Jonathon now, an exchange as private as their lovemaking had been.

So she filled her mind with thoughts of the child she carried. She sat embroidering clothing for him as she and Joanna watched Will's antics. Suddenly, she felt a strange sensation, and she stopped. She sat very still; she felt it again. A fluttering, a tiny sensation that whispered of a presence known of but, until now, imperceptible. Emily sat and waited, eyes focused on nothing, all her senses focused within. Joanna noticed her stillness.

"Emily, what is it?"

Emily looked at her, her eyes shining.

"Joanna, I felt my baby move! He is real. Our child is real."

Joanna knew the miracle of this moment. She rose and went to Emily and embraced her.

"Of course he is real," she laughed. "But I understand what you mean."

"Joanna—" she began. Her sentence was interrupted by a distant, faint sound. They both looked toward the window, hoping to recognize the sound of David's horse. But he was not due home until the end of the week at the earliest. Hope turned into dread as the sound grew into the pounding, terrifying rhythm of many horses.

The women looked at each other in alarm as Joanna sprang to the bell rope, summoning Dulcie, while Emily crossed to Jonathon's study. She found the key to the gun cabinet in the top desk drawer and quickly unlocked the cabinet. She loaded a pistol and rejoined Joanna in the main hall as the pounding roar halted outside the front door. They heard a clear voice call out commands, and then the heavy brass knocker echoed in the hallway. Dulcie hurried by with William and disappeared into the back of the house.

Emily's legs trembled so that she could barely walk to the door. She fumbled with the latch and handed Joanna her pistol. Smoothing her hair, she opened the door and gasped at the sight of a troop of British soldiers covering the drive. The officer in charge saluted smartly, catching Emily by surprise, causing her to blink and step back.

"Good evening. Do I address Mrs. Jonathon Brentwood?" The words snapped out of his mouth briskly, mirroring his salute.

"Yes, sir. May I be of some help?" Emily's curiosity was piqued enough to somewhat diminish her fear.

"I have a warrant for the arrest of your husband, Captain Jonathon Brentwood, on charges of treason, conspiracy and assault on an officer of the king."

Emily recoiled at his words as her mind struggled to make sense of them. Frowning at the officer, incomprehension clouded her face. The image of Jonathon's body being hauled into the British skiff assaulted her with fresh anguish, and confusion battled anger at the cruelty of his words.

"How dare you come here and mock my sorrow," she seethed.

The officer exchanged a meaningful look with his men. Turning back to Emily, he repeated his statement more insistently.

"I have a warrant for the arrest of your husband, Captain Jonathon Brentwood, on charges of treason, conspiracy and assault on an officer of the king."

The ramification of his words began to dawn on her, and her mind began to race at their meaning. If what he said was true then . . . Jonathon was alive! How could that be? She saw him murdered and carried off. She stared at the officer, his words ringing in her ears. The shock was too much, and she saw only grayness surround him as she felt herself beginning to black out. *No! You must be strong,"* she told herself. *"You must hang on."*

"Mrs. Brentwood? Mrs. Brentwood!" His voice echoed at her from far away, but she pulled up all her strength, invigorated by the cold night air and the one thought that exploded in her mind: *Jonathon must be alive!*

"Forgive me, officer, could you explain your meaning?" Emily finally asked. She needed more information; she must divert them from wherever Jonathon was hiding. But where could he be?

"Please do not try to stall us, Mrs. Brentwood. We have come to arrest Captain Brentwood, and any interference on your part is also punishable by law."

"Is this a pitiless joke, officer? I saw my husband shot and killed with my own eyes. I saw the British soldiers recover his body from the sea. You are too cruel!" Emily exclaimed.

The officer gazed at Emily gauging her sincerity. Coming to a decision, he spoke harshly.

"Mrs. Brentwood, I see through your attempt at deception. Captain Brentwood escaped the prison weeks ago. We believe, of course, that he took refuge here. We will not leave until we find him, arrest him, and return him to Norfolk for hanging."

She knew Joanna heard the news, for she felt the woman's hand tighten on hers as it held the door open. She squeezed it in conspiratorial celebration while both women maintained a composed exterior. She silently motioned for the pistol and hid it in her skirts.

"Mrs. Brentwood, please ask your husband to come out. It will be easier on everyone," the officer said firmly.

"My husband is not here," Emily answered. Her voice seemed to come down to her through a long tunnel. She knew she spoke the words, but faintness overtook her, and she balanced on the edge of consciousness.

"Mrs. Brentwood," the officer's voice rang out harshly, "I am afraid we shall have to search the house."

"You have no right—" Emily protested.

The officer motioned to his men, and the soldiers began to dismount. In one swift move Emily swung her pistol up and fired just above their heads, the blast piercing the wintry night. The horses shied at the noise, and the soldiers ducked and dismounted in disarray. Leaping off of his horse and rushing toward Emily, the officer grabbed the pistol. He swung her arm back, pivoting her and thrusting her to the floor. His pistol was out and aimed at her head.

"Now, Mrs. Brentwood, we shall look for your husband," he sneered.

He slowly drew his gun back and replaced it in his belt. Joanna ran to Emily and helped her to her feet. Men brushed past them and began to search through the rooms, overturning furniture and roughly grabbing at drapes and doors. Others searched the outbuildings and the grounds. They rousted slaves from their quarters, shoving them with their rifle butts.

In the house, Joanna and Emily sat together on the settee under the watchful eye of the officer.

"It will not take my men long to find your husband, Mrs. Brentwood. It would have been much easier on him had he simply surrendered. Now my men may have to get . . . forceful." Standing, he made his way across the room and poured brandy from the crystal decanter. His icy stare took in the furnishings, then the women.

"I believe we shall spend the night," he murmured.

Just then Dulcie entered with William. Her eyes were wide with fright and she hurried to Joanna who rose, composed, belying her pounding heart. She took William from the servant and held him close. The officer's eyes had watched the transaction carefully, noting which woman took the child. He would get Brentwood whatever it took.

Two men entered the room and saluted.

"We do not see any sign of him, sir." The taller of the two spoke. "We have searched the house, the grounds . . . everywhere."

The officer slammed his glass down causing the women to

jump. Will began to cry and Joanna tried to hush him. The men talked over the commotion until, enraged, the officer shouted.

"Shut that child up!"

Will cried all the louder. The officer strode across the room toward them. Emily stepped between the man and Joanna.

"Sir, the child is hungry. Let us retire to the next room. Then you and your men can discuss your plans, and the child can be fed." Her blue eyes were steel, boring into his.

The officer looked at her ready to refuse her request, but as if on cue, William burst into a louder cry than before. The officer looked over at the child, then back at Emily.

"Of course," he said coldly. "But do not leave the next room until I send for you."

The women quickly moved into the next room and closed the door. They embraced and began to laugh and cry in the same breath.

"He is alive! Joanna, he is alive!" Emily whispered excitedly.

"Emily, it is a miracle. How can it be so?" Joanna exclaimed softly.

"I do not know, Joanna. I saw him get shot and fall into the sea. I saw British soldiers take him away. Even Mr. Gates gave up hope." Tears glistened in Emily's eyes as she spoke. "Where could he be, I wonder? I hope he is safe."

The women continued to speculate as Joanna nursed William. He settled down and eventually fell fast asleep. Emily could hardly contain herself. She paced the room and poked at the fire constantly. She wanted to flee from here, ride out and search the countryside for her beloved Jonathon.

In a while the officer came into the room. He looked agitated and impatient.

"Mrs. Brentwood, I insist you tell me where your husband is immediately," he said harshly.

"I do not know where he is," she answered honestly.

"We know he is not on his ship. He must have returned here. It will be much easier on all concerned if you simply tell us where to find him," the man said threateningly.

"Sir," Emily said firmly. "I do not know where he is. I saw him last in Norfolk. He has not returned to Brentwood Manor."

"Then we will wait here for him," he answered.

The women exchanged glances, both appalled at the thought of having these men trample all over Brentwood Manor. If Jonathon did return, it would mean certain death for him.

"Surely you have more important things to attend than this," Emily said.

"More important than capturing a traitor to the king?" he replied haughtily.

The words rang in Emily's head. Was it not she who had flung that accusation at Jonathon just a few months ago? Now his life hinged on that accusation. And somehow those words did not make sense to her anymore.

"Sir, we do not have enough food and provisions to house you and your men," Joanna spoke up. "We barely have enough to feed ourselves these days."

Emily almost blurted out that it was thanks to parliament's stranglehold. My God, she thought, I am becoming a damn patriot. She smiled inwardly.

"Your slaves look well-tended. I am sure they will last a while if they are not given as many table scraps," he shot back at her.

Emily's heart pounded with rage. The impertinent fool! Who did he think he was?

"After all," he continued, "you are doing this for the king's troops, and Mrs. Brentwood's sympathies toward us are well known in the area."

Emily felt flushed with shame. He walked over to her and ran his finger along her jaw.

"In fact, Mrs. Brentwood, I was expecting a much warmer

welcome than this." His voice was soft and menacing.

Emily drew back, fighting off the urge to slap his face.

"It is late, sir. We would like to retire," she said as she walked toward Joanna and William. "You may stay the night; tomorrow you must leave. I assume you are prepared to sleep out of doors." She stared at him coldly.

"You are delightful. No wonder Brentwood was captivated by you," the officer laughed. "You give me orders while my troop of armed men waits outside for my orders." His faced changed instantly, a frown replacing the sly smile. "But you forget who is in charge here. We will leave when I give the order to do so and not before. It would be in your best interest, Mrs. Brentwood, to remember who it is that gives the orders."

Emily was furious, but she was also aware of the reality of the situation. To give in to her temper could endanger her life as well as that of her child, Joanna, and Will. And Jonathon. She hated this helpless feeling; she hated being ordered around by this officer who demanded his way without regard to the needs or wants of others.

Much as parliament had been doing to the colonies.

Chapter 12

The icy wind whipped around the buildings and through the trees, moaning beneath a pale, white moon. A lone figure crouched beside the south wing of the Wren Building. Inside, the last hymn faded into the night as students and faculty of the College of William and Mary began to depart the evening service. Men buttoned their coats and secured their hats as they left the chapel; voices called farewells and groups parted, heading home to warm hearths and hearty suppers.

The figure crouched animal-like, ready to spring on its prey, while at the same time, remaining concealed. His ears strained to hear the voice or name of one student in particular.

"Andrew, you bear! I thought you were going to miss service tonight," a youthful voice bellowed.

"*Shhh.* Do you want to get me in trouble?" Andrew responded good-naturedly. The two companions hurried merrily toward the boarding house where they roomed.

The silent figure moved forward and peered into the dark; seeing no one else about, he moved ahead, then stopped, hunched noiselessly against a tree, and listened. Satisfied that all had departed, he followed the two young men, moving silently in the shadows.

"Andrew, it is good to hear you laugh again. I know what a terrible ordeal your family has been through. I am sorry about your brother-in-law," the youth said earnestly.

Andrew swallowed hard several times to rid his throat of the too familiar, painful tightness. His only respite had been moments of forgetting, conscious battles to think of other things, to go on.

"Thanks, Peter," he croaked.

They had arrived at their boarding house, the glow of warmth and firelight hastening their steps to the door. On opening it, the welcome aroma of beef pie and fresh biscuits spurred them on even more quickly. The door closed behind them shutting out the noise and warmth inside, leaving the cold quiet of the night to the stranger in the shadows. He waited until the brick house was blanketed in silence, its windows dark. Then the figure stamped his feet to circulate the blood and shock them from the cold. The icy wind had died down to a constant whisper of cold breath from the north that bit through the woolen layers that protected the silent watcher. From his post he was fairly certain which room belonged to Andrew Wentworth, and he was confident of getting to it without any difficulty.

*

He crept stealthily across the deserted road and slipped into the shadows of the house. Finding the back door, he examined the latch and easily dismantled it. Then, with a furtive glance about, he quietly swung the door inward and crept into the back hall of the boarding house. To his right embers burned on the kitchen hearth; to his left a door was closed on the plump woman who ran the establishment. Her gentle snoring floated through the door and urged him forward.

Gradually his eyes adjusted to the dark enabling him to make out the forms of the furnishings. He skulked to the front hall and the stairs that led up to the boarders' rooms.

One shape had not been evident, since it was so close to the ground. The intruder took a step and instinctively pulled away as the high-pitched screech of an affronted cat broke the stillness. Caught off balance, the stranger reeled to his right and tipped a slender stand, sending a plant crashing to the floor.

The snoring ceased and was replaced by the sound of rustling and scuffling. Noting a half-sized closet door beneath the stairs, the figure dashed to it, concealing himself just as the landlady emerged. Nightcap askew, she held a candle in one hand, a pistol in the other.

She crept forward cautiously and, seeing the plant, exclaimed, "Elmer, you have attacked my fern again! What shall I do with you, you naughty tiger?"

Scolding the cat, she picked it up, nestled it in her pistol-toting arm and took it to her room.

"We shall clean this mess up first thing in the morning," she yawned as she closed the door behind her.

Slowly, the half-door opened and the silent figure emerged. Closing the door, he sidestepped the broken pottery, tested the first step, and then with catlike precision mounted cautiously, noiselessly. He looked at the position of the doors and calculated their placement from his view outside. Nodding in silent assent, he crossed the hall to the door on his far right. His gloved hand turned the brass doorknob, and he inched the door in. Stepping inside, he closed the door behind himself. Across the room, lying curled on the bed, lay Andrew, sound asleep.

The figure crossed to the boy and reached toward his head, then pulled his hand away. He crouched beside the boy, studying his face. With instinctive awareness, Andrew slowly awakened. He jumped at the sight of the figure beside his bed, paralyzed with fear for he could only make out a shadowy form. The figure clamped a hand over Andrew's mouth, preventing any sound from escaping.

Had anyone been in the room below, he would have heard the muffled sound of a body slump to the floor.

*

The presence of the British soldiers was unnerving for the women, so Emily and Joanna decided to share a room. Will was sound asleep when they retired, but Joanna slept fitfully and Emily was unable to sleep at all. One thought possessed her throughout the night: *Jonathon was alive!*

At dawn Emily rose and went to the window. The soldiers had camped on the beautiful lawns of the manor. The horses had dug up the grass and made a mess of the flowerbeds. Emily sighed and let the curtain drop. She stretched and looked at Will in envy. He slept peacefully unaware of the threat lurking just outside.

Emily went down to breakfast, not feeling hungry, but knowing she must eat for the child she carried. She had felt its determined movements again, making its presence known. That and the hope of Jonathon being alive filled her with a swelling feeling of joy. But the ominous presence of the British tempered her elation.

Dulcie was laying out the ham and bread when Emily entered.

"It's no good, Miss Emily. No good at all. Them soldiers all over the place, eatin' all our food," she shook her head in dismay.

"They will be gone soon, Dulcie," Emily said, not believing it herself. She looked up feeling the woman's eyes on her. "What is it, Dulcie?"

"They sayin' that Master Jonathon is alive," Dulcie replied gently.

"Yes, I know."

"How can that be, Miss Emily, when you saw him die yourself?" she asked in a whisper.

"I saw him shot. I saw him fall into the sea. I saw the British pull him into their skiff. I do not know; he must have still been alive," she answered, her heart soaring at the thought, but remaining calm in appearance.

The officer entered and greeted them.

"Good morning, Mrs. Brentwood. I trust you slept well?"

"When do you leave, sir?" she asked, ignoring his question.

"We leave when I give the order," he stated flatly.

Emily glowered at him.

"I realized this morning that I have not introduced myself. I am Captain Arthur Walters," he bowed before sitting at the head of the table.

"Captain," Emily said disinterestedly.

"Come, Mrs. Brentwood, the hospitality of the Brentwoods is

known far and wide. Surely you can do better than that."

"Your presence is an intrusion, Captain. You are not invited guests, and your continued stay is most unwelcome. Surely you can see why my welcome is less than warm."

Rising, he walked over to her chair and stood behind it. Emily froze as she felt his presence so near. He placed his hand on the back of her chair, his fingers just touching her shoulders.

"Perhaps if your welcome were warmer it would be easier on Captain Brentwood when we catch him," he said in a smooth voice.

Emily felt sick; she shivered.

"Well, I see my words have some effect on you. You may seem cold on the exterior, but I imagine there is a passion that burns within you," he said as he leaned nearer to her ear.

"That is something you can imagine for the rest of your life, if you so choose, Captain. But it is not something you will ever know for certain," Emily said coldly.

"Do not be so sure, . . . " he began, but pulled away and returned to his chair as approaching footsteps sounded in the hall.

Joanna entered and noted the look of repulsion that was in Emily's eyes. She looked from her to the officer and silently understood. The man bowed to them and left.

"Joanna, do not leave me alone with that horrible man!" Emily cried.

"What did he do to you?" Joanna asked.

"Oh, he said vile things. He tried to seduce me in exchange for leniency for Jonathon. Oh, he is repugnant!"

Joanna put her arm around Emily's shoulder, and Emily shuddered, recounting the exchange. The women ate breakfast quickly and sat together in the parlor. They contemplated ways to get rid of the soldiers, even knowing they were powerless to do so.

"When is David due back?" Emily asked. "Do you think he will be able to do anything?"

"He would be one man against all of them. Perhaps he will see them in time to go back for reinforcements. Oh, Emily, when will this end?"

*

For Emily and Joanna, the next few days were filled with tension and fear. The soldiers had obviously set up a camp for a long stay, and the grounds were being ruined. Food supplies were dwindling fast, and the women wondered how they would feed everyone on what little remained.

Emily went to the smokehouse to check on supplies. The day was unusually mild, and it felt invigorating to be out in the sun even for this short walk. The promise of spring floated in the fresh scent of the air.

When she entered the smokehouse, no one was there, so she began to take stock of the supplies herself. A sense of being observed overcame her, and she hurried through the remainder of her task. She had an unusual urge to run, to get out in the sun and be where other people were. Then she heard a twig crack outside as if it had been stepped on, and she abandoned her counting and went to the door. As she reached for the handle, the door swung open. Standing before her was Captain Walters. Emily gasped and stepped back.

"So, I see you are ensuring our comfort," he said. "Making sure we are well fed and comfortable? The perfect hostess. However, Mrs. Brentwood, one of your guests has a particular request and only you can be of assistance."

As he spoke, he stepped inside and closed the door behind him. Emily backed up to keep her distance from him. He approached her slowly.

"I think you should cooperate, Mrs. Brentwood. It might save your husband's neck from the gallows. Just think—you might save him from swinging in the wind. Have you ever seen a hanging? It is not pleasant, but most interesting the way the body jerks when it drops, the snapping sound of the neck breaking . . . But, no more of this kind of talk; our conversation should put us more in the mood to become better acquainted."

He stood before her, his breath brushing her hair as he spoke. His eyes roamed up and down her body making her feel undressed.

"I have no wish to become any better acquainted with you, Captain. The only thing I wish to see is your back as you leave my home," Emily snapped, trying to still her trembling.

"You shall see more than that before this day is through," he whispered.

He pulled her to him and bent his mouth to hers. Emily turned away, and he grabbed the back of her head, pulling her by the hair until she faced him.

"You can be kinder to your guests than that, Mrs. Brentwood," he seethed.

"I hate you!" she screamed at him.

"I knew there was fire in you," he laughed.

He pulled her close and forced his mouth down on hers.

She tried to turn away, but his grip on her hair tightened until she thought he would pull it out. She struggled to get away from him but he tightened his arm around her. Finally, he pulled away and let her go so suddenly that she stumbled backward almost losing her balance. Steadying herself at a table behind her, she reached back and her hand touched the wooden handle of a tool. Her fingers clasped it instinctively, though she could not identify what it was.

He moved toward her.

"So, you like rough play?" he sneered. "I can play rough games."

He drew his hand back and slapped her across the face. She cried out at the sting of the blow, her cheek ablaze where he struck her. Anger flared in his eyes, and Emily's heart pounded.

He reached back again, and she steadied herself for the next blow. But he stopped.

"This is no good," he said hoarsely. "I must try something else."

His hands reached for the clasp on her cape. Deftly he unfastened it and let the wrap drop to the dirt floor. He ran a finger from her jaw, down along her neck to the top of the swell of her breasts. He traced the swell and stopped. Emily's breath was shallow, but she tried to hold her breath so her bosom would not move against his finger.

"That is more suitable, Mrs. Brentwood. Calm yourself and allow your guest his pleasure," he taunted.

"I will allow you nothing!" she spat.

He placed his finger in the top of her bodice.

"Then I will simply take what you will not give," he threatened.

With one movement he ripped the top of her dress roughly grabbing her breast. Emily grabbed the tool in her hand, brought it around and swung it at his head. He was taken by surprise and moved into it. She struck him with the meat cleaver on his shoulder near the base of his neck. The leather strap of his uniform impeded some of the impact, but the blow was still severe. Stunned, he fell to the floor. She turned the cleaver to the blunt side and hit him soundly on the head.

Blood oozed from his shoulder, and he tried to rise. He teetered dizzily, and then fell to the dirt floor, unconscious. Emily flew to the door and stepped out. She fastened the latch from the outside and raced to the house clutching the bodice of her dress to her, her knees so weak they could barely support her. She stumbled and fell once, covering her dress with dirt. She rose and wiped the tears from her eyes so she could see where she was going, streaking more dirt across her face. When she reached the house, she called frantically for Joanna.

Dulcie saw her first and exclaimed in shock.

"Miss Emily, what on earth happened?"

Emily collapsed into a chair by the hearth. She felt faint from running and tried to catch her breath. Her chest heaved and the torn material dropped. Dulcie sucked in her breath, her eyes filled with horror.

"Who did this to you?" she demanded.

"Dulcie," Emily gasped, "get Joanna quickly!"

Dulcie hurried toward the front of the house calling Joanna's name. Soon the two women rushed back into the room. Emily had recovered enough to realize the impact of what she had done. Her body trembled as a result of the encounter with the captain, and in fear of its ramifications.

Joanna ran to her and held her quivering form.

"Was it Captain Walters?" she asked, already knowing the answer.

Emily nodded dumbly. Dulcie brought a basin of warm water and began to wash the dirt from the girl's face. The girl winced when Dulcie brushed the spot where she had been struck. Dulcie gasped in horror when she saw the bright red bruise under the smeared dirt.

"What did he do to you?" she exclaimed. Joanna saw the mark too, through tears of outrage.

"We must do something about him. Joanna. Send for Dr. Anderson quickly," she demanded.

Joanna nodded to Dulcie and the woman hurried off. Joanna took over cleaning Emily's face and gently dabbed the tender area.

"We must check on him," Joanna said.

Emily nodded and the two went back to the smokehouse. They peered into the window and saw the officer lying on the floor.

"Is he breathing?" Emily asked.

"I cannot tell from here," Joanna answered. "Emily, we must go in and tend him. If he dies, they will hang you."

Emily looked at her with eyes wide with fear. "All right," she assented.

They unlatched the door and entered the room. Emily picked up the cleaver that lay where she had dropped it. Joanna bent down over the captain and felt his pulse; it was weak. Noting that he was still alive, she breathed a sigh of relief. Quickly she unbuttoned his coat and ripped open his shirt, tearing it into strips and pressing them against the gaping wound.

"He has lost a great deal of blood," she observed. Emily could barely look at him.

"We have to move him inside, Emily; we have to get some of his men to move him."

"They will punish me for this! Joanna, I am so frightened," Emily cried.

"If we can save his life, it will be better. Emily, he attacked you. That is plain to see. Even they have a code of conduct to uphold." She looked sympathetically at Emily. "We must go to them with you in this condition."

Emily began to protest, holding the material closer to her bosom.

"Emily, they must see what he has done to you . . . and what he intended to do."

Dulcie found them and informed them that someone had gone for the doctor.

"Them soldiers want to know who is sick. I told them Miss Emily was feelin' ill. They're on their way to the house, Miss Joanna. What should I do?"

Joanna thought a moment. She looked at Emily for a time. Finally, Emily nodded.

"Bring them here, Dulcie," Joanna said firmly.

"Miss Joanna, you think that's a good idea?" she protested.

Emily nodded. Dulcie shrugged her shoulders and left. Soon she returned followed by two soldiers. They entered the smokehouse and took in the scene. One of them dropped to his knees beside the captain and began to tend his wounds. The other looked at Emily and then back at the wounded man. It was clear what had happened.

They carried the captain to the house and up to one of the bedrooms. Dulcie brought water and clean linens, and the one who tended him in the smokehouse gave her instructions on preparing some items he needed. She hurried off, and he rolled up his sleeves and turned back to his captain.

The captain's breath was shallow, his face ashen. Emily and Joanna stood aside watching the soldier's ministrations. He worked quickly, cleaned the wound and bound it. When Dulcie returned with the items he had requested, he made a thick poultice, applied it to the wound, and then bound it again. When he was finished, he turned to the women.

"I do not know if he will live or not. There is another regiment nearby. We have sent for the officer in charge there. He will have to make the decision about what charges will be brought," he explained.

"Charges?" Joanna asked.

"If he dies, ma'am."

"He attacked her!" Joanna cried out, enraged.

"He is an officer of the king, ma'am. She is the wife of a traitor."

Joanna looked at Emily whose eyes were filled with fear. The other soldier who had come upon the scene stepped into the room.

"Tim, here, will stay with you ladies at all times until the other officer arrives," he said.

Tim opened the door for the women to exit the room. They went to Emily's room where Dulcie had fresh water and linens laid out for her. As Emily washed and changed into a fresh gown, Joanna stayed with her and they spoke in low tones, knowing that Tim stood just outside the door.

"Joanna, I am frightened," Emily cried softly.

"It will be all right. Everything will be all right. That soldier seems to know what he is doing, and Dr. Anderson will be here soon. Captain Walters will live, Emily." Joanna comforted her.

They were allowed to go downstairs, and Dulcie met them.

"I fixed some dinner for you," she said.

In the dining room, neither could eat. They played with the food on their plates for a time until Dulcie tired of urging them to eat. Finally, they retired to the parlor.

Dr. Anderson arrived in the early evening and examined the captain. He was impressed by the care the soldier had given him and said there was little else he could do. It would be merely waiting now to see if the captain were strong enough to pull through.

Emily tossed and turned throughout the night. When she dreamed, it was nightmares about being confined in a British jail. When she awoke, she was covered with sweat and her heart raced.

She rose with the dawn and paced her room until Joanna awoke. Together they checked on the captain. The same soldier was attending him, and they were relieved to know that he was still alive. He lay back against the pillow, his face pale, and his breath shallow. The soldier informed them that he had been much the same throughout the night.

"The fact that he is still alive this morning is a good sign; however, he still is in danger of death," he explained.

Although afraid to hope, Emily felt more encouraged than she had the previous day, and she whispered silent prayers for the man who had attacked her.

The women ate a light breakfast and took Will out for a brief walk. The bright sunshine was discordant with the mood they were in, but the weather was mild, and both felt a need for fresh air.

"Joanna," Emily said, "even if Captain Walters lives, I shall still face charges of some sort."

"I have thought of that, too, Emily," she answered. "I wish David were here. Perhaps we could whisk you away and hide you somewhere."

"That would only put all of you in danger," Emily replied. "Perhaps if the captain lives he will drop charges in order to save face."

"It seems that there should be some code of conduct that officers must observe," Joanna agreed.

They returned to the house and sat in the parlor. The presence of the soldiers made movement on the grounds uncomfortable, so they spent most of their time inside. They rang for tea, and as Dulcie brought it in, they heard horses approaching.

Emily saw three riders coming up the drive; all were adorned in the scarlet of the British troops. The officer of the other regiment was here to decide what charges she would face. She trembled, and her stomach lurched. She turned to Joanna, who put her arms around her.

They watched the officer and his men approach the camp and dismount to speak to the soldiers. One soldier gestured to the house, speaking animatedly. The officer who seemed to be in charge nodded and spoke with them for a while. Then the three turned and rode toward the house.

Emily looked at Joanna in dread; tears filled her eyes. She brushed them away, straightened her shoulders, and answered the door. Joanna followed, holding her head high in an obvious effort to appear calm. Emily smoothed her skirts, brushed a wisp of hair from her eyes and opened the door. Amazement overtook her as she stared into the eyes of Michael Dennings. He had changed considerably since that day in her London parlor when he had proposed to her. He stood tall and striking in his officer's red uniform. An air of command enveloped him, and his eyes held a maturity that war adds to every man who endures it. He was no longer the naive, innocent Michael she had known.

"Michael?" she whispered.

His eyes conveyed a warning, and he shook his head so slightly that only Emily could perceive his message to her.

"Mrs. Brentwood, I am Captain Michael Dennings, and I am here to speak to you about the incident in which a fellow officer was very seriously injured," he said in a loud, clear voice.

Emily was bewildered. The scene seemed so bizarre. Here was Michael Dennings, her lifelong friend, dressed as a British officer and speaking to her as if she were a stranger. Surely this was all a bad dream. All of it—Jonathon's capture, Captain Walters's attack on her, Michael's coldness—surely, this must be a dream. Panic gripped her, and she began to sway. Joanna was behind her in a moment steadying her balance.

"Emily, I am here," she whispered urgently. "It will be all right; stay calm."

Joanna's voice had a soothing quality that revived her. She took a deep breath and closed her eyes. When she opened them she found Michael's upon her. There was no coldness there, rather a look of concern and anxiety.

"Mrs. Brentwood," he said, "perhaps we can discuss this matter inside."

"Of . . . of course," she stammered.

She stepped back to allow him to enter. He started toward the door and paused when his men followed him.

"You two wait out here," he ordered. The soldiers looked at each other in confusion.

Michael proceeded into the manor, and the door closed behind them.

When they were safely in the drawing room, Michael exploded.

"Emily, what has happened?"

Joanna jumped in surprise. She looked at the young officer in bewilderment, then at Emily.

"Joanna, may I present Michael Dennings, a dear friend of mine from London."

Joanna appeared startled at the name. Perhaps she remembered Emily speaking of him as the boy she nearly married to escape leaving England. He no longer was a boy, but a handsome young man, albeit in the uniform of the British army.

"How do you do, Captain Dennings," she said.

Michael bowed to Joanna then quickly looked back at Emily.

"What has happened here? I have been told that you almost murdered Walters," he said. "Where is he?"

They led him up to the room where Captain Walters lay. The captain looked just as he had that morning. The same soldier still tended him and explained to Michael the treatment he had administered. Michael nodded, then stepped to the bed and felt the captain's pulse. He looked anxiously at Emily.

"This is quite serious," he said quietly. "How did it happen, Mrs. Brentwood?"

Emily was distressed by the coldness in his voice. She explained the confrontation in the smokehouse, and the way she had defended herself. When she finished, he turned to the soldier and asked him to corroborate her story.

"I did not see any of this, sir," he answered. "All I know is that when I arrived, Captain Walters lay unconscious in a pool of blood; Mrs. Brentwood stood over him, and a blood-spattered meat cleaver lay beside him."

"Mrs. Brentwood, did Captain Walters threaten you with a weapon?" Michael asked.

"Why, not exactly . . . " she began. "But he had his pistol in his belt—"

"In his belt, not ready for use?"

"Well, yes . . . that is . . . no," she stammered in confusion. She noticed that Joanna had left the room. Where was she? Emily desperately needed her right now.

"Well, you simply attacked him, then, for no reason?" Michael demanded.

"No reason! He was about to rape me! I was defending myself—"

"That is your word against his, Mrs. Brentwood."

Emily could not believe this nightmare. Was Michael so bitter about her rejection of his proposal that he would see her imprisoned or, worse yet, hanged? She could not believe this of him.

"No, Captain Dennings, here is some evidence," Joanna said from the doorway. She carried in Emily's torn dress and handed it to the officer. His face blanched when he saw the ripped material. He glanced at Emily, anger showing in his eyes. He replaced it quickly with a cold, flinty stare.

"Let us return to the drawing room to discuss this further," Michael suggested.

The soldier who tended Captain Walters gave Emily a smug smile. She brushed past him and followed Joanna and Michael to the stairs. Her mind raced as they descended. She must get Michael to believe her story. If he did not, she would surely be sent to prison.

"Would you care for tea, Captain Dennings?" Joanna asked as they entered the drawing room. She rang for Dulcie at Michael's assent.

Emily stood by the hearth trembling and needing its warmth. Michael walked to the windows to check on his men, and then crossed to the drawing room door and closed it. He strode to Emily and put his hands on her shoulders.

"Em, are you all right?" he asked anxiously.

Emily collapsed into his arms in relief and sobbed.

"Oh, Michael, why did you frighten me so? Why did you treat me so cruelly?" she cried.

"I had to, Em. If this does not look like a fair and objective decision on my part, they will send for someone else to decide your fate. No one must know that you are my friend." He shot a warning look at Joanna.

"You can trust Joanna, Michael," Emily reassured him.

Michael looked down at her tenderly. He gently touched the bruise on her face. Anger filled him again.

"Walters has a reputation for this," he spat. "I would like to go up and finish the job you started."

"Michael, please," Emily said.

Dulcie entered, and Michael quickly stepped away from Emily and sat down. They sat back and relaxed with their tea.

Emily explained again what had happened. Michael listened intently, his eyes blazing.

"We shall have to do this carefully, Em. Above all, do not let on that you know me."

After tea, Michael returned to his men, and Emily and Joanna relaxed a bit. Perhaps Emily would be saved after all.

*

Captain Walters improved the next day and even regained consciousness briefly. Captain Dennings informed his men that they would remain for a time to see if Captain Walters would improve enough to tell his side of the story. The soldier who tended him continued giving Emily smug smiles that communicated his conviction that she would pay for injuring his captain.

Three days later, Walters had improved enough to stay alert for some time and was strong enough to be questioned. Michael dismissed the attending soldier and talked to Walters alone. He was with him for some time, and when he emerged he immediately sought Emily and Joanna in the drawing room. Again he checked the windows and closed the door. He sat beside Emily on the settee and took her hand.

"I have talked to Walters," he said to her. "He was very weak, but very determined to see you punished."

Emily's heart sank.

"Oh, Michael, where will they send me? Michael, I am going to have a child. How can I go to prison if I am going to have a child?" she cried.

Michael's glance inadvertently dropped to her waistline. He looked back up at her and blushed in embarrassment. He would not have noticed on his own, but now it was evident that Emily's trim waistline had filled out.

"You will not go to prison, Em," he promised. "You see Walters and I sampled many a tavern together. One night he outdid himself on ale, and there was an accident with a young prostitute. I was not there when it happened; he told me about it later . . . She did not survive, and her family brought charges against him. Of course, as a British officer he was able to have the charges dismissed, but not without a severe warning. In any event, I reminded him of it today. I doubt that he will charge you with any crime. In fact, I had the distinct impression he would like to leave Brentwood Manor as soon as possible."

Emily threw her arms around Michael.

"You are a dear, dear friend!" she cried. "Oh, Michael, how can I ever thank you?"

"By taking good care of yourself and that babe. Congratulations, Emily," he grinned, and then looked at her soberly. "Mine is one of the groups assigned to find Jonathon, Emily. If you know where he is, tell him to avoid the southeast coast. That is where they are concentrating."

Emily's eyes shone with gratitude; she clasped his hand.

"Actually, Michael, until these troops arrived, we believed Jonathon to be dead. With my own eyes I saw him shot, saw his body fall into the sea, and saw his body dragged into a skiff by the British. I could not believe it when Captain Walters said they were searching for him. When this conflict is over between us, Michael, I hope you will come back and visit as a friend," she said sincerely.

"The conflict is between us, Emily? You side with the patriots?" he asked in surprise.

"I side with whoever is victimized by a stronger, tyrannical power, Michael. This was a source of bitterness between Jonathon and me, but now I understand what the colonies have been fighting for."

*

The next afternoon David arrived with a group of armed men, Randy among them. They rode up the drive and halted at the camp. Michael came out to greet them.

"What are you doing here?" David demanded hotly.

"We are under orders to search for Jonathon Brentwood," Michael replied.

"You and your men pack up and get out as soon as—"

Emily and Joanna had come out of the manor when they saw him arrive. Joanna broke into a run.

"David! David, you are home!" He dismounted as she ran to him. He caught her up in his arms.

"Are you all right, Joanna?" he demanded.

"Yes, darling. Please come inside," she asked.

"No. I intend to get these men out of here—"

"David, please. You do not understand. Please come inside."

"Yes, David. Randy, you too," Emily added.

The two men followed them inside leaving the others to stare down the British.

"Please explain!" David demanded.

"Jonathon is alive!" Emily exclaimed.

"We had heard rumor of that in town. But no one knows where he is. He has disappeared," Randy said.

"Emily was attacked by one of the soldiers," Joanna blurted out. The men froze. "Emily—" Randy crossed over to her, taking her hand.

"I am all right, Randy. But I made him pay. He lies upstairs recovering from his wound."

The men looked at each other in apprehension, the ramifications apparent to them.

"Emily, did he—" David did not know how to finish the sentence.

"No, David."

A look of relief crossed his face, and then concern returned.

At a knock on the door, Dulcie ushered in Michael. David stiffened at his presence, and Randy clenched and unclenched his fists. Michael looked apprehensively at Emily.

"I trust these people with my life, Michael," she said softly.

"Then you had best introduce us before they carry out whatever they are plotting at this moment," he suggested.

"Of, course," she laughed. "Randy, David, this is my dear friend, Michael Dennings."

"Oh, the one you almost—" David stopped at a stern look from Joanna. "Oh . . . well . . . It is a pleasure," he finally managed.

Emily explained to them Michael's protection of her, and they began to relax. She also told them of Michael's warning about the search for Jonathon.

"The Raleigh Tavern was abuzz with news of his escape," Randy explained. "He received a severe wound to his side, but only a flesh wound at his temple. It stunned him, but did not stop him. Not our Jonathon. Gates has half his crew searching, but no one has turned up a clue as to his whereabouts."

"They traced him quite a distance out of Norfolk, but lost his trail after a day," Michael explained.

Speculation about Jonathon continued until suppertime, when they invited Michael to join them.

"Thank you, but I must, at all costs, appear at odds with all of you," he replied. "Walters is steadily improving, and with luck we will be away from here the day after tomorrow. I will, however, return someday to accept Emily's most gracious offer."

Emily escorted him to the door, but paused before opening it.

"Michael—" She blushed and looked down.

"I know, Emily," he said quietly.

"I am so sorry that I hurt you, and now you save my life when you could have . . . I can never thank you enough."

"Emily, I will always carry you in my heart." He looked down uncomfortably, and then looked into her eyes. "I could not bear to see you hurt. Brentwood is a lucky man." He kissed her cheek then opened the door. Emily watched his soldiers salute him, and he jammed on his tricorn as if leaving in anger. She whispered a prayer of thanksgiving for his friendship.

*

True to his word, Michael ordered Captain Walters carried out to one of the wagons, and the regiment set out for Williamsburg two days later.

A sense of peace pervaded the house at their absence and spirits rose at the thought of Jonathon's survival. Randy remained with them for several days to reassure himself that no redcoats had lingered.

They sat at supper one evening when they heard a carriage approach. Rising, David went to the door to greet the guest and returned to the dining room with Deidre. They all were shocked at her appearance. Her usually carefully coiffed hair was disheveled, pinned haphazardly and hanging in her face. No color highlighted her cheeks, which were drawn, attesting to her hunger. Her eyes were dull, her mouth slack. Looking around the room, she raised her hands in a helpless gesture.

"I have nowhere to go," she stated simply. "The slaves have fled, the food is gone, my home is mortgaged to the British, and they refuse to allow me to remain."

There was no spark of defiance; no fight remained in the beaten woman. The room was quiet as each digested this news. Joanna looked at Emily. It was her decision; it was her home.

Emily rose from her chair and went to Deidre. She put an arm around the woman's frail shoulders.

"Come and eat, Deidre. Of course you have somewhere to go. You will stay right here with us," she said softly.

Deidre looked into her eyes. "I—"

Emily shook her head imperceptibly.

Deidre looked at her with what appeared to be a mixture of disbelief and gratitude.

They all resumed eating supper.

*

Life had become more agreeable at the manor, but Emily grew more impatient and anxious about Jonathon each day. The weather had remained mild, so she took many walks and busied herself with the gardens to try to calm her thoughts.

She was on the veranda when she saw a carriage rolling up the drive. Hastening out to meet it, she hoped it would bear news of Jonathon. She exclaimed in surprise when she saw her brother alight.

"Andrew!" she cried as she ran up to embrace him.

"Em!" he caught her up and swung her around.

"Drew, be careful," she said, laughing. "I have such good news, Drew. Jonathon is alive! But I do not know where he is. Have you heard anything of him?"

"Em, I must talk to you. Come for a ride with me," he urged.

"What is it, Drew?" she asked, concerned.

"Just come with me, Em," he insisted.

"Drew—"

"I must talk to you about an important decision I find myself faced with. I trust your judgment, Em."

She paused for a moment.

"All right. Let me get my wrap," she agreed.

Emily ran into Joanna in the hall.

"Whose carriage is that?" she asked Emily.

"It is Drew. He needs to discuss something with me, something urgent. I hope he is not planning to marry already!" Emily exclaimed.

Joanna laughed.

"Well, have a pleasant ride."

The air was brisk, but the sun warmed their faces as they rode along. Emily pressed Andrew, but he said he would reveal his news at the right time. They rode for quite a while as Emily related the story of Captain Walters and Michael Dennings to him.

"Drew, how far must we ride before you tell me what this is about?" she implored.

"Just a little farther, Em."

Soon they came to a small clearing, and Emily recognized the cabin where she and Jonathon had spent their first night. Memories of their lovemaking flooded her, and her heart raced. She had refused to allow herself those memories for so long, too painful to bear while she believed Jonathon dead. But now she let them wash over her like warm, gentle waves. She blushed at them and was suddenly very warm. She turned to look at Andrew. His face was covered with a wide grin.

"Andrew, what—?"

He helped her down and led her to the cabin door. He opened it, and she stepped inside. Her eyes took a moment to adjust from the brilliant sun outside to the dimly lit room. When they did, she saw a figure lying on the bed.

Her heart stopped, and she could not breathe. Her knees buckled, and Andrew supported her weight.

"Jonathon! Jonathon!" She ran to the bed.

"Love," he whispered as she buried her head in his chest. "My beautiful Em."

She looked up at him through her tears. Her hands stroked his face and chest, their desire for the feel of his body unquenchable.

He pulled her forward and kissed her long and full. His mouth on hers was the sweetest sensation she had ever known.

Emily laughed and cried. She barely noticed Andrew's quiet exit; she presumed he would return to Brentwood Manor to share the news.

*

Once her eyes had adjusted to the darkened room, Emily saw how pale and weak Jonathon looked. Concern gripped her.

"Jonathon, we must get Dr. Anderson to look at you," she insisted.

"You are the best medicine for me, Em," he argued.

"Oh, Jonathon. I cannot believe you are really here!" She bent to kiss his lips. "What happened? How did you get here? How did Andrew find you?"

"Stop, stop! I shall answer your questions later, love. But right now I feel the need for some tender ministrations." He chuckled.

"I do not think your health is quite ready for that, Jonathon," Emily scolded.

"Well, we could explore just what my health is ready for, Mrs. Brentwood."

"I can see the British were not able to tame you," she teased.

"Only you have ever been able to tame me, love."

CPSIA information can be obtained at www.ICGtesting.com
Printed in the USA
LVOW101754040912

297321LV00015B/12/P

9 781440 550621